FINDING YOU

BY EMMA NICHOLS

Britain's Next
BESTSELLER

First published in 2017 by:

Britain's Next Bestseller
An imprint of Live It Publishing
27 Old Gloucester Road
London, United Kingdom.
WC1N 3AX

www.bnbsbooks.co.uk

To keep in touch with the latest news from Emma Nichols
and her writing please visit:

www.emmanicholsauthor.com
www.facebook.com/EmmaNicholsAuthor
www.twitter.com/ENichols_Author

Available in paperback and digital.
ISBN: 9781521750490

Thanks

I would like to thank the wonderful Kiki Archer and Jae
for their continued inspiration and great advice that has helped
me to get my work to this point. Thanks also to those who
have read, suffered, and read again to ensure the story
is the best it can be. And finally, to my partner Murielle whose
creative genius informed the plot, right about just before I lost
it! Thank you to all who read this story and its sequel,
Remember Us. I hope you enjoy it, as much as I did writing it.

Dedication

To mum. Always in my heart.

1.

'You look like shit!' Never one to mince her words, Rowena's maternal eyes surveyed her key client with a compassion that didn't match her direct manner. 'Come on.' She softened her tone. 'Coffee?' Swinging her motherly arm around Anna's shoulders and squeezing her tightly, she walked her to the office two-seater, plonked her into the deep red-leather couch, and approached the Nespresso coffee machine without waiting for an affirmation. Woman on a mission, she selected the soft, creamy, Linizio blend for its soothing properties. She popped the pod into the machine, snapped the mechanism shut, and pressed the lungo button. There was something reassuring about the hiss and pop, followed by the gentle trickle and delicate aroma. Rowena breathed in the nutty, caramel scent for the seventeen seconds it took the coffee to spill into the cup. Staring out the window across the Paris landscape, she reflected on the damp, grey, Monday morning weather, and the uncharacteristically depressed state of her client. 'So, honey, what's up?'

Anna shrugged as her eyes lowered to her intertwined fidgeting fingers. Rowena handed the delicate cup to her and perched, half a cheek of her post-menopausal expansive bottom, on the soft couch. The cushions huffed under the pressure and she watched, patiently, as a delicate trickle gathered pace down Anna's face. Anna had sworn to herself she was past crying having sobbed her way through the best part of Friday afternoon, and spent the weekend processing the situation in her own mind. Rage building inside her, tempered by sadness, she slumped. She hadn't expected to react like this in front of her agent - not that Rowena would think any less of her for bursting into tears. It wasn't about that. Reaching out, the kind, puffy hand took back the cup, which was beginning to shake with the sobs and in danger of spilling. The soft hands pulled Anna into a comforting hug, stroked her hair, and eased her into a natural rocking rhythm that occupied the silence.

As the sobs eased and her breathing returned to normal, Anna pulled her red-rimmed eyes and blotchy face out of the heat of the busty embrace. 'Mum's got cancer and I've fallen in love with someone I will never see again.' The words spilled from Anna before she could censor her thoughts and she froze at her own utterance. It seemed wholly inappropriate to talk about her mum and Lauren in the same breath and she noticed a sinking feeling in her gut. She hadn't realised until now the impact meeting Lauren had had on her. The words had come from somewhere deeper than her conscious, and shocked her. She wished she had asked for the Corsican woman's business card. *Idiot*, she chastised herself. *In love with a woman I will never see again.* She played the words over and over hoping the overwhelming sense of loss would leave soon. It didn't.

'Shit. Shit. Shit!' Rowena jerked backwards, the cheek of her bottom almost losing complete contact with the couch, the cushions creating a tidal wave with the sudden movement. Anna's slight frame swayed with the after-shock. Clammy hands pressed against her round, paling, face and red painted lips. Rowena gasped in horror. Her heart sunk heavily into the pit of her stomach as the word 'cancer' repeated its mantra of doom through her head. She had known Anna's mum, Lisa Taylor, since their college days. They had studied at Oxford together, Rowena majoring in Design and Business Studies, whilst Lisa majored in Art and Design. Fleeting memories of their drunken exploits and solidarity at student gatherings appeared in her mind's eye at the thought of her impending death, reminding her of the many good times they had shared together. Sadness overshadowed the pleasant memories.

'Breast cancer,' Anna clarified without being asked.

2

When Lisa and Vivian underwent their commitment ceremony shortly after leaving University, Rowena had been there to give her away, beaming with pride as her friends openly fought against the societal norms of their time. She had known Anna since birth too, held her within hours of her entry into the world. As a young girl, her own daughter had spent many hours following Anna in adoration. She was the older sister Eva didn't have. They were like family back then, and this news cut Rowena deeply.

Rowena grimaced and tutted, hauled herself up in the seat, and shook her head violently back and forth. Her worst fear had just darkened an already dull Monday. Her friend was dying. Even though she couldn't allow herself to think that way, the vibrating that had started inside her body had already reached her hands. 'Hell Anna, when did she find out? Why didn't you stay in London?' *What's the prognosis? How's she coping? How's Viv handling it?* So many questions Rowena wanted to ask. As her eyes assessed Anna she was reminded of the young girl who would climb trees, graze her knees, and get Eva into all sorts of trouble. Many a time Rowena had wiped off mud and blood, and applied a sticky plaster to her wounds. Anna would give her a beaming smile with those light steel-blue eyes. So full of life and adventure, she would jump up shake herself off and resume the role-play that had caused the accident in the first instance. She mourned the loss of that carefree child as she observed the pain on her adult face. Sadness compressed her ribs and she breathed in hard to try to relieve the pressure.

'Friday. She discovered a lump a few weeks ago.' Anna stared into space. 'Typically, didn't tell me.' She huffed at her mum's independence. 'Viv got her seen quickly. They've recommended a lumpectomy, so that's scheduled for next week. I'm sure they'll get the best treatment possible,' she said, looking to Rowena, her eyes seeking something...

reassurance maybe. 'There isn't much I can do right now,' she shrugged at the helplessness she felt. 'Being there would just drive me crazy with worry. I need to work.' Anna's pragmatic tone had Viv written all over it. But even so, there was no hiding the distress. Vivian Cartwright had also studied at Oxford but a few years before Lisa and Rowena. Now a retired Doctor she had contacts that were useful and kept up-to-date with advances in the medical profession. She was genuinely passionate about the industry and often called upon as a guest lecturer at her old university. Neither woman was under any illusion that Viv was the right person to act in Lisa's interests.

'You're right. Viv is more capable of dealing with this than anyone I know. I'm sure she'll get the best treatment available.' They stared into the grey Paris morning, the flicker of car lights weaving slowly through the busy streets going unnoticed as the two women mulled over their thoughts. 'Hmm. So.' Rowena wriggled, groaning and puffing as she shifted her bulk to her - too small - feet. Anna was thrown back in the seat on the wave, but hardly noticed. The expansive dress had ridden up Rowena's thighs and she flapped at it to cover the exposed flesh as Anna brought herself effortlessly to stand, reaching out her arm to support the floundering woman as she righted herself. 'This won't get us anywhere,' she said authoritatively, fighting back the pounding in her temples.

Anna picked the tepid coffee off the low table and downed it in one, shuddering at both temperature and taste as the bitter after-taste assaulted her taste buds. *Yuk.*

Sighing deeply, she wrestled with the mixed emotions rumbling around her mind and body. Whilst she was definitely still in shock following the call from Viv on Friday, she was also overwhelmed, and even more disturbed, by what had followed. *Can you fall in love with someone you don't know?* Under current circumstances, she felt bad about the tingling warmth that invaded her body as she drifted to the events of the Friday evening. Of course, she could have been acting out, in denial, seeking solace, misreading the gaze - the smile - that had passed between her and Lauren. Though that would be completely out of character, she was usually a good judge of people. Stranger things have happened in the face of adversity she thought, as she reflected on the events of the evening.

2.

She had exited the warmth of the London art gallery into the autumnal early evening chill that penetrated effortlessly through to her bones. She may as well have been naked, so little effect were her clothes having. That thought had amused her and a chuckle rippled lightly in her chest as she considered the impact of that sort of attention on her career as an artist. Maybe it was the tiredness catching up with her, the early flight from Paris and she the fact that she hadn't stopped for lunch. It was also the end of a sequence of torturous weeks. Long hours completing her private work in Paris, whilst also curating a portrait display for the boutique gallery in London. Before the news about her mum she had felt excited, exhilarated, even though the display wasn't perfect. But since that devastating call from Viv, her attitude had changed and she had quickly become irritated at the slightest imperfection.

She had taken her time to place the final canvas on the wall, eyeing every centimeter of its subtle detail. The old woman's face crevassed by the depth of her experience over time, as the circles of a tree trunk, said she had lived for many years and lived well. Her eyes sparkled, not unlike those of a child. Though absent of innocence they conveyed wisdom and... freedom. Her mother's skin was much softer with fewer lines than this old woman, she had pondered. Her mother may never reach an age... she had carefully positioned the piece in its rightful place. Her hands shaking, eyes tightening, she held back the tears. Excusing herself she had gone to the ladies' toilet and sobbed uncontrollably.

Splashing water on her face to regain her composure sufficiently, she had returned to her work. Politely rejecting the offer to a pre-launch party with her colleagues. She couldn't muster the enthusiasm, even though the distraction might have helped in some way. Her heart ached, wounded, bleeding at the immediate future her mum faced. The longer term she couldn't even begin to contemplate - though her mind had clearly gone there to show her a negative future. Death. She had instantly wished it were her who had been diagnosed. She could take away the pain and suffering, wrap it up inside herself and free her mum to live forever. That would be easy, and preferable to facing a potential future without her.

Goose bumps spread up her arms at the sight of the crew-cut, dark haired man as he swaggered past her in a white t-shirt and tight-fitting jeans, arms flailing into his mobile phone. Spots of icy rain hit her face and she winced. She pulled the mock-fur lined hood of her coat up over her ears in response. Wrapping her arms around her body she stood, fighting for her balance on the cobbled London side street, pondering her next move, looking for a street name to orientate her. Unconsciously she caressed the outside of her right breast. The wind stung her face and burned her eyes so she turned out of its path, sighing at the immediate relief. Touching her nose, its tip was cold, and a trickle was forming just short of its exit. She swiped it with the back of her hand. It was unusually chilly for mid-September, she mused, as she scanned her phone for somewhere locally to eat.

7pm. She needed to numb her senses, to hide in an alcoholic haze for a few hours, and to get warm. The local bar was packed out, people spilling into the street already well on their way to drunken oblivion. She didn't seek that. The smell of smoke and sweaty bodies as she moved through the sprawling mass caused her to choke. She wanted quiet, calm, and her own space - not so easy to find on a Friday night in one of the liveliest capitals of the World. In Paris, she would have known exactly where to go - a quiet bistro in the Spanish quarter. She envisioned it. As she twisted and turned down the cobbled side alleys the spots of rain increased. Getting heavier, the downpour focused her attention, and she dived towards a small but cavernous Italian restaurant. It wasn't the place her phone was directing her to, but she didn't want to get any wetter on top of the cold she was already feeling. A bell jingled as she opened the door, and she was thrown back by a wave of heat and the scent of mixed spices. It's dark interior, red slate floor with sandstone brick separating alcoves and subtle individual table lights, felt quaint... and quiet. *Perfect*.

'Ciao signorina.' The tall dark waiter held the door, shifting sideways as she bustled her way through the opening and out of the cold rain. His smile was warm, welcoming, and unhurried. He held her face with his compassionate eyes assessing her. 'Do you have a reservation?' he asked softly. The idea, even though reasonable on a Friday evening, hadn't occurred to her.

Tensing, she turned towards the door. Her shoulders rose to her ears and irritation was quick to surface. 'Sorry, I don't. I...'

'Wait signorina.' His words stopped her just as her hand reached for the brass door handle. She glanced over her shoulder and raised a weak, grateful smile.

'Let me make a quick call. I will find a quiet table for you.' The tall young waiter waved her into the restaurant, whilst he moved to the bar and picked up the phone.

'Thank you,' she said. Sighing deeply, comforted at the thought that she wouldn't need to face the outside any time soon, the irritation disappearing as quickly as it had appeared. Her eyes watered as they adjusted to the warmth.

Speaking in Italian, the words rolling smoothly off his tongue, Anna watched as he nodded his head and waved his free arm as he spoke - like the man in the street, she noted. Ending the call, he approached Anna with a broad grin that lit up his face. His soft blue eyes sparkled. 'Allow me to take your coat please.' He held out his hand. Shaking the short duffle coat gently over the mat, he then placed the coat respectfully on one of the hooks by the door. 'Follow me please,' he said, directing Anna to the back of the restaurant.

'Thank you,' she said. The waiter led the way through the restaurant to a lower level cave hosting two small rustic wooden tables and black leather-clad bench seats. Sinking into the seat her jaw tensed, and then softened as she adjusted to the initially cold material, before relaxing a little into the couch. Taking the embossed leather case menu that was offered to her she placed it unopened on the table. The delicate sweet smell of freesias, the simple multi-colour centrepiece adorning the table, caught her attention momentarily.

'Can I get you a drink signorina?' The waiter stood, lightly to attention, patiently awaiting instruction.

'Could I have a large Gin and Tonic please?' She breathed deeply, her eyes resting on the kind waiter, trying to raise a smile. She failed. Nodding his head in affirmation, he turned and left her to her thoughts. She felt comforted that warmth had begun to filter through her upper body, but her lower legs, below her coat line, and feet, were still damp from the downpour. Moving to rub her legs to warm them, she knocked her shoulder on the side of the table. 'Shit.' She cursed, massaging the sore point just as the waiter re-appeared. 'Sorry,' she apologised, wincing.

He placed the tall glass containing the large shot of alcohol and ice onto the table, together with the small bottle of tonic and a small saucer with slices of lemon and lime. 'I can recommend the vegetarian Lasagne alla Norma, or the Malloreddus, of course. Traditional Sardinian durum wheat pasta with fresh sausages and tomato sauce,' he said, with a genuine passion for the food, before leaving her table to attend to the ringing of the front door bell.

She poured the tonic into the glass and added a slice of lime. Watching her actions, she felt the light spray on her hand as the fizzy drink released small bubbles into the air. Sipping the sparkling, zesty drink, the bubbles tickling her nose, she savoured the tingling sensation in her mouth, and derived pleasure from the immediate effect of the alcohol on her empty stomach. Her eyes scanned the quaint environment, realising for the first time the intoxicating aroma's emanating from the kitchen. Garlic, herbs, cheese and salami fused to create a homely authentic feel. She found herself entranced by the cosy cavern and soft music, welcoming the distraction from her thoughts. She had no desire to rush. She had nowhere to go. Taking another long sip of the chilled drink, her eyes closed.

*

'Thanks Naz.' The soft deep tone, slightly gravelly, pulled Anna instantly out of her reverie. Her eyes flicked open and she sat bolt upright. Clearing her throat, she noticed the tall, elegant, woman with dark wavy hair, and dark eyes resting on her. Her breath caught in her throat at the woman's intense smile.

Even though the woman dressed casually, something in the way she carried herself exuded confidence and stature, and Anna became aware she had been staring open mouthed. For how long she didn't know, but heat had risen into her cheeks and she felt a genuine smile penetrate her face as she lowered her eyes.

'Thanks.' The dark eyes shone as she touched the waiter's arm with familiarity. Anna found herself imagining that tender touch on her arm. She shuddered. Sitting delicately the woman ordered a glass of Livon Friulano in a low, easy voice that sang in Anna's ears, and vibrated down her spine. Mesmerised, Anna reached for her drink, fumbled, and sent the tall glass tumbling, instantly pulling her out of her indulgent trance.

'Shit!' Standing quickly, flustered and flapping, she tried to avoid the trailing fluid further soaking her already wet trousers. 'I'm so sorry,' she apologised, wincing for the second time since entering the restaurant. Wiping herself down with the pristine white table napkin, she became aware of the woman holding back a chuckle. Anna's eyes locked with the stranger, sensing the lightness in her brown eyes, seeing the humour in the situation, she too began to giggle.

'I have been known to do that myself.' The woman held out her hand, offering her napkin to Anna as she stood and breached the gap between them. 'I'm Lauren', she said, moving closer to shake hands whilst the mopping ensued. 'Seems you are absent of a drink. Would you like to join me in a glass of wine?' She touched the waiter on the arm again before Anna could respond. Anna noticed her long, strong fingers, with their surprisingly delicate touch. She struggled to swallow. 'Can you make that a bottle of Friulano please Naz. I think we're going to need it.'

Anna had opened her mouth with every intention of declining the generous offer from the stranger, but her voice had deserted her. She could feel her heart in her throat and the flowery, soapy scent emanating from Lauren had already infiltrated her body in a delightful and unexpected way.

'Anna,' she replied, mustering a quietly controlled voice in a vain attempt not to give away her crumbling internal reality. *Who is this woman to have this effect on me?* 'That's very kind, but I can't possibly...'

'No. I insist. It's no imposition,' Lauren interrupted, with her gentle, yet commanding tone. 'You are down a drink and I am down a date, so your company would be most welcome... unless you would rather dine alone of course?'

Lauren's look seemed to question why one might want to eat alone.

Anna could feel the insistent dark brown eyes as if they were caressing her physically, and that smile... there was something lustful about that smile. The sensual warmth, enchanting - entrancing - Anna found herself nodding in acceptance of the offer.

'Please do join me. Have you ordered?'

'No, I was just about to go with the recommended speciality, Malloreddus.'

'Excellent choice.' Lauren's eyes never moved from Anna as they spoke.

'You eat here regularly?' Anna asked. Lauren certainly seemed very familiar with the staff and menu.

'It's my favourite place in the whole of London.' Lauren oozed passion for the quaint Italian. 'And, I'm a big fan of authentic Italian food. What about you, what do you like Anna?'

Anna wasn't sure if there were undertones she should be picking up on, especially the deliberate way Lauren had used her name... and those penetrating eyes.

'I'm a fan of great food. French, Italian, Spanish.'

The waiter approached with the wine and an ice bucket. Placing the chilled bucket at the side of the table he held the label in front of the two women.

'Would you like to try the wine?' he asked, directing the bottle at Lauren who pointed to Anna's glass.

'Please, I know this wine well. Would you like to try it?' Lauren smiled and nodded encouragingly.

The clean, well-balanced, natural acidity teased Anna's taste buds, widening the smile that was fast becoming a permanent feature in the company of this woman. Anna became aware that Lauren was watching her intently. Her dark eyes seemed to have adopted a lighter, hazel brown colour.

Her smooth, tanned skin showed few ageing lines that served only to enhance her innate attractiveness. Well crafted, natural lips - absent of botox - seemed expressive and seductive. Yes, her lips and her mouth, Anna thought, as she sampled the deliciously delicate, dry wine on their behalf, oblivious to its taste. The lingering gaze was creating significant, pleasant, discomfort. Anna returned her glass to the table and nodded her approval.

The waiter poured both women a glass, returning the bottle to the ice. 'Would you ladies like to order?' he asked, politely enquiring, hands resting behind his back.

Lauren looked at her companion, nodded her affirmation and sought confirmation of Anna's previously stated preference. 'The antipasti is excellent here. Would you like to share?' Lauren's eyes held Anna's with curiosity.

'Sure, and the Malloreddus for me please,' Anna addressed the waiter directly.

'I'll have the same, thank you Naz.' The waiter smiled and took the two menus with him.

As they settled into easy conversation, Anna discovered that Lauren was a lawyer working in the City. She had moved from Corsica to undertake her training in London and had worked there pretty much ever since. She had been mentored for partnership in her organisation. Anna surmised that she was diligent, conscientious, and, from her manner, humble. She wanted to know more about the stunning, kind woman. She had been stood up by a client, for which she was actually thankful. After a long and stressful week, the thought of entertaining well into the night hadn't filled her with joy, she revealed. Disappointingly for Anna, she had a partner who had just been elected by the Conservative Party to represent Brighton & Hove. They had been together for 10 years, though from what Anna could gather Lauren seemed to spend most of her time in London rather than Brighton. As Lauren talked about her relationship Anna became acutely aware of the absence of passion in Lauren's eyes. Pride, sure. Love, yes - the sort of love that bonds people over time. Love that gives the illusion of compatibility and longevity but with no real sense of fire or lust, she mused. She had watched Lauren's eyes dull and her mouth barely raise a smile as she spoke. On the other hand, when Lauren talked about her work she oozed passion. There was definitely a detectable difference, Anna observed. As the evening progressed, Lauren held Anna's gaze with greater intensity. There was something else behind those dark hazel eyes. She didn't ask but she felt touched by them.

Anna had talked about her mum's diagnosis. She found it quite cathartic sharing her feelings and thoughts with Lauren. She had been understanding, compassionate and considerate, asking questions rather than giving advice. At one-point Lauren had reached out and touched Anna's hand, gently stroking across her knuckles as she spoke. The perplexing sensations shooting through Anna's body wrestled with her need for the tenderness of touch, creating an absence of thought and sudden inexplicable silence between them. Anna looked longingly at Lauren for a moment, her attention drawn to those perfect lips. Lauren smiled knowingly. Anna had felt truly listened to, in a way that she never experienced with her ex, Sophie. She talked about the fact that Sophie had cheated on her. As a pro tennis player, Sophie had taken both her status and the opportunities that presented themselves one step too far. Her relationship with Sophie had been kept out of the public eye so when the news of Sophie's love life had been plastered all over social media - without reference to Anna - and the images revealed Sophie kissing her doubles partner in a clearly passionate embrace, Anna had simply text her, wishing her farewell. Sophie hadn't responded to the text. That was in July. Wimbledon. Right on the doorstep, Anna reflected, and anger fused in her chest at the raw memory.

The food had been excellent and after they had slowly worked their way through a second bottle of wine - chatting the night away - both women reluctantly agreed it was time to leave. Lauren had insisted on paying and Anna had already begun to realise that Lauren generally got what she wanted in life. She smiled at the realisation. Highly successful, exceptionally attractive with dark wavy hair sweeping around her olive skin, and what appeared to be a perfectly athletic build - and she was taken! Anna had sighed at the cold, hard truth, as they had been the last to leave the restaurant.

'I'm staying just around the corner, at the Marriott,' Anna said, as they stepped into the night's chill, moving towards Lauren as if to hug her goodnight.

'I'll walk you, if that's okay. I could do with a little fresh air.' Lauren took Anna's arm without engaging in a hug and slowly walked them in the direction Anna had pointed. They had walked in comfortable silence, like old friends, soaking up the city's Friday nightlife. The streets were still bustling as people bounced their way from bar to nightclub - from inebriated to unconsciousness. The autumn chill seemed to heighten Anna's desire for human contact. With Lauren's arm linking through hers she shivered noticeably.

'Are you okay?' Lauren asked with genuine concern.
'It's chilly,' Anna said, feeling anything but cold. She couldn't go there she told herself. To act on how she was feeling would violate her values, even though her body was crying out to be held and touched by Lauren. She couldn't do to Lauren's partner what had been done to her. That was assuming Lauren even felt the same way. She sensed she did. She had tensed involuntarily under the impact of that thought.

The tall building with its glass-fronted façade and revolving doors appeared too quickly. 'Thank you for a lovely evening.' Anna reluctantly released the arm holding her and locked onto Lauren's dark eyes. 'That was most unexpected,' she said. She didn't feel ready to leave the company that had made time pass in a flash, made her forget about her mum, and put a deep and genuine smile on her face. 'In a pleasant way, I mean.'

'Can I have your number? We could catch up again when you're in London?' Lauren said. She had looked vulnerable in that moment and against her better judgement Anna had conceded, handing her a business card.

She hadn't asked Lauren for her number. She didn't trust herself not to try to take things where they couldn't go. Anna moved in for a farewell hug. Brushing cheek-to-cheek, heat flared though her face at the brief touch. As she pulled back, Lauren held her arms tightly, the intensity of her dark eyes scorching her skin, tingling sensations firing though her body. *No, please don't kiss me.* For a moment, her eyes closed to avoid being sucked in. She couldn't...

Anna felt the warmth of Lauren's breath on her lips before the lightest of touch that immediately penetrated her soul. Like the gentlest blow that left her pleasantly winded, the pain exquisite. Absent of rational thought, her will lost in some distant notion of doing the right thing, time stood still. The temporary blindness lifted in an instant, as Lauren eased out of the chaste kiss, the tenderness remaining as she held Anna's eyes with her own, releasing a breath that said so much. Anna stumbled, jolted, temporarily torn as a wave of consciousness filtered through her. Her heart raced, her head spun, and her legs barely held her weight. A wave of guilt jarred her and she pulled back, instantly feeling the distance as a well of loneliness sitting heavily in her gut.

'Thank you for your company Anna,' Lauren had said, using her name in that deliberately seductive tone again. Anna turned and dived through the revolving doors. Standing on the inside for what seemed like an eternity, she had eventually turned around, looked over her shoulder, sadness overwhelming her. Lauren was gone.

3.

'Ashes to ashes, dust to dust.' The Priest's deep voice echoed across the private plot on the western most side of the mountain. The grey, thundery, wet drizzle - uncharacteristic Corsican weather for the time of year - seemed a perfect reflection of the state of affairs that had just befallen the Vincenti family. The small gathering of close friends, family, business associates, all heads bowed, dressed in black, stood silently as the coffin was lowered into the ground. Stifled sobs pushed through the silence as Lauren's mother stood, stone-faced, watching. She stepped closer, threw a single white rose onto the coffin then stepped back, taking hold of the arm of their estate manager for stability. Antoine Fiorelli had been working alongside Petru Vincenti since leaving school at sixteen. He had learned from the master vigneron now lying in the box in front of them all. His eyes were wet with tears and swollen. He bowed his head at the box and threw in a second white rose. It landed across the rose Petru's wife had just thrown, forming a cross at the head of the coffin.

Lauren had received the call from Antoine on the Saturday afternoon and had booked a flight to Paris that evening with a follow-on flight to Ajaccio on the Sunday morning. Standing in the cold damp Corsican air, staring at the box in the ground with its gold ornate handles - *he would have hated those* - she had never felt more alone. She felt a world away from her unexpected Friday evening experience. Anna had stirred something in her and she didn't know how she felt about that.

A painfully intense shiver rode her body and heavy tears burned the back of her eyes, but she could not cry. She had missed the ceremony lost in her thoughts. So many questions she needed answers to. *What possessed her father to commit suicide? Was it suicide or was he killed?* At fifty-six, he was a still a young man. He had been fit, active, and very much alive the last time she had seen him. Lauren was still staring at the solid wooden box below her feet, earth scattered loosely across its surface and the two white roses, long after the other guests had departed. Only the two gravediggers stood a professional distance from the spot waiting patiently for her to leave so they could finish their work. Petru's grave had been positioned between his parents and her younger sister Corry in their family plot, within the shadow of the notably tall eucalyptus tree. Lauren glanced towards her sister's headstone and closed her burning eyes.

Leaning against the white skin of the eucalyptus for support, she looked out across the cloud-darkened valley, feeling overwhelmed by emotion. She didn't tolerate negative feelings and the depth of them took her by surprise. She could not stop the tears that followed so she allowed them to blend with the misty damp climate that was already wetting her face. She felt sobered by the emotional onslaught, and drained. Staring out at the storm, sweeping its way across the mountain range, her vulnerability struck her. She shivered, a cold and thick buzzing sensation passed through her body.

She had always been aware that life was short. The untimely death of her grandfather and younger sister had driven her to take up Law and live in London. She had been unable to face living in a place that blew up innocent people in the name of retribution. The attack had specifically targeted her grandfather for his historical activities, being formally known as a Corsican Godfather. Although long since retired, the hit had been undertaken as retribution for the past, maintaining the feud between the Germani and Colonna families. They hadn't realised that Corry was in the back of the car. A single bullet was all it took, and the car veered off the road and down the side of the steep cliff. Even if the shot hadn't killed him outright, neither would have survived the fall.

The car exploded on impact. Lauren's world had changed in that moment.

The damp chill was starting to penetrate her awareness, her clothes wet through from the constant drizzle now descending as heavy rain. The wind was getting up, decreasing the temperature by ten or more degrees. Shivering, she walked slowly and reluctantly up the side of the hill towards her family home.

The Vincenti mansion was set in an expansive plot. Outbuildings turned into self-contained workers' homes and the 40-ha vineyard rising from the Rizzanese river had been in the family for generations. Though adapted and renovated over the decades, their home still retained the traditional features - small shuttered windows, a large wood burning stove in the living room, dark wood interior fittings and deep-set fire-places in each of the other main rooms.

Located in the Sartène region, the Domain Ferdicci had recently evolved into a very popular regional wine, also benefiting from international demand, courtesy of her father's passion and devotion. With everything going so well, suicide just didn't make sense. Stepping into the entrance hall, Lauren could hear the voices of the guests, mostly deep voices. Polite conversation and sombre tone reflected the disbelief that this life had come to a sudden and unexpected end.

Lauren climbed the stairs with a heavy heart and entered her bedroom. She couldn't face the wake right now, and in any event, she needed to change into dry clothes. The scent of roses and lavender graced her senses as she opened the door to her childhood bedroom. The king-size bed seemed smaller than she remembered. She hadn't been back home for a while, she realised. A plain cream coloured throw covered the puffed-up quilt, and with stacked crimson red pillows Lauren felt drawn to curl up inside until the nightmare was over. Instead, she walked hastily into the en-suite and violently wretched into the pristine white bowl. Bilious fluid burned her mouth and nose. Sinking steadily to the floor, tears flooded her eyes and she sobbed uncontrollably.

As the nausea passed and the tears stopped, Lauren tentatively rose to her feet. Shivering, she removed her clothes and stepped into the walk-in shower. The blasting heat caressed her face and she relaxed into its warmth. Soaking up the refreshing feeling, raising the heat and pressure, she moved around the shower to allow her shoulders and neck to receive the same pounding massage. It felt good. Her thoughts drifted to the Friday evening. *Anna, Anna, Anna. What have you done to me?* Lauren had been unable to think of anything else, until the phone call had collided with her fantasy, jolting her into a reality she didn't want to face - the death of her father.

As she brought to mind their parting hug and the electric brush of cheek on cheek, the pulsing in her clit and shaking in her legs, that had nearly brought her to her knees then, she felt the need to relieve herself - to try to sweep the memories of that delicious moment from her mind. They would never see each other again. Anna had made her intentions clear by not asking for her phone number. Taking the showerhead in hand and adjusting the pressure, Lauren leaned her back into the white tiled walls and applied the pressure where she needed it most. As the orgasm rose quickly within her, Anna's steel-blue eyes and the burning touch they shared consumed her mind. *Anna.* The name escaped her as she tipped over the edge. Revelling momentarily in the welcome release, she felt far from satisfied. Towelling dry, she walked into her bedroom and pulled on her black fitted jeans, white shirt and onyx cufflinks. She felt the need to shift the mood from the all-black funeral attire, but out of respect for her mother's traditional outlook couldn't go as far as she, *and her father*, would have liked.

4.

Lauren ambled into the main reception room, the larger of two such rooms in the house and the one most often used for formal events over the years. The lower level walls decked in African Walnut would have been overpowering in any other room, but the size of the room carried the dark wood well. Lauren noted the deep red country style curtains. They hadn't changed in all the time Lauren remembered. She smiled at the familiarity; the slightly musty scent in the corner closest to the patio windows where the damp still penetrated the wall there and the strong essence of rose emanating from the pot pourri - probably to cover the mouldy smell, Lauren thought. In spite of this being her family home, she felt out of place. It had been over a year since she had set foot in Corsica and even longer since she had visited her parents. Glancing around the room, the people were familiar of course, but she had nothing in common with them. She felt like a stranger in her family home. She sighed and strolled across the room towards her mother.

'Ms Vincenti, we are terribly sorry for your loss.' The dark, shorthaired man approached Lauren as she took a glass of Champagne from the silver tray presented to her.

'Thank you.' Lauren nodded to the waiter before turning to the man trying to get her attention. 'Yes, it's all very sudden,' she responded. She watched the man as he virtually hopped from one foot to the other, fiddling his hands in front of his body.

'Sorry. Jean-Claude Canazzi,' he said, holding out a limp, sweaty hand. Lauren took it, giving a firm shake, and his whole upper body seemed to move with the small action. 'I am the solicitor dealing with your father's estate,' he almost stuttered.

'How can I help?' she asked, without enthusiasm.

'I need to arrange to meet with you before the reading of the will. I apologise for the timing of my approach. It is a matter of urgency that your father insisted upon. He said you would understand.'

'Of course. How about tomorrow morning? I can come to your office.' Lauren sipped the chilled fizzy drink, recalling that she would have preferred a glass of their estate wine. She faked a smile and nodded, seeking his response. Jean-Claude nodded.

The Canazzis had been her father's appointed solicitors for all matters relating to business, and life, for as long as she had known. Their fathers, and fathers before them had been friends and work associates. They were considered part of the wider Vincenti family.

'And call me Lauren, please,' she said, holding out her hand again to seal the arrangement.

'That will be perfect Ms... Lauren,' he said, blushing as he shook her hand more firmly this time. '11 o'clock?'

'Perfect.' Lauren smiled graciously as she excused herself to continue her hosting duties. She moved across the room with elegance, aware of the eyes in the room scanning her.

She spotted her mother talking to the priest who had conducted the service - seeking solace in his words no doubt, aligning her pain with verses of the bible that seemed to flow from his holiness with such certainty as to be moderately convincing, Lauren surmised sardonically. Just the sight of her mother riled her. Dressed in black, head to foot, there was no questioning the source of her designer clothes. *Why did she need to wear D&G to the funeral? She makes it look like a bloody fashion parade*, Lauren mused, incensed that her mother had put herself at the centre of attention... again. Some things never change, she reflected, as she diverted her walk away from the occupied woman. The priest's lips twitched towards Lauren, with tacit agreement that their worlds were light years apart. Lauren returned the acknowledgement with equal measure of tolerance.

She had long since stopped believing in any form of religion and questioned the idea of an after-life. The idea of heaven and hell seemed quite preposterous to her. Her mother, however, was deeply entrenched in the Catholic faith, though selectively attending mass, her donations to the church amply made up for her absence on a Sunday morning. Lauren had at times been frustrated with her mother's insistence on the biblical truth, especially in matters to do with her lifestyle and sexuality. But over the years she had also come to realise that, for her mother, the level of comfort and security *believing* gave her, outweighed the pain she had to personally endure, courtesy of her mother's protestations. Lauren smiled half-heartedly as she caught her mother's painted grin. They would have time to catch up later. Lauren needed some air.

She stepped out the French doors onto the grey tiled patio. Looking out through the arched border to the main gardens she could see the lone eucalyptus where her father and sister now slept, eternally. Breathing deeply, enjoying the softening effect on her body of the air filling her lungs, her eyes wandered down the valley as a wave of sadness hit her senses. The weather had shifted and the sun was beginning to show itself through heavy white clouds. The temperature was rising and the warmth a welcome contrast to the cold London weather of just a few days ago. Perhaps tomorrow would be sunny and dry. Lost in her musings, the light tap on her shoulder made her jump out of her skin.

'Jesus!' Champagne sploshed over the edge of her glass and she dived backwards to avoid the spillage, which bounced off the grey slate tiles onto her leather boots.

'Hi... Sorry.' The familiar voice was accompanied by a strong grip on her shoulder and a snigger. Turning Lauren, the arms swept around her into a warm embrace. 'I've missed you. How are you?'

'Carla. My God. It's been...' Lauren held her old friend at arm's length while she looked her up and down. 'You look great. How are you?' She pulled her in for another hug. The contact felt good. They had always done proper hugs - open, warm, connected... and always platonic. They had been friends since Maternelle and had been through school, college, and high school together. Carla had gone off to study psychiatry and Lauren had moved to London to study law. They hadn't seen each other a great deal since Lauren's move, but they didn't need to. Their connection was timeless and the envy of most couples in intimate relationships.

'I'm sorry I missed the ceremony. OMG. How are you sweetheart?' Carla oozed love as she pulled her friend in for another squeeze. It took every effort for Lauren to hold the tears back that pressed so hard for release.

'I'm... okay,' Lauren said, her voice starting to betray her. Carla held her friend firmly and gently, and a sense of knowing passed between them.

Carla had lost her mother in a traffic accident when they were both children. Lauren had been there for her then, but as young children they had just played games together in silence. Lauren had cuddled her friend when she had called for her mum after falling and banging her knee. She had cried a lot then and Lauren had cried with her. Then they had sat for what seemed like ages, holding hands, staring at nothing in particular until the tears had been forgotten and play had resumed.

Breaking the silence, 'Can I get you another drink?' Carla asked. 'I do feel a bit responsible for you not finishing this one.' She smiled as her eyes focused on the splash marks on Lauren's boots.

Composing herself and wiping at an errant tear, Lauren smiled, momentarily thrown back to Anna's flustered state as she had sent her drink flying on the previous Friday. She slugged the last of her Champagne and placed the empty glass on the patio wall. 'Actually, I think I'm ready for something stronger.' Linking arms, she led Carla back through the house, into the living room, and to the bar.

*

'Let's go for lunch.' Rowena looked into the eyes of her young protégé, recognising the need for a break. After the revelation about Anna's mum they had started work on a photography project requested by one of Anna's avid collectors. The morning had flown by and the weather had cleared. Paris was coming alive for the midday diners - locals and tourists sampling the delights of traditionally presented, microwave cooked cuisine, cheap house wines and a genuinely unhurried culture. No one rushed lunch so no one even bothered trying to go out for a quick snack. 'I have another proposal I want to run past you,' Rowena casually mentioned, as she grabbed her light jacket and bag.

Anna rubbed her sore eyes as she pulled them away from the images, which were beginning to merge into one blob after hours of consideration. 'Sure, I'm starving.' Other than the delectable meal she had shared with Lauren on the Friday evening she hadn't had much of an appetite over the weekend. She had paid an impromptu visit to her parents' house on the Saturday morning, before heading to the airport for her flight back to Paris early Sunday morning. Lisa had been in the throes of a commissioned portrait of the newest edition to the Royal family and Vivian deeply engrossed in the latest medical advances in breast cancer treatments. She would not rest until she had all the facts and details.

Lisa immersed herself in her passion not to get away from the truth, but because there was nothing she could do in that moment that would make any difference to the reality she faced. Anna had sat quietly and watched her mother at work. Forever her inspiration and mentor, she had been awestruck at the ease with which her mum transformed the formal image on the photograph in front of her to the canvas - enhancing it - capturing the unseen, she transferred the newly emerging character through intuition and insight. The transformation conveyed something beyond the image - the life. The energy. The aura.

'That's truly amazing,' Anna said softly whilst totally absorbed in the creation.

'Yes, she has something about her, doesn't she?' Her mother spoke as if the baby had been the one to create the masterpiece in progress. 'Such a gorgeous baby.' She softly traced her fingers over the face on the photograph, touching something deep within the tiny new-born that she would later transfer to the canvas. Both women sat, absorbed - lost in their own mental reflection - united in their common appreciation.

'Drink you two?' Vivian asked, gently drawing them back into current space and time. As they both turned, she was taken aback by the stunning similarity between birth mother and daughter. A wry smile crossed her face as she glanced lovingly at her two favourite women.

'Is it too early for a glass of wine?' Lisa asked, winking at Anna as a cheeky smile crossed her lips.

'Coming up.' Vivian took the question as a clear instruction. It was midday somewhere in the world, she reasoned.

The three women had chatted easily, enjoying a glass of chilled Sauvignon before heading out to the local tapas bar for a casual picky lunch. Anna had taken the opportunity to mention her chance meeting with Lauren and how enchanted she had been by the kindness of the tall, elegant, stranger. Even though she skipped most of the detail about how she felt towards the Corsican woman, her body confessed all. Without saying a word both her mums had exchanged knowing glances and smiles. The fact that Lauren was already with another woman didn't preclude the fact that this chance liaison could evolve into something special for their daughter. They always hoped. They had never seen Anna as taken by another woman as she seemed to be by this Lauren. Even though she had been devoted to Sophie, neither of them had seen that relationship lasting.

'Mutually incompatible,' Vivian had stated categorically. 'The woman has an ego that she will trip over at some point and our Anna just isn't like that.'

She had been right of course. Even though the breaking news was no surprise to any of them, including Anna, they could see that their daughter had been deeply hurt by the affair. Perhaps this liaison would be the beginning of a new and exciting chapter for Anna. Her mums were definite believers in love at first sight - how could they not - they were a positive example of it.

Anna had left her mums after their lazy lunch, heading back to her hotel to pack for her early morning flight. She had been somewhat reassured that her mums were living life as normal, but something she had noticed in Vivian's eyes, as she had looked up from the laptop screen to welcome Anna, portrayed the gravity of the situation and an indication of what the next few months might entail. It was fleeting, but it was enough. Looking at her phone, unconsciously stroking the screen, Lauren's dark penetrating eyes and soft smile appeared in her mind and she wondered if she would ever hear from her again. The idea that she might not drifted past her consciousness accompanied by a depth of sadness she hadn't realised existed in her. *Why hadn't she taken her card? She's married that's why. I can't go there, even if I wanted to... and I really do want to!* Releasing a deep sigh, squeezing and pocketing her phone, she had showered quickly and grabbed an early night. But those long hours had been haunted by a restless, tormented sleep.

'So, what's the proposal?' Anna asked as they sat at the red linen clothed table, the waiter reeling off the Table d'hôte options, of which they were already familiar. Selecting the Foie Gras de Canard, followed by the stir-fried black sausage and house red wine, Rowena looked questioningly at Anna, as if assessing her emotional suitability for the task she was about to present. 'Well?' Anna said, impatiently.

'It will involve you being based in Corsica for three months,' she said, deliberately fronting the proposition with the potential barrier to Anna agreeing to the project. With her mum's situation Rowena reasoned that Anna might be thinking about staying closer to home, and although Corsica wasn't that much further South, it was still more of a faff getting into London during the winter months than it was going directly from Paris.

'Ouch!' Anna's initial response and pinched look reinforced Rowena's initial concern. Her eyes lowered to her phone resting on the table. She needed a distraction, she reasoned to herself. 'Okay, tell me more.'

Rowena could see Anna processing the possibility rapidly. One of the things she liked about Anna, as had drawn her to be best friends with Lisa over the years, was her ability to adapt rather than block opportunities. No matter what was going on in her life she would always give suggestions due consideration, finding solutions rather than reasons why she couldn't undertake something. It was also one of the characteristics that had led her to be successful in her work. Pragmatism and adaptability were unusual characteristics in 'creatives', in Rowena's experience, so when you found them in a talented artist you knew you had something special to work with.

'Well, the call came in last week from Antoine Fiorelli. He's the estate manager for the Vincenti Vineyard. He wants to commission a portrait for his boss's wife, or I should say now ex-boss's wife, Valerie Vincenti. They are big vignerons in the Sartène region. It's a delicate situation. Mrs Vincenti had wanted to commission you for her and her husband, but he died unexpectedly. I got a call from Mr Fiorelli to say that she is even more adamant that she wants to go ahead with the commission, and she still wants it to be of her and her husband. She asked if you could work from a photo of him? Of course, I told him you could. It's a delicate situation.' Rowena sounded apologetic. Most normal people would put a halt on things following a sudden death, but clearly Mrs Vincenti was anything but normal in that respect.

'I need to think about it.' Anna wasn't sure what the bad feeling that briefly touched her was about, but she needed to process the idea of undertaking this work. She needed time to consider the consequences.

'They will of course accommodate you while you're there and they're willing to pay, handsomely.' Anna stared out the window, unaffected by both points. Rowena broke the spell, 'How's the food?' Innocuous, the comment shifted the focus of attention and they continued chatting about the safe topic of the photography project.

Anna's thoughts drifted again to her mum's portrayal of the baby, her life-threatening condition, this man's sudden death. *How short this life is*. Suddenly, she felt unfulfilled. Empty. Alone. For all the beauty that surrounded her, the unconditional love of her parents and her agent, her friends, her work, her gorgeous barn and all that she had invested in it, she felt horribly isolated and lonely. The insecurity that struck her sat like a heavy ball in the pit of her stomach. She had to work hard to give her full attention to the conversation and lift herself from the overwhelming sense of self-pity.

'I'll do it.' The words were out before Anna realised. 'I'll do Corsica', she said, confirming which project she was referring to. She didn't know why her mind had suddenly - and without consultation with her - just agreed to the project, but she knew she had to trust some deeper instinct. She smiled with smug contentment at her ability to drive out the loneliness and replace it with a meaningful project. Immortalising her wealthy client through art, she pondered. As the artist, it also immortalised her of course - although some part of her deeply rejected that idea.

5

Lauren took the short drive into town, enjoying the warmth of the new day as the sun reflected through the windscreen of her car and heated her face. It must be 25-degrees already, she considered, as she wiped at the small beads of sweat forming at the edge of her temples. The transformation in the weather from the previous day was indicative of the area and never ceased to amaze her. Antoine would be pleased, she thought. Warm dry weather moving into late autumn would assist the picking process and ensure the healthiest crop possible - and that was good for the wine and good for business. She found herself nodding at her musing as she pulled into the tight parking spot at the front of the Solicitor's building. Sitting in the stilled car, her heart was beating faster than she had appreciated and she felt a little short of breath. She was aware of how stressful it was speaking to a person of the law since her clients often appeared anxious and flustered at their first meeting with her. She hadn't expected to feel the same way though and smiled wryly at her body's response.

Easing herself out of the car she entered the building, its darkness was accentuated by the brightness of the sun outside and it took her eyes a while to adjust to the change. She followed the brass sign on the internal corridor wall and headed for the second floor. She opened the door and stepped into a small reception area. There was no receptionist, but a coffee machine, low-level table, and dark brown faux-leather couch adorned the dark space.

'Good morning Ms Vincenti.' Jean-Claude Canazzi stepped out of an adjacent room and addressed Lauren with the formality with which he felt comfortable. In his own surroundings, he was almost assertive.

'Good morning Mr Canazzi.' He moved to air kiss her cheek on each side then indicated with his hand to the coffee machine as he walked towards it.

'Can I get you a coffee?'

'Thank you,' she nodded. 'Espresso two sugars please.' Lauren needed the adrenaline rush and energy push after a restless night. She had not been looking forward to this meeting, and the after effects of the wake were beginning to take their toll on her mentally and emotionally. She looked as grey and tired as she felt. She was also feeling disconcerted at the underlying tension residing in her chest, that she couldn't seem to shake, and wondered if she was going down with some wretched bug. The last thing she needed was to be delayed too long getting back to London. She had a caseload building and a court appearance to make in a couple of weeks. She needed to get things wrapped up here and get back to work.

Handing her the small bone china cup and saucer, the aroma of the strong brew already started to awaken Lauren to the reason for her meeting.

'You have something for me I take it?' Her tone was flat but there was also something in her voice that meant business.

'Yes. Please.' He walked from the coffee machine through the frosted glass door, with his name written in an old-school style calligraphic black print, indicating for Lauren to follow him.

His mahogany desk and black leather director's chair were clearly features of the otherwise sparsely decorated, small room. Two black leather chairs in front of the desk, a water cooler humming in the corner, and a framed picture sat on his desk.

'Please take a seat,' he indicated to Lauren with his hand as he moved around his desk. The bridge between them reinforced the formal nature of their meeting and was clearly more comfortable for the young man. Reaching down he picked up the only item on the desk and handed Lauren the envelope with her name on it. *Angelica Lorenza Vincenti.* She recognised the writing as of her father's hand and fought hard to stop the burning in her eyes from becoming the tears that she wanted to shed.

'I will leave you to read the letter. I am truly sorry for your loss.' Jean-Claude's respectful tone raised the briefest, though somewhat forced smile from his client. 'I will be outside if there is anything you wish to discuss, unless of course you would like to take the letter home and read it? We can always arrange another meeting should you wish to discuss the contents?' he suggested, sensing that Lauren might prefer to take more time than he was able to give, given his meeting schedule for the day. 'Your father was a remarkable man, Ms Vincenti,' he added.

'Thank you, I think I will take it home if you don't mind?' Relieved at the opportunity to reflect on the contents in her own space and time, leaving the unfinished coffee on the coaster on the side of the man's desk, she rose from the chair, a trance-like state carrying her on a wave of disbelief back to her car.

*

Sitting in the swing seat, facing the eucalyptus tree - rocking gently to and fro - the haunting wind whistled across the valley, bridging the gap between this life and the next. Consumed by the rhythmic sound, the letter sitting unopened, Lauren sipped the chilled white wine as if waiting for a direct instruction from her father to open and read it. Her stomach told her she didn't feel ready to face the contents. Maybe she never would.

She had arrived back from the Solicitor's to her mother vigorously rearranging the downstairs living space. Furniture that had sat in the same place for decades was now being uprooted, disposed of, or reincarnated. Artwork that had adorned the walls was being removed, carefully wrapped, and stored. The overwhelming transformation of the place felt too soon for Lauren - the reality of death had to be faced not swept away like it had never happened. She was aware that organising and controlling activities gave one a sense of purpose, but the need to redesign the space she had called home for so long just didn't feel right.

'I've commissioned a family portrait,' Valerie had stated abruptly. 'I do hope you will sit for it?' The idea, presented as a statement rather than question, left Lauren cold. In spite of the requirement for her to *perform* in court, she hated being photographed, let alone sitting for a painting. *I'm not sure I can do that.* She just shrugged her shoulders, non-committal, not wishing to get into any conversation that would result in her inadequacies being thrown in her face. Her mother had a knack of reminding Lauren of her need to present the right image at all times. Aristocratic, Valerie was a stickler for social correctness, especially as the rules applied to 'master-servant' relationships. Family portraits were an essential feature for landed gentry and she had certainly bought that ticket. Lauren despaired. Unable to face the makeover taking place around her, as she stood in the foyer, she had needed space and left the house.

Wandering through the cellar she had grabbed a bottle of her father's favourite wine, in the hope that it might enable her to connect to his absent form. Favouring a simple clear glass over their ornate crystal collections, she had taken herself into the garden. From there she had privately toasted her father, the spirit of the tall eucalyptus tree responding directly to her, swaying in the autumn breeze. She could feel her father's presence: calming, reassuring. Looking down she sighed deeply. Picking up the envelope, carefully unsealing it, she pulled the family crest embossed paper from its sleeve. The hand that had written the words seemed disturbingly strong and confident, not weak or distressed, as she might have expected. Somehow it would have been easier to accept suicide if it had been the latter, she thought.

My Dearest Lauren,

I firstly need to ask your forgiveness for my cowardice. You may never understand the reasons for me taking my own life, though some things will become clearer over time, I am sure. I could not speak to you about my plans and for that I may reside in eternal sorrow. However, I need you to trust my judgment that this outcome was right for all concerned. As painful as I know this will feel, please know that I always loved you and, if there is a life after this, I always will.

All will become clear in my will, but I need you to head up the business Lauren. I know you have your own interests in Law and I am sure you will be able to maintain some level of involvement in your current work. Antoine is more than capable of running the day-to-day activities. He holds my passion for the vines and knows better than anyone how to take care of them - how to nurture them. However, he doesn't have your head for business, neither is he interested in such matters. He is a good man - the best. Please look after him. He is to all intents and purposes family. He also has a thirty per cent share in the business. Ownership and the majority shareholding must stay with a Vincenti - and I trust you in this matter. You are a lot like me and you are very smart. You will easily learn anything that you don't already know. I can only hope that one day you also develop a passion for the vines. They will serve you well.

Your mother will be taken care of. I set up a trust fund for her a long time ago so she will never need or want for anything. I have, however, left everything I own to you, including our family home. I know you will allow Valerie to live there, should she wish, until she dies. We have essentially lived independently for some years now, but I have always cared for her deeply. She is the mother of my daughters and for that I will always love her.

If I can give any words of wisdom they would be these... Be true to your heart Lauren and fear not the consequences. Life is too short.

All my love,
Papa

Lauren froze. Tension and heat rising through her body she stepped off the swing seat. Her eyes scanned the surroundings in all directions, as if seeking the answers, as her feet agitatedly paced up and down. She reread the letter, shaking her head in disbelief. She wanted to scream. *How could taking your own life be the answer to anything?* They had never discussed her taking any role in the business. *Why hadn't he talked to her? Why? Why? Why?* Incensed, she emptied her glass, swallowing without tasting, and instantly refilled it. Her hands were shaking violently and she looked at them like a stranger to the events unfolding. Breathe. Stop, she told herself. She looked searchingly at her father's tree, with flailing arms - still no answers. The eucalyptus rustled effortlessly with the wind, rhythmically, undisturbed by Lauren's heightened emotional state. Lauren speedily downed the second glass of wine, trying to calm herself - staring into space. With vacant composure, she refilled her glass again, walked through the lawns to sit under the tree, and allowed her eyes to feast on the valley below, at the vines that dominated the landscape in front of her across the chalky slopes and down to the river.

'They are beautiful, no?' The soft, smooth, tones in Antoine's slow steady voice gently stirred Lauren from contemplation. It was now close to dusk and she was shivering. Antoine placed the grey jacket he had been carrying around her shoulders. She felt herself breathe into the additional layer of warmth and the reassuring touch of his hands on her shoulders as he rested the jacket around her. She hadn't remembered finishing the wine, but both bottle and glass were empty and she felt more subdued - resigned even. 'You are cold, Lauren?' As the gentle man looked intently at her, for the first time Lauren became aware of something in his eyes - eyes that carried such emotion were calling to her - longing for what? He looked down the valley towards the vines, stretching his arms out indicating the vast expanse of her father's creation, and smiled knowingly. 'Beautiful.' His eyes had darkened by the time he addressed her again. 'It is very sad that he is gone.'

'Yes,' she confirmed, leaning into the warmth of his body for a few moments, as his arms embraced her. The hold was one of compassion and unified sharing of an experience - grief.

'I can show you around later this week if you would like to see your father's work?' There was pride in Antoine's voice, and without acknowledgement of his own part in the success of the Vineyard over the years. *The best,* her father had said in his letter.

'Thank you, I would like that.' She smiled warmly at the kind-hearted man before her. She had much to learn. As she held Antoine's deep blue eyes with her own, her thoughts drifted fleetingly back to Anna. The tingle low in her belly and weakness in her legs was brief, but didn't go unnoticed. Picking up the empty bottle and glass, she linked her arm through Antoine's and they meandered slowly, in step, back to the house. Surprised to feel an assured sense of comfort in the arm of this man, she allowed herself to absorb the much-needed feelings without further analysis.

*

'I need to return to London. I have work there,' Lauren said, as her mother ordered the antique mahogany drinks cabinet relocated from the living room to what had previously been the library.

'Of course you do darling. I'm not sure what possessed your father to leave the business in your hands. I mean. You know nothing about running a vineyard.' Her mother's indignant tone grated, even though there was some truth in the words she spoke. 'And you can't possibly live here with...' she hadn't finished, but her face conveyed her unarticulated thoughts. It never even occurred to Valerie to ask about Rachel - Lauren's partner of 10 years. Lauren didn't know whether to laugh at the ignorance or be angry at her mother's inability to accept her for who she was. As she watched her mother, longing for things to be different between them and knowing they never would, she knew she couldn't stay.

Valerie had sat stiffly in the Solicitor's office as the will had been read. She never so much as flinched. No one would know how Valerie Vincenti truly felt and that's how she liked to play it. Lauren hoped that the trust fund had appeased an otherwise difficult situation, but she wouldn't find out her mother's true feelings until they were behind closed doors.

The stiffness was still present in her demeanour when they entered the newly dressed living room, her mouth pinched into tight lips and her jaw sitting rigid, creating sharp edges to her features. Valerie poured herself a glass of Champagne from one of the open bottles resting in the chiller cabinet. To the external world she had taken the news admirably. To those who knew her, she was deeply wounded.

Her mother wasn't a greedy person. She was, however, complex. Flamboyant in nature, with expectations based on her status in life, she was also a very private person. To reveal her emotions would be considered an intolerable weakness. She had never known what it was like to need something and not be able to acquire it. The idea of needing something would be preposterous to her - being a place reserved for those less fortunate in life. To Valerie her position in the Vincenti family was a matter of the *right of birth*, and in that respect, she had been lucky.

'I've asked the solicitors if there's any way we can appeal. He must have been out of his mind.' Valerie grumbled. Inwardly infuriated at her exclusion from her husband's estate - mostly on principle. The five million Euro trust fund was some compensation for the sorry state of affairs, but not if she were evicted from her home. She glared at Lauren for a response. Sipping her drink, Lauren had neither the will nor the energy to engage with her mother, knowing her father's last wishes had been for Valerie to remain in the house should she wish to do so. She would always honour his wishes.

'It's your house mother,' Lauren clarified to avoid any pretence that might destroy their already fragile relationship. 'I have no intention of living here.'

Lauren had no need for the house. Although it was familiar of course, she didn't warm to the property. It held too many memories of which she would prefer not to be reminded. She had her place in London, her own income and a substantial fund already set up. Her father had certainly ensured they both had their financial independence. A flash of anger whipped, unchecked, through Lauren at the thought of her father. It was the least he could do, she supposed, although a feeling of disgust seemed to overwhelm her senses. No amount of money would ever compensate for his absence; never compensate for the fact that she had not been given a choice in the matter - she just had to deal with his *independent* decision to take his own life. *What sort of a father does that to the people they love?*

Valerie stopped fiddling with the furniture and held her daughter's eyes momentarily, grateful for the reassurance her daughter had offered. Lauren held her gaze. She sighed and her heart felt heavy as something unspoken passed between them. Lauren was her father's daughter and for Valerie therein lay the problem.

Forcing a smile, she cleared her throat. 'Thank you,' she said in a formal tone, maintaining the barrier between them, before busying herself with organising the move of the writing desk and chair, which would now sit in the new study room. Lauren nodded, overwhelmed with emptiness and a desire to feel loved by this woman - her mother - just once.

6.

Lauren looked intently at her phone and the white business card in her hand. Her finger tenderly followed the raised lettering on the card. Anna Taylor-Cartwright. The person was imprinted in her mind and body as the name was on the card. She smiled to herself as she traced each number with her index finger, playing out the pros and cons of contacting Anna in her mind. She bit the inside of her lip and stared out of her bedroom window. The sun had started to rise up from the earth, throwing out a pink flow of light across the horizon. Above the sun, the clear blue sky was presenting itself to the day. Not a cloud in sight, just a single wisp of white where an aircraft had left a short trail perched high in the sky. Lauren watched as the pink steadily disappeared and the white sun appeared in full, occupying its rightful place. Pressing the card between her thumb and finger she placed it on the table and picked up her phone. Heading towards the door, she shoved it in the back pocket of her jeans, resolved that it would be for the better to not contact Anna. Not now. Not ever. Her heart didn't agree, but she would deal with that by occupying herself fully in her work. She needed to get back to London. The determined thought persisted as she descended the staircase and followed the scent of coffee.

'Morning mother.'

Valerie sat at the dining table reading the paper as she ate the buffet breakfast that had been laid out on the table for them both. 'Morning darling,' she responded, waving her hand rather than looking up from the newspaper. Finishing the article that had consumed her, she glanced up and nodded. 'Sleep well?' she asked.

'Fine.' Lauren waved her head back and forth as she poured herself a coffee from the steaming pot and sat at the table opposite her mother.

'Hmm,' Valerie mumbled.

She had slept fitfully, but her mother didn't need to know - or care to know - the details. Rereading the letter from her father, her mind had gone into overdrive, and without resolution. She had then given her attention to Anna, which had made matters worse as her body had responded, leaving her thoroughly frustrated on every level of her being. She had paced the room, stared out of her window at the thousands of tiny lights in the night sky, and then bathed. At one point, she had even resorted to exercising in her room to relieve the tension, all with little effect. Eventually, having exhausted herself, she had drifted into sleep in the early hours. It must have been only three-hours before the rising sun had woken her.

'Are you going to the vineyard?'

'Yes,' she said, sipping at the strong, hot coffee.

Valerie stopped reading and folded the paper neatly. 'Good,' she said, rising from the chair. 'You'll have a nice day. Will I see you for supper?' she asked.

'Sure.' Lauren's eyes pressed Valerie for some form of emotional connection, but her needs did not register as her mother turned efficiently and paced out of the room.

Lauren rested her elbows on the table and continued to sip at her drink. Looking at the spread on the table, she had lost her appetite. Placing the cup down on the white linen tablecloth she rose out of the chair and strode out of the room, determined not to let her mother's lack of responsiveness affect her mood. Grabbing the car keys, she closed the front door behind her and stepped into the warm sun. It felt good, she noted, and a smile formed as she clicked the lock to the car door.

*

'Good morning.' Lauren's cheery voice was a reflection of the sunny warm day that was emerging as she stepped into the vineyard office building.

'Temperatures could hit thirty-one today,' Antoine remarked.

'Such a beautiful day,' she smiled. The short drive had given Lauren the space to think. Maybe for the first time in a long time, she had really seen the beauty of the natural landscape; rugged rocks, trees, ferns, late autumn flowers, the soft scents moving on a warm breeze - *what's not to love?* She had mused as she steered the car down the narrow winding mountainous roads.

'It is a beautiful day.' His soft tones warmed Lauren as much as the sun's rays had. She beamed at him in return. She liked Antoine. He reminded her of the drive, as if he were a part of the natural landscape. He seemed to blend in in that way - at one with it all. And he was clearly dependable, she thought. She could understand why her father trusted him.

Even though he had been working for them for twenty plus years, Lauren had had very little to do with the vineyard and their previous meetings had been quite formal. She was, after all, the daughter of the boss - and that meant keeping a respectful distance. Unpretentious, he simply went about his work as if it were the most natural thing in the world. He didn't need any instructions. In fact, she wondered if he needed anyone at all. He resonated self-sufficiency, quiet self-assurance, and she felt comfortable in his presence.

'Shall we go?' Antoine voiced excitedly. 'I think you will love the vines.'

'Right.' Lauren recoiled in a teasing manner. She didn't know how she felt about the vineyard, or the vines. It had never occurred to her to find out either. She would play along and follow her father's wishes as best she could, but secretly she was hoping Antoine would pick up the pieces. 'I'm ready,' she nodded, linking her arm through his.

As they exited the office, he began to induct her into the process of wine making, a lot of which she was familiar with, but that didn't matter. First, highlighting, broadly, the processes the grapes undertook at each stage of their evolution, before going into more detail about the grapes themselves. As he came to life, enthralling her with his knowledge - he reminded her of her own performances in court - she couldn't help but notice the sparkle shimmering through those deep blue eyes. He was in love with the vines, that much was clear, and as she became more deeply engrossed in his words - his passion - she too was beginning to feel different. Lighter. Contented. She had no desire to return to the house. Now, she was looking forward to exploring the vines... with Antoine.

Row upon row, a green carpet covered the chalky landscape. Standing like soldiers at a height a bit short of Antoine's five-feet seven-inches, the leaves clothed bunch after bunch of succulent deep-red grapes. The grapes pressed firmly together like penguins in a huddle protecting each other from the elements, full of juice, ripe for picking. Lauren marvelled at the size of the operation ahead of them. Each bunch would be hand-picked... with love, he had said. The picking process alone would take days of long hours and hard labour. But the result would be perfection in the making. The prediction was that they would reap the best harvest yet, weather permitting. The last few weeks of autumn were of paramount importance to the health of the crop, damp could lead to disease and any promise of a great harvest would be thwarted. They would pray for dry warm weather late into October. Lauren's eyes watered as she imagined her father being there to see it.

7.

Anna stepped back and assessed the canvas with a critical eye. She was almost happy, but. The ringing of her phone pulled her away, wet brush in one hand she flicked the screen with her thumb and pressed the mobile to her ear. 'Hi Rowena.' Her concentration was still fixed on the painting as she spoke.

'How's my favourite artist?'

'My mother's your favourite artist,' she corrected.

'That was then, this is now,' Rowena sniggered. 'Sunday.'

'Sunday what?' Anna asked. She was still engrossed in her thoughts and beginning to feel frustrated at her inability to see what the work needed. She was barely paying attention to the call. 'Urrgh,' she grunted out loud.

'O...k...ay,' Rowena stretched the word out in a tone implying the outburst had nothing to do with her call.

Anna stopped looking at the canvas and moved to stare at the sunset out the loft window. The instantly refreshing scene lightened her mood. 'Sorry, just trying to get the Johnstone piece right and something's missing,' she said.

'Ah. Well maybe a change of scenery will help?'

'Mmm... maybe?' Anna mulled over the idea. She had also been working long hours to get the photography project finished and truth be told, distracting herself from her thoughts of Lauren. The painting was lacking something... or maybe she was, and she couldn't work out what. The client was happy with progress and timescales weren't an issue. The last couple of weeks had taken their toll and she was feeling drained and uninspired. Maybe a change of scenery would help, she reasoned.

'So, Sunday. Can you fly out Sunday to meet with Mrs Vincenti? There are seats, I've checked,' Rowena pre-empted as she sipped her G&T following a hectic week jostling artists' egos, project scope creep and picky buyers with an inflated idea of the value of their Euro.

'Okay...'

'I love you,' Rowena interrupted excitedly. She had predicted that Anna would agree without too much pressurising.

'What time's the flight?'

'8.30.' Anna groaned. 'It's a short flight and you can enjoy the gorgeous scenery there, instead of the rain here,' Rowena chirped convincingly. The meeting's at 12.30.'

'Right,' Anna mumbled.

'Excellent. I'll email you the details then you can check in online,' Rowena said.

'Thanks.' Anna was genuinely grateful not to have to think about admin details, which generally drove her insane. It was much easier to just turn up and do what she did best. She would happily suffer Rowena's short notice than have to deal with it all herself.

Ending the call, she cleaned up and wandered down to the kitchen. Unscrewing the top of the chilled Sauvignon she poured a glass, savouring the fresh aroma and sharp taste on her tongue. She took the wine to her en-suite and ran a deep, hot bath. Sipping her wine, watching the bubbles form, taking in the lavender scent infusing the bathroom, she drifted to thoughts of her dinner date just a week earlier. Warmth spread through her body and she checked her phone - nothing. Feeling frustrated that she hadn't asked for Lauren's details, she stared longingly at the glass in her hand, rubbing her thumb up the condensation that had formed on its surface and twirling the stem in her fingers. The heaviness in her heart made its presence known as her pulse thumped slowly in her chest forcing her to breathe deeply. *Lauren.* Carefully stepping into the hot suds, she lowered herself slowly until her body was fully submerged, her deep sigh causing a light wave to travel down the tub. Lauren filled her thoughts as she endeavoured, but failed, to relax.

*

She grabbed her hand luggage and shut the door of the barn, stepping quickly into the waiting taxi. Dark and cold, Autumn moving into Winter, the crisp clear early morning chill shocked even the sleepiest early morning traveller into wakefulness. The driver took the small bag and placed it in the boot, on principle. 'Going anywhere nice?' he said, the standard line to all his customers heading for the airport - conversation for the sake of it.

'Ajaccio,' Anna replied, though her preference was to sit in silence for the journey as she allowed her eyes to adjust to the waking day.

'Nice. My cousin lived there for a bit, before moving to the mainland,' the driver revealed. 'Nice weather, great beaches, humble people,' he continued with his limited facts about the island. 'Holiday?' he pressed.

'No.' Anna's abruptness was clear indication that the chat had finished for her.

The driver turned the radio station up a fraction and continued, in silence, the smooth journey to Orly airport. It was still dark when they arrived, but the hustle and bustle of people moving into and out of the airport created a lively buzz, in which Anna could lose herself. She tipped the driver five Euros, out of guilt for her lack of interaction, thanked him, and moved through to departures. She had checked in online so it was a swift move through baggage checking. She grabbed a seat at the Café Gascon and ordered a double espresso. Adding one sugar and a dash of milk she sat and watched the world go by, glancing now and then at the screen for her departure gate. Her thoughts drifted to the woman she wanted to touch - the woman who hadn't been too far from the front of her mind the whole week. Tormented at her inability to shake off the sensual images of the dark stranger, she searched her phone for law firms in London, hoping to find a picture of Lauren somewhere.

*

She watched out of the small aircraft window at the changing scenery. The clouds cleared, blue sea merged with blue sky, differentiated only by its shade. The stunning mountainous terrain of Corsica soon presented itself. The aircraft followed the standard route through the sweeping valley, landing effortlessly on the warm dry tarmac. The mid-morning warmth and light breeze was a welcome break from the now cool, and wet, Parisian weather.

With no security check and no baggage to collect Anna exited quickly into the arrivals hall. The board with her name on it caught her eye and she walked towards the short, stocky, tanned man with a big white smile, holding it aloft. Offering her hand, she was taken aback by the soft, warm grip - expecting something far rougher given his stature. 'Hello... Ms Taylor-Cartwright?' he asked, in a soft singsong tone of voice, before stepping in to air kiss her on both cheeks.

'Yes, hello. You must be Antoine?' she asked. 'Anna. Please call me Anna,' she insisted as the man reached to take the small case from her hand.

'Anna, lovely to meet you.' He smiled as he turned and walked towards the parking machine, slotted the coins, and took the stamped ticket. Leading them to the parked Mitsubishi Outlander, Anna could feel the gentle heat softening her body. The breeze felt refreshing yet there was also something haunting in it too. There was something about this place that touched her in a way she wasn't expecting. Beyond the hustle and bustle, the car fumes and dust, her eyes widened at the natural beauty of the place. A calm expanse of sea bordered mountain ranges on both sides of the valley in which the air landing strip blended with its natural surround; lush green foliage merged effortlessly with the parched grey-white earth and golden sands. *Beautiful.*

The hour and forty-minute journey from Ajaccio to the Sartène had taken Anna's breath away. Her eyes feasted on the oak, pine, and broadleaf deciduous trees lining the narrow winding roads, sweeping up from the valley floor as they climbed, descended and climbed again. The drive up from the Rizzanese through row upon row of vines, like soldiers in battle formation, had elicited excitement from Antoine as he explained a little of the history of the Vincenti vineyard. She could sense the pride and passion in his voice, and something else she noted but couldn't name.

Stopping in front of the Vincenti family home, he stepped out of the car and opened the door for Anna. 'Welcome,' he beamed, pointing towards the house. Taking her bag, he directed her through the front door. 'Would you like to freshen up? Madame Valerie will be in the living room shortly.'

'Sure, thank you,' she nodded, as her eyes scanned the front of the large traditional country home with its white shutters obscuring the sun from invading the house.

She followed Antoine into the large foyer reception with central stairs sweeping in both directions at its apex. The dark wood feature with ornately carved balustrades probably dated back to the original build. Anna sucked in the air through pursed lips, as she admired the original works of art adorning the walls, and the matching Napoleon sculptures standing either side of the stairs.

Antoine led her to an en-suite bedroom on the first-floor. The bathroom comprised a large walk in shower, square bath, double-sink and toilet. The pristine white, modern, suite was quite unexpected in the otherwise traditionally decorated house. The suite was complimented by a blue accent wall and abstract painting - drawing on shades of blue, green and grey - resembling a stormy sea at night. Together it worked, she thought.

'When you are ready Madame will be in the living room downstairs, at the end on the right.' He indicated with his hand as he spoke. 'There is no rush.'

'Thank you,' she smiled graciously, genuinely warmed by his friendly welcome and the recognition that having spent half a day travelling she would feel more comfortable after freshening up and changing her clothes.

The hot spray felt good, the soapy lather cleansing and the large white, Egyptian cotton, towels comforting. She picked up the lavender scent as she held the warm, soft, cloth against her face for a few moments. Already she felt more relaxed than she had in a while. Looking at herself in the mirror, she noticed the dark rings, for the first time. Burning the candle at both ends was now showing in her face. Breathing deeply, she vowed to get a grip of her life and take some time out. *Perhaps she would take a holiday whilst she was here?*

8

Casually dressed in faded jeans, white open neck shirt and a burgundy-red stylish waistcoat, Anna stepped into the long corridor. The simple off-white painted upper walls highlighted the pictures that were set along the length of the corridor. Family portraits going back several generations seemed to peer at each passer by - a little freaky - overseers of their heritage. It was like a museum, she smiled inwardly.

'Come in.' The sharp tone alerted her senses and she felt herself jump slightly. She reached for the handle on the dark, heavy, wooden door, and rose up to her full height of five-feet, seven-inches.

Entering with a confidence she didn't feel; her stride was stopped instantly at the sight of the woman about to greet her. She faltered and her breath caught in her throat.

'Welcome Anna.' The dark brown eyes greeted her but the smile seemed distant, though softened within seconds. 'I'm Valerie Vincenti,' the woman said, as she held out her hands to clasp Anna's shoulders for a traditional French greeting. The hauntingly familiar dark brown eyes, brown wavy hair - longer than Lauren's she noted - struck her instantly. The resemblance was remarkable and unexpected. Anna struggled for the breath caught in her dry throat and froze, unable to return the greeting with any conviction. She was shaking. 'Are you alright darling?' The dark eyes held gentle concern as they looked at her paling face. 'You look like you've seen a ghost,' Valerie laughed haughtily, not looking for a particular response. 'Please do come through. I hope you had a comfortable trip. I'm very excited that you could come. You were highly recommended,' she remarked, pointing at the large lounge chairs for Anna to sit. 'Can I get you a drink? I'm having Champagne darling. We have gin, whiskey, vodka, wine

- what will you take?' Valerie continued to ramble as she poured the fizzy drink for herself.

Regaining her composure, and staring at the remarkable resemblance of this stranger to the woman she had met only a few weeks ago, Anna sat tentatively. 'Thank you, Champagne please.' She was still staring. Taking the drink offered, she noted the slender hands and long fingers, and shivered.

'I'm so excited you agreed to meet. I'm sure your agent has briefed you, but I think it's important for us to connect if we're going to be working together for a while, don't you?' Valerie asked, almost rhetorically.

'Yes, of course.' Anna mumbled as she took a sip and the bubbles lightly tickled her nostrils.

'I also think it's important you get a feel for us as a family, our home, our work. I want the portrait to reveal the depth of our relationship and love for each other. And since my husband has sadly passed away...' she drifted off, her eyes moving from Anna out to the bay window and the gardens beyond.

'Yes, I agree,' Anna said, filling the short space as the older woman composed herself, her grief still apparent in her expression, even though it appeared she was working hard not to show it. 'It will be a pleasure to get to know your family and this beautiful place a little better.'

Valerie studied the younger woman for a moment. She liked her. Vulnerable, compassionate, perceptive, creative... and professional, she nodded at her assessment. She already knew she would enjoy working with her. Something about Anna felt very agreeable. She was easy to be around - a little subdued initially, but that just endeared her even more. 'I have a lot of photographs of my husband that I would like you to look through at your leisure. Then perhaps we can discuss the details of the work, once you've gathered your thoughts of course?'

'Yes, of course,' Anna caught a glint in the woman's eyes as she spoke with excitement about the project. Clearly, getting the right image of her husband was a key and everything else would fit around that, she figured.

'Now, how about a spot of lunch? You must be starved.' Valerie stated, slotting her arm through Anna's like an old friend and guiding her through a door into the classic dining room. Leaving her at the dining table, Champagne in hand, she stepped into the adjoining kitchen.

Anna observed, five places were set, yet the table could seat twenty comfortably. The white linen tablecloth and ornate crystal glasses were neatly presented on the solid oak surface. Silver cutlery indicated that several courses would be served. The white wine sat chilling in the ice bucket at the head of the table and an open bottle of red wine rested on the sideboard.

Anna turned as she heard voices outside the room getting louder. The door from the main corridor opened and Antoine entered the room, his soft smile engaging the artist in an instant. As he moved in to air-kiss her on each cheek, Anna's breath caught and she froze. Over his shoulder two women strolled lazily into the room. Antoine released her from his embrace, still holding her shoulders, and saw the instant exchange in her eyes. Turning to see the object of interest, Lauren looked ghostlike. Sharp heat rose instantly and uncontrollably through Anna, her legs began to shake and her heart raced. She struggled to think, or form any words, as her cheeks reddened. Lauren too, looked as if she were struggling to compose herself.

Time stood still as the two women locked eyes and stared intently at each other, momentarily oblivious to the other people in the room.

Antoine nodded towards Lauren. 'Meet Anna, our artist,' he said winking, knowing full well the two women had met before - even if in a previous lifetime.

'Hello again.' Lauren's calm confidence restored, she made no secret of the fact that they already knew each other.

The second woman, Anna noticed, was stunning. Her long, straight, dark hair and light blue piercing eyes seemed to undress her as she looked from Anna to Lauren with a hint of amusement. 'You two know each other I take it?' The woman looked questioningly towards Lauren as she stepped in to shake hands with Anna. 'Hi Anna, I'm Rachel, Lauren's partner. Lovely to meet you,' she said, clearly staking her claim.

Anna felt the sinking pain, heavy in her gut, as she glanced towards Lauren, who was already walking towards the side-cabinet and reaching for the bottle of red wine.

'Yes, we met a few weeks ago,' Anna confirmed quietly, as she took Rachel's firm hand. Feeling struck by a whirlwind, she took in the stunning woman's gaze and smiled, captivated by her dominating presence and sharp eyes. 'I understand you're in politics?' she said, steadying herself.

'Wow, you obviously know something about me and I know nothing about you. But, that's not unusual. Lauren hardly tells me anything,' Rachel remarked pointedly, as she raised her eyebrows whilst catching Lauren's eyes. Lauren just glared in response.

'Shall we sit?' Valerie asked, returning from the kitchen waving her arms towards the table. 'Anna, please sit here.' She pointed to the chair on the right of the head of the table. 'Antoine here - opposite Anna - and you two ladies can take your pick.'

Lauren placed the red wine in the centre of the table and took the seat next to Anna, watched ruefully by Rachel. 'So, did I hear that you already know my daughter?' Valerie had overheard the conversation as she entered the room. 'What a coincidence! How did you meet?'

'It's a long story mother,' Lauren interjected, to protect Anna from the potential inquisition about to ensue, and conscious that she might not want to talk about her personal life with a room of strangers.

'I look forward to hearing about that one later, eh Lauren?' Rachel gibed, with more than a hint of cynicism in her voice. She had clearly picked up on something unspoken between her wife and Anna and she wasn't going to let it drop that easily.

'Wine?' Lauren offered, holding up the chilled white wine in anticipation.

'Thank you,' Anna nodded approvingly, feeling a little overawed. Lauren filled her glass before handing the bottle to Valerie. She picked up the red wine, pouring Antoine and Rachel a glass before filling her own. Antoine cleared his throat, invading the near painful silence.

'Well, Anna will be spending some time getting to know our family before she embarks on a portrait I have commissioned,' Valerie stated in a commanding tone as she poured her wine, looking intently at Antoine and her daughter and scanning Rachel fleetingly. The blatant disregard for her daughter's partner didn't go unnoticed by Anna. 'If you could all oblige Anna, that would be appreciated.'

'Of course we will mother.' Lauren spoke for them all, smiling warmly as her eyes met Anna's. 'I'll give Anna the guided tour after lunch.'

Anna had to work hard not to blush again. She reached for her glass and sipped at the deliciously chilled wine, instantly taken back to that fateful Friday night. 'Thank you.' She smiled, trying not to make eye contact for fear that Rachel could read her mind and aware that her body was giving her deepest desires away too easily.

*

Rachel had quickly turned the conversation onto the topic of British politics, for which Anna had been grateful. Antoine and Valerie entered into a lively discussion about French governmental issues, the handling of the recent terrorist atrocities, immigration - and the legalising of gay marriage in France, to which Valerie was clearly opposed. Lunch had turned into late afternoon, as wine had been followed by Cognac and coffee. Rachel had made an impromptu visit to Corsica, taking advantage of a short break in her busy schedule, before attending a European Conference in Paris. It had also enabled her to give her condolences in person, having been unable to make the funeral. She would be leaving early in the morning, for which Anna felt instantly relieved. As Anna stood from the table she felt a little light-headed and more than a little tipsy.

Rachel cornered Valerie, both women now with a large glass of Cognac in hand, and retired to the living room, still debating the ethics of spin in political campaigning and male dominance in politics. At least they agreed on something. Antoine smiled at the two remaining women and excused himself with work he needed to catch up on before the week began in earnest.

'Shall we start the tour? I don't know about you, but I could do with some fresh air,' Lauren said. The slightly gravelly voice, together with the impact of alcohol on her nervous system, sent a tingle down Anna's spine.

'I'm not sure how long I'll last,' she said, stifling a giggle. 'I feel quite drunk. Are lunches always this...'

'Boozy?'

'Yes.'

'Not always, but definitely on special occasions,' Lauren confirmed. Her honest, broad smile caused Anna to throb with longing as she stared at the mouth she desperately wanted to kiss. 'Come. Let's wander and I'll show you the grounds. See how you feel...' she indicated to Anna to follow her as she led the way into the gardens.

'That's an amazing tree.' Anna pointed towards the tall, lone, eucalyptus tree silhouetted against the low setting sun.

'Yes it is.' Anna noticed Lauren's tone had shifted to melancholic and her eyes searched the horizon.

'I'm really sorry about your father,' she said, softly.

It was the first time Anna had felt it appropriate to say anything to the woman who had patiently sat listening to her talk through her mum's situation only weeks earlier. She felt genuinely upset and distressed for the woman she realised she had fallen hopelessly in love with. Lauren's eyes sparkled with wet, as tears of remembrance pushed to the surface.

'Hey,' Anna moved towards her. Wanting to take the pain away, she gently pulled her into a light embrace. Lauren accepted the warmth of the hug, melting into Anna's arms, which affected her more deeply than she could have anticipated. She absorbed the genuine concern and affection that was being lavished on her. She felt safe. Home.

'Come.' Lauren said, still husky from the sudden rise in emotion. Reluctantly pulling back from the embrace, she linked arms with Anna. They walked in comfortable silence toward the tall tree, stared out over the valley and took in the last remnants of light. The soft strength of their interconnecting arms steadied both women, silently affirming their deeper relationship to each other.

Slowly releasing each other, Anna immediately felt the absence at a non-physical level. She watched Lauren as she surveyed her family's resting place. *You're beautiful.*

'You're staring,' the husky voice, subtly different from a few moments earlier, turned to face her with eyes that were saying something she hadn't yet spoken in words. Lauren struggled to breathe as she feasted on the dark steel-blue eyes that exposed her where she stood. Her body weakened with lust whilst her mind pricked her conscience. Her partner was currently debating with her mother and here she was lusting - no, falling in love - with another woman. She corrected her thoughts. Truth was, she liked Anna staring at her - a lot - and she liked staring at Anna. 'You're beautiful.' The words had escaped, over-riding her conscience. The smile - open and revealing - froze Anna's gaze. Lauren looked away and into the darkening sky, at nothing in particular, and a sudden burst of warmth filled her body.

'I was thinking the same thing,' Anna said, her slightly drunk state loosening her inhibitions. She was feeling brave - more than. She was drawn to Lauren in a way that she never had been with any other woman, and in this moment unsure if she could refrain from doing what she had wanted to do from the moment they parted, outside her hotel in London. 'I want to kiss you,' she said, looking longingly at Lauren as the truth tumbled seductively from her lips. 'But I can't. You're married and your partner is talking to your mother right now. It's a little surreal.' As Anna brought her mind back to the reality of their situation, looking back up towards the house, she felt anxious, embarrassed, and very aroused. 'I'm sorry... I think I've had a little too much to drink.' She gave a smile that raised a barrier to the intimacy they had just shared. She couldn't act on her desires. Not now, not ever.

'Don't be sorry. I've wanted to kiss you since you spilt your drink,' Lauren revealed as she tenderly pressed Anna's hand briefly, with her own warm fingers. Anna bit down on her lips. Working hard to prevent her legs from buckling beneath her, a surge of energy hit her low in her womb.

'Urrhh...' she failed to stifle the guttural sound whilst wanting to take Lauren... now, against the tree. Anna backed away suddenly, hoping the space would ease the desire she was struggling to contain. It didn't.

'Come. I need to show you around this place. My mother will test you later you know,' Lauren said, lightened the mood.

Will you stop telling me to come? It's really not helping me take my mind, and body, off wanting to fuck you here and now. Oh my God, I'm in trouble. Anna cleared her throat to banish the invasive thoughts from her mind. 'Right... coming.' She stammered, tilting her head at her own words, as she followed Lauren, preserving a short physical distance between them.

9

'I can't do this?' Anna blurted to her agent as she regarded the verdant valley that dominated the area. Dressed in a fine white shirt and fitted jeans, she savoured the light breeze that rustled the fading green leaves of the eucalyptus under which she stood, mobile in hand. She was thankful for the mild temperature. It would make the winter feel shorter when she got back to Paris. It was ten degrees cooler there, and also wet, according to Rowena who had complained bitterly and professed her jealousy at Anna's fate.

'Why? What's happened? Is Lisa...'

'Mum's fine,' Anna interrupted her. 'It's hard to explain.'

'Try me,' Rowena said with a hint of sternness, needing answers. It was most unlike her protégé to have issues with a project, especially once she had committed to doing it. Something must have happened, and she needed to know what that something was.

Breathing deeply and knowing she wouldn't get away with a flippant response, she brought Rowena up to date - recounting her original meeting with Lauren, the mutual declarations of the previous evening and Rachel. Lauren's partner had left for Paris on the early flight out of Ajaccio and Lauren had taken her to the airport. She was yet to return.

Anna had wandered around the grounds alone, soaking up the atmosphere in daylight, which was like nothing she had ever experienced before. A spiritual feeling seemed to embrace the place. There was a softness and warmth that transcended the temperate climate, yielding a deep sense of contentment and peace. It was quite bizarre. Why someone would take their own life was beyond her too, but that was what Lauren's father had done and she could see... feel... the pain in her friend as if it were her own. How she longed to take that pain away, hold the woman close, and protect her from the outside world.

'How can I stay? I don't trust myself,' Anna confessed.

'It's not just about you though, is it? It's not like you can force her into doing something she doesn't want to do.' Rowena countered.

'I know, but what about Rachel? They're married for Christ sake.' Anna paced heavily up and down the garden in exasperation, rubbing her fingers firmly across her forehead.

'I know. It's a tough one, but she's not really your problem either. That's for Lauren to sort out,' Rowena said, reassuringly supportive of her surrogate daughter. 'And it sounds as if... Lauren is more into you than she is her wife?'

'Yes, but...'

'There are no buts. Just the *butt* you need to get back to work. Worst case, you can harness this energy to create spectacular art and another exceptionally satisfied customer.' Rowena's pragmatic approach, trying to focus Anna to project her lust filled feelings onto the canvas, caused Anna to smile wryly.

'Funny,' she sighed as she smiled. 'I can probably do that,' she said, unsure whether she believed herself or not. Envisaging Lauren sitting for her - translating her beauty to the canvas - she could do that... couldn't she? She could focus on creating that transformation, rather than being distracted by the impact the exquisite woman had on her physically.

'You're going to wear that patch of grass out,' the husky voice said causing Anna to jump out of her skin.

'Got to go. I'll chat later okay?' Anna clicked her phone off abruptly and she turned to face the penetrating gaze of Lauren. Feeling more than a little ungrounded by her presence, she froze.

'Sorry, I interrupted you. I didn't realise you were on the phone,' Lauren said sincerely, raising her hands as if to back off.

'No. It's okay. It was my agent and we were finished anyway... You look... lovely.' Anna faltered as she spoke softly, unable to take her eyes off the deep brown gaze and wavy dark brown hair that perfectly framed Lauren's tanned face. High cheekbones and a narrow chin complemented her fit, athletic frame. *Gorgeous.* Heat flushed through her body, colouring her own cheeks as she pocketed her phone. Linking her fingers together at the front of her body, she twitched and fidgeted. Lauren smiled encouragingly as she surveyed the pleasant discomfort her presence had caused.

'I make you uncomfortable?' she questioned, with a wry smile.

'Only in a good way.' Anna's unabashed response surprised herself. 'If I don't find something to do with my hands, I won't be held responsible for them,' she smiled seductively, enjoying their flirtatious interaction. Perhaps this was the way she could handle the situation. *If they were openly flirtatious they wouldn't need to act on their feelings?* It was a start. Flirting with Lauren felt so good.

'I need to show you the vineyard,' Lauren said more seriously, drawing Anna's concentration back to the business at hand. 'Mother is at some social event in Ajaccio today so she won't be back until this evening,' Lauren confirmed. 'So, if you're good to go?' she motioned towards the house. 'I'm still learning the ropes, so Antoine will give you a guided tour and explain some of the history. I'll take you to lunch. To be honest with you, I haven't been involved in my father's business... until now of course. I'm not sure what will happen moving forward. I've still got my day job to do, so I'll be back to London as soon as I can.' Lauren reeled off the words at a pace. Anna's heart sunk - the forthcoming absence - she hadn't factored in that she might miss Lauren if she weren't around. But she would, more than she cared to admit.

'Are you planning to sit for the portrait?' Anna asked hesitantly. Lauren had given the impression that she wasn't keen on sitting let alone having any form of representation of herself adorning the walls of their family home. 'Or will I need to work from a photograph of you too?' she pushed, leaving no room for doubt that Anna intended to ensure Lauren was transformed onto the canvas along with her parents.

'Maybe?' Lauren smiled with hesitation, answering neither question. There it was again, that emotion. Anna had seen a flickering of it several times before. *Whatever it is it runs deep*. Catching Anna lost in reflective thought, Lauren laughed softly. 'Of course I'll sit for you.' There, she had committed herself. Anna beamed as their eyes locked. 'Naked of course,' Lauren teased mercilessly, as she opened the car door for Anna. Heat exploded through her and there was no stopping the strong blush that burst onto her face. Lauren laughed huskily as she took the driver's seat. 'I'm looking forward to it already,' she winked cheekily as she turned the engine over. She too was burning.

*

'So, what do you think?' Lauren questioned as Antoine and Anna sauntered into the office and gentle warm air filtered through the doorway into the air-conditioned room.

Antoine smiled, 'I think she'll do great,' he chirped.

'Ha ha.' Lauren countered.

'It's beautiful,' Anna said. Having been Fiorelli'd for the morning she looked beautiful. Angelic. Touched by the vines. It happened, Lauren reflected as she fixed her eyes on the subtle shift in the sexy fair-haired woman's aura. *Fuck, if she wasn't hot enough before. Jesus, she is enchanting.* The pulsing

64

sensation in Lauren's black jeans thrust her into standing and she moved quickly to the water cooler to distract herself for a brief moment.

'It is something special,' she said as she sipped the cool water. It wasn't having much of a cooling effect, but it did allow her to regain control of her broken voice.

Antoine looked from one woman to the other and smiled. 'Right, I'll be back after lunch. See you both then?'

'Sure,' Lauren nodded in affirmation as Anna gave the man an honest, full-on, hug.

'Thank you.' Her genuine appreciation touched Lauren, causing her to sip furiously at the cold water and hop subtly from foot to foot. Anna was positively glowing.

As Antoine turned and made his exit, Lauren offered her a glass of water. Smiling seductively, 'Hot?' she said, nearly hoarse.

'Very,' Anna teased, brushing her fingers against the hand holding the glass before taking it into her own hand. She sipped the cool water. Eyes locked on Lauren's, lips teasing the fluid gently. Lauren gulped, grabbed the car keys and stepped out the door, suddenly in a rush - the image of Anna's lips pressed against her own doing nothing for her sense of self-control. *How the fuck can I sit in front of this woman without jumping her bones - let alone for the length of time it will take her to paint?*

*

'How's your mum doing?' Lauren asked as they were shown to a wooden table on the terrace of the bergerie, with spectacular views overlooking the valley and down to the sea.

'She's fine. She doesn't fuss about these things. Just gets on with life, and her work. She's amazing,' Anna reflected.

'She sounds it. You clearly love her,' Lauren was enamoured by the emotion Anna showed when talking about her mum. So different from her relationship with her own mother, which was stiff, formal, and with an undercurrent of *never good enough* that seemed to overshadow any love and affection that might exist between them. She took the offered menu, with a weak smile, the sadness she felt towards her relationship with her mother apparent in her sudden withdrawal.

'Your mother is quite funny,' Anna said, as she pondered the options.

'Funny? That's not how I would describe her. Detached, aloof, bigoted are terms that come to mind... but not funny,' Lauren said in seriousness, her eyes remaining firmly on the menu in her hand.

'Yes, I know she comes across that way, but it's all a front you know. She's old school. Traditional,' Anna mused, 'Matriarchal'. The description caused a raise in the eyebrows of her companion as she flicked between Anna's face and her menu. 'But deep down.' Anna quizzed.

'Seriously?' Lauren looked up and caught the smiling blue eyes that were reaching into her soul across the short space between them. She couldn't prevent the love that filled her in that moment from radiating out.

'Yes seriously.' Anna responded with emphasis. 'What do you recommend?' she said changing the subject.

Thankful for the shift away from the conversation about her mother - and more particularly about her failed relationship with her mother, Lauren gave due attention to the menu. 'You can't go wrong with the brochettes - they're cooked on a wood fire here, and the daily special tarte is also good - aubergine, tomatoes and the local cheese.'

'Sounds perfect,' Anna said, caught by the sight of Lauren biting into her bottom lip as she pondered the options.

Shivering slightly, she turned her attention to the view. 'Spectacular,' she whispered, as if talking to herself.

'You are,' Lauren responded, her eyes darkening as the object of her *spectacular* looked directly at her. The silence between them spoke a language they both understood loud and clear.

'Would you like to order, ladies?' the waiter interjected, pad and pencil in hand.

Lauren placed their order without taking her eyes off Anna. Finishing the order with a bottle of the house rose, she turned briefly to the tall, tanned man, handed over the menu and thanked him with a smile. 'Are you cold?' Lauren said with an edge of concern, given the temperature was close to thirty degrees, recalling the shiver a moment earlier.

'No. I'm definitely not cold.' Anna breathed deeply and fidgeted in her seat. She knew she couldn't sustain the distance between them, with the intensity of longing so clearly fusing them together at every interaction. She would explode. Perhaps talking about it would help, she rationalised. 'I'm sorry,' she began quietly, 'I just find you so god damned attractive. I can't take my eyes off you and I want to make love to you - and I know it's not going to happen. I think I would be better off leaving. You're with Rachel and I don't want to get in the way of that,' Anna rattled off her thoughts in quick time.

'Hey, slow down,' Lauren said softly, reaching to take Anna's hand. 'If it helps I feel the same way as you. I've wanted to make love to you since I walked into the dining room on Sunday. I want to hold you every time I see you... And those lips are so fucking kissable. It's killing me.' Lauren confessed with a sardonic laugh. 'I need to tell you about Rachel and me.'

'So, tell me?' She figured, if she knew how much Lauren loved Rachel and how good they were together perhaps it would be easier to maintain a distance and be professional about her work there. Otherwise, she might need to turn down the job and leave. Perhaps that would be the best option anyway. She could speak with Rowena and let Valerie know her decision to leave in the morning. Then she could return to her barn and work, and leave the two women in peace. Thoughts spiralling, Anna had missed what Lauren was saying. 'Sorry, I just missed what you said completely,' she confessed.

'I'm not in love with Rachel,' Lauren repeated. 'We met twelve-years ago. We… I thought we were in love and I have no doubt she loves me in some way. But we are not in love. At least, I'm not.' Lauren sat back in her seat staring out at the vast expanse as she spoke - matter of fact and rational in tone. 'She was just getting serious about her political career and we met at a private function. High powered people of industry and government making deals over champagne and canapés. Cutting a long story short, we got together, got married, and the connection with me has been good for her career ever since - out-lesbian, committed, lawyer-wife - but as for a relationship? I guess at best I would describe it as formal, detached, but convenient.' The loneliness in Lauren's voice froze her in space and time, wrenching at Anna's heart. She leaned in and squeezed the lifeless, limp hand. The warmth of the touch started a glow in Lauren and she tensed under the tender caressing fingers - raising her from the depths of her reflection.

'I'm so sorry,' Anna said, battling with feelings of guilt and sorrow, and the cocktail of lust and love upon which she really wanted to act. 'I shouldn't have pressed you.'

Pulling herself out of the trance, Lauren sat taller and smiled in earnest, but a distance remained and a barrier had been raised. 'No. It's fine. I have known for some time that Rachel and I aren't working. I just haven't had the need to do anything about it.' But things were far from fine. Lauren smiled, but her eyes didn't.

10.

'We need to talk.' Lauren's decisive tone grated.

'Hi lover, how are you?' Rachel mocked.

'Sorry, I didn't mean to be abrupt,' Lauren backed down instantly. Rachel had a habit of achieving that with her. She was the only person Lauren had come across, other than her mother, who made her feel inferior and unworthy. She hated herself for how she reacted around her wife, how she conceded when she should defend herself. It irked her that she felt weak, in a way that she never did in court defending her clients. She tried to breathe but the tightness in her throat choked her.

'What do we need to talk about?' Rachel said with a disinterested huff, taking control of the conversation.

'Us?'

'What about us?' Rachel's ears pricked up and her tone shifted to one of vague amusement, bordering on defensiveness.

'It's not working. Our relationship. We're not working,' Lauren reiterated, her eyes searching the ceiling as she held the phone tentatively to her ear, bracing herself for the response, tears pressing her eyes, her heart thumping through her chest.

'What do you mean, it's not working?' Rachel seemed genuinely perplexed. 'Are you serious? You really want to have this conversation over the fucking phone?' she demanded, anger rising sharply in her tone.

'No, not particularly,' Lauren almost whimpered. 'But given I have no idea when we'll see each other next it's something we need to address.'

'Since when? What's the rush all of a sudden? We're fine. We've been fine, until now, apparently,' Rachel questioned, searching for the cause of the sudden change of heart in her wife. Although she was quite adept at handling curveballs in her line of work, she was always well scripted for them, with a line of responses to handle all potential challenges. This was different.

As she processed Lauren's sudden change in attitude, the energy between her and the artist at dinner, the fact that they had already met. 'It's her, isn't it?' Not waiting for confirmation, 'Oh my god. I should have seen that one coming. You cannot be fucking serious. Have you slept with her?' Rachel accused rather than questioned, as she paced her room with greater intent. 'I can't have this conversation now. I have an event I need to attend in half-an-hour. I'll speak to you tomorrow.' The decisive words were immediately followed by the ringing tone at Lauren's ear.

Fuck, that wasn't what I expected. Tears burst through the intense brown eyes - frustration, sadness and despair driving the flow, as Lauren slumped onto her bed and stared out the window, at nothing.

*

'Good evening darling.' Valerie greeted Lauren with an uncharacteristic smile as she entered the living room for their customary pre-dinner drinks. 'Kir Royale?' she offered, indicating the Champagne bottle in her hand before she caught sight of Lauren. 'You look ghastly. Are you going down with something?' Valerie observed as she poured the drink.

'Thanks,' Lauren responded, taking the drink from her mother, feeling depressed from the earlier telephone call and her subsequent musing. She didn't know whether to feel pleased at the fact that she had addressed their relationship issue or concerned that Rachel didn't even realise they had a problem. She had misjudged her wife's response completely and then, after the call, gone on to reflect on the reality of her situation - it wasn't pretty. Had she really slept through the last ten-years? She had of course been party to their bland arrangement, but to what end? Had she been seduced by the idea of the trophy, or the woman herself? Did she have such low expectations of relationships? She had never felt anything for Rachel as she did for Anna. She had never felt a real connection with her, just an arrangement - a contract. Fun had turned to formality quickly, their lives dictated by events, meeting schedules, long hours and haughty conversations. Had her relationship really been as flat as she was now feeling? 'How was your day?' Lauren asked, in an attempt to direct the attention to her mother's favourite subject.

'Fabulous darling. Utterly fabulous,' Valerie's animation took Lauren by complete surprise. Even though she was still sporting black attire most of the time, her mood was certainly far from morose. She even had a sparkle in her eyes that Lauren hadn't noticed before. 'How about you?' Valerie asked.

'I'm getting divorced,' Lauren spoke the words as if to cement her thoughts. Even though she hadn't expressly asked for a divorce, she knew it was only a matter of time and process. She couldn't back down now.

'Oh... I see,' her mother's unemotional, clipped, response and lack of desire for any further detail, or expansion of her feelings, summed up, in Lauren's mind, her mother's thoughts about her marriage. Valerie had never really accepted her daughter's sexuality, hoping it was just a phase, openly stating that she didn't think it right for two women to get married. Her Catholic conditioning wouldn't allow her to think any differently, even if she wanted to. Christ, she still introduced her wife of ten-years as a *friend*. What had Anna said? Old school. Traditional. Matriarchal. Lauren looked towards her mother as she fixed herself another Kir Royale. Yes, she was traditional, fixed in her ways. But, she was also looking older in spite of her newly found liveliness, and it dawned on Lauren that they had never really talked - daughter to mother - adult to adult. She would have liked that. She smiled weakly as her mother looked up and walked towards her, drink in hand.

'Anna,' Valerie said, beaming, ignoring Lauren, with a genuinely delighted smile as the artist entered the room. Valerie re-directed her walk to take Anna by the arm and led her to the bar. 'What can I get you?'

Watching her mother with Anna, she couldn't help but notice how different she was with her compared to Rachel. She wondered if her mother would be as openly pleasant and engaging if she knew Anna and she were in a relationship. After all, that's what she wanted and it seemed Anna wanted that too.

'Evening Anna,' Lauren spoke softly, weary from the emotional roller coaster she felt she had been riding - for how long she couldn't say, but the impact of the last few weeks hit her like a train. The room began to spin and the voices slurred, merging into one, as the ringing in her ears escalated. She thought she had found a ledge for her drink and a seat, but the smashing of glass was the last thing she heard before she blacked out and collapsed to the floor.

Both women screeched instantly the shattering glass and heavy thud hit their ears. Scared eyes appraised the scene in an instant as they both bolted to Lauren's side. Blood was seeping from her head and her eyes were blinking as if waking from deep sleep.

'Oh my god, darling, what happened?' Valerie asked, brushing the wavy hair back from the sweating pale face and glazed eyes staring up at her.

'Lauren.' Anna's voice trembled in panic and tears hit the back of her eyes as she tried to get close, but withheld the real touch that she wanted to express. Anna's eyes searched

Lauren intently, checking for any other obvious injuries. She began to apply all the first aid she knew, even though it might not be needed. 'Speak to me Lauren. Can you hear me?' she said in the firmest voice she could muster. Lauren tried to lift herself off the floor and groaned as she moved.

'Lie still sweetheart.' Valerie's soft voice was of little comfort to Lauren's ears.

Anna moved her hands down the prone body, as she remembered from her certification course many years ago, squeezing section-by-section, hoping not to find pain. *This wasn't how I imagined our first touch to be.* Lauren smiled mischievously at the soft touch, a moan escaping as Anna checked the top of her thighs. 'Did it hurt?' she asked, full of concern.

'Mmm. Not exactly,' Lauren smirked and opened one eye as the sensation raced through her body. A wry smile appeared as the dark brown eye locked onto Anna's. 'Ouch!' Lauren winced as Anna pressed a sore point, pursing her lips with mock disdain. As she winced she felt the throbbing pain in her head and reached for the spot. 'Fuck!' she complained, now fully aware of the real pain.

'You have a cut on your head. I don't think there are any other injuries, though you'll have bruises in other places,' Anna said, confirming her diagnosis with a relieved grin. 'Do you know what happened?'

'I must have fainted.'

'I'm calling the Doctor immediately. You need to get checked out,' Valerie said purposefully.

'I'll be fine.'

'No. I agree with Valerie,' Anna nodded in affirmation. 'You look dreadful and that cut needs properly taking care of. You might need stitches?'

'I'll go to the walk-in clinic then.'

'Darling. A Vincenti does not go to a walk-in clinic. And

you don't look well enough to get in a car. I will call Henri now,' Valerie ordered, marching out of the room as she spoke.

Anna reached out and gently stroked Lauren's face. Avoiding the cut on the side of her head, she eased her fingers through the loose wavy locks, cupping her cheek and running her thumb delicately over the pale, dry lips. Watching her own movements, lavishing in the response her fingers elicited in Lauren, she hadn't noticed Lauren's eyes shift from their dark brown to near black. The look made her shiver. Her hands were shaking and her body followed, as tears rolled uncontrollably down her face. 'You scared me,' she whispered.

Lauren reached up and held the wet cheeks. Eyes that Anna didn't think could get any darker just did. Bewitched, she was caught in the energy that passed between them, and she knew there was no escape. The connection she felt could not be explained and she had never felt this way about anyone, ever. It scared her. Lauren scared her. No, losing Lauren scared her more than anything, and she didn't like that feeling.

'I'm sorry,' Lauren declared quietly, as she softly wiped at rogue tears that refused to be abated.

'Sshhh. You need to rest.' Anna tried to deflect the chat unable to take in the depth of emotion she was feeling.

'Bollocks. I know what I need,' Lauren's bravery was swiftly thwarted as she tried to move. 'Shit, that hurts,' she whined. Anna leapt to support the movement as Lauren fell back to the floor, taking Anna with her.

'Henri is on his way,' the authoritative voice declared as Valerie strutted back into the room, pausing momentarily to take in the scene.

Pulling herself quickly off Lauren, Anna apologised, 'Sorry, I was just... helping.'

Valerie waved a dismissive hand as she walked towards the injured party. 'How are you feeling darling? Where does it hurt?' Not waiting for a response, but looking Lauren up and down, she continued. 'Shall we get you onto the couch? It will be more comfortable there. Henri will be here in about fifteen-minutes. Can I get you a drink? Isn't Cognac supposed to be the thing?' The words came tumbling faster than Lauren could respond, but the concern didn't go unnoticed and she smiled lovingly at her mother.

'It's okay, mother. Comfort would be good, but no Cognac thanks.'

'I'll have the Cognac then,' her mother said, as she strode to the bar. 'Anna?'

'I'm fine thank you.' Anna smiled warmly towards Lauren, joining her in her temporary sobriety. She reached down to provide support, putting her arm around Lauren's waist and easing her gently to her feet. With the feel of the taut warm skin under the soft white shirt, wanting to squeeze and explore the supple flesh, she pulled away quickly as soon as Lauren was seated. Coughing to ease the tension in her throat and dryness in her mouth, she looked back to the bar. 'On second thoughts could I have a Macallan please?' Anna puffed out the compressed air as she moved to join Valerie at the bar, returning with a glass of water for Lauren whose eyes had closed, but with a smile that remained.

*

'She'll be fine,' Henri confirmed as he completed his assessment and sutured the small cut. 'There shouldn't be any concussion, but keep an eye on her until the morning,' he advised, as he packed up his bag.

'Thank you Henri. I hope this didn't disturb your evening?' Valerie gushed, fluttering her eyelids and smiling broadly as she placed a large Cognac in the older man's hand. He took the glass and swigged the burning liquid with ease.

'No problem at all, Valerie. I'm glad you called,' he said, his voice lingering on her name with just an ounce of something, clearly encouraging the flirtatiousness between them. 'Glad to help,' he said. Smiling he turned to the two women watching and bid his farewell. Valerie followed him, close to heel.

'Were they just flirting?' Anna asked as she turned to face Lauren who was now sat on the lounger, leaning her head against the large, soft cushions.

'I doubt it,' Lauren said, deadpan. *Her mother didn't flirt.*

'You need to look after yourself,' Anna pointed out, her serious tone heightened by the concerned look in her deep steel-blue eyes.

'Yes.' She had been working stupid hours in London before arriving in Corsica. Her father's suicide had hit her hard, and the dawning realisation that her relationship had been a farce the past ten-years was the straw that had broken the camel's back. If she were truly honest, she hadn't felt well for a while. Stress did that to you, she reasoned. And, whilst she had a reputation for handling situations that would cause grown men to fold, she felt tired. Drained. Her normally sharp thinking had been foggy for some time, which had resulted in her having to work harder to maintain the status quo. Her sleep had been, at best, broken with many a night spent working through her hideous caseload. *Was it really worth pushing for Partner?* She had needed to maintain that work at a distance over the past couple of weeks, whilst also learning about her father's business - her business - during the daylight hours. She needed to be in London and she needed to be here and right now she didn't have the energy for either.

'Let's start that now then?' Anna said, breaking Lauren's reverie.

'What? Sorry, I drifted.' Lauren smiled apologetically.

'Bath. Candles. Bubble bath?'

'Will you sit with me while I bathe?' Lauren asked, with a weary sadness in her voice.

'Yes. I need to keep an eye on you tonight, remember. Doctor's orders,' Anna responded, with a lighter tone and kindness in her eyes. Taking Lauren by the hand, she gently helped her to her feet. Gripping her arm firmly they took a slow walk up the stairs.

*

Lauren stepped carefully into the hot bubbles, the lavender scent delivering a much-needed soothing effect. Her head thumped and an overwhelming sense of tiredness consumed her. Anna had placed the scented candles on the ledges around the large, white, freestanding bath. Soft lighting created the intended ambience - relaxing and calming. Leaving Lauren to get changed and into the bath, she had gone to the kitchen, even though Lauren had protested that she wasn't hungry and didn't need to eat.

Lauren groaned in pleasure as the bubbles and warmth enveloped and comforted her aching body. Resting her head into the designed curve in the bath, eyes closed, she was blissfully unaware of the woman watching her with affection.

Anna had tiptoed into the room, plate in hand, and sat quietly, on the white, wooden chair. The small cut on Lauren's tanned skin stood out - raw, angry - and the dark rings under her eyes seemed more obvious than she had previously noticed. She watched the easy, rhythmical, breathing create a gentle sway in the water, and the absence of any facial expression exposed the smooth, stress-free, blissful state of sleep. Smiling lovingly at the youthful appearance, she found herself breathing softly, in tune with the woman who had stolen her heart from first sight. Sitting back in the chair, plate on the side of the bath, she closed her eyes and allowed herself to be captivated by the lavender scent infusing the room.

Anna opened her eyes suddenly to the sploshing and spluttering sound, as Lauren lifted herself up out of the water having submerged to the point of potential drowning.

'Shit, are you okay?' She jumped up out of the chair.

Lauren chuckled as she rose from the unofficial baptism, 'I thought you were looking after me?' she teased with a broad smile and twinkle in her eyes. 'Remind me to wear water wings next time?'

'Ha ha! Sorry, I dropped off.'

'Brrr. It's getting cold in here.' Lauren shivered as she began to rise and step out of the bath, reaching for the white bathrobe that Anna had laid out for her. Anna averted her gaze, but not before she had taken in the pert breasts and athletic form. She could feel her nipples pressing hard against her soft, pink-cotton blouse, as electric shocks pulsated through her into her tight jeans.

'Sorry.' The husky voice turned to face her. Smiling, lust filled eyes called out to the darkening blue-pools. Anna picked up the still untouched plate and made a swift exit into the cooler air of the bedroom. Lauren followed her as she wrapped the robe around her body.

'You need to eat something,' she stuttered, diverting the energy to the innocuous topic of food, in hope of regaining some control. Lauren took a pace closer, holding the intensity between them. Anna's shaking hands seemed to amuse her.

Reaching her hand up slowly, she took one of the crackers, bit into it, and smiled. 'Happy?' she said. Her voice, ragged with desire, all the while her eyes tracing Anna's face, breasts, hips and back up again. Anna felt undressed, undone and unable to move. The force of the energy between them fixed her to the spot. If Lauren kissed her now, she would be powerless to do anything other than kiss her back. Deeply.

'Thank you,' she virtually croaked, mesmerised by the sumptuous mouth taking in the bland food. *How can a cracker appear so seductive?* Anna giggled inwardly at the thought as she attempted to give her attention to the cracker, rather than the mouth that was tempting her. Turning, she put the plate of food on the small table. As soon as it was down, Lauren took her gently by the arm, spinning her back to face her.

'Thank you for taking care of me,' she said with sincere gratitude. 'I really don't want to be alone tonight.' The vulnerability in her voice sobered Anna instantly. Pulling Lauren into a full body hug, with the touch of those sensual lips brushing her neck, Anna ignored her body's reaction to the contact and focused on providing the support that Lauren needed.

'You're welcome,' she sighed into the hold. *Restraint, restraint, restraint.* She repeated the mantra to herself in some vain attempt to tame the rising sensations through her body. Pulling back gently from the embrace, she looked at Lauren. 'Bed,' she ordered.

'Is that an offer?' Lauren teased, with intentions that she was in no fit state to deliver.

'Funny lady! Bed,' Anna demanded, pointing authoritatively at the king-size bed. The deep red cushions, set on the crisp white, deeply filled quilt, called to her. She would stay, but she doubted she would sleep.

Lauren huffed as she turned towards the bed. Dropping her robe she stepped forward, pulled back the covers, and slid her naked body into the large welcoming space. In spite of their overtly sexual banter, Lauren's head hit the pillow with a deep sigh of contentment and within seconds the soft rhythmical breathing had returned. Anna moved to sit on the cream leather chaise longue, to watch from a safe distance.

'Where are you going?' The sleepy voice quizzed from beneath the covers.

'I'm going to rest...'

'No. Please. There's room in here, not on the couch,' the voice mumbled as her hand patted the vast, unoccupied, space to her side.

Anna walked around the bed, pulled off her jeans, and tentatively climbed in. With her back facing the sleeping woman, she clung to the edge and tried to sleep.

11

'Morning darling.' Valerie's chirpy voice pierced the silence in the dining room. 'How are you feeling? How's your head?' She touched her daughter lightly on the shoulder, squeezing and rubbing as she spoke.

'Apart from a sore head, I'm feeling a bit better thanks.' Lauren certainly felt more refreshed after sleeping soundly for ten-hours.

'That's good. Anna looked after you well it seems?' Her mother's raised eyebrows and questioning intonation - seeking answers to unasked questions - caused the heat to surface in Lauren's face, like the child who knows they have been caught out.

'She did,' Lauren confirmed, smiling with a level of sensitivity that her mother had never witnessed in her daughter when speaking about Rachel.

'Good. Seems she's good for you. I like her.' The comment surprised Lauren, who choked on the croissant she had just bitten into.

'Sorry,' she apologised, trying to regain her breath, sipping the piping hot coffee and burning her tongue.

'Morning,' Anna breezed into the dining room beaming a smile at both women. She had skipped out of Lauren's bed in the early hours of the morning in order to get some sleep in her own room, not wanting to risk waking next to Lauren for fear she wouldn't be able to control the urge to kiss her. The loose fitting white t-shirt, open black cardigan and fitted black trousers, caught Lauren's breath. She couldn't stop the colour rising to her cheeks. 'How's the wounded warrior feeling?' she eyed Lauren with a jovial countenance, whilst taking Valerie's shoulders in her hands for a more traditional greeting, kissing each cheek.

'Fine thank you.' She stood to greet Anna, their lingering hold saying more than they realised. Valerie watched briefly before giving her attention to the buffet awaiting them.

'Coffee?' she offered.

'Thank you,' Anna nodded and moved to take the filled cup, before taking a seat at the table opposite Lauren.

'We have some time scheduled together today,' Valerie said, gently prompting Anna of the formal nature of her visit. 'I trust you enjoyed exploring yesterday?'

'Yes of course. The vineyard is really quite special, and this house... Perhaps we could go through the photographs today? I have some ideas I would like to run by you,' Anna said with enthusiasm. Her earlier concerns about her ability to undertake the project escaped her mind when she focused her attention on the beauty of the place and how she might do justice to the owners through the portrait.

'Wonderful. I can't wait to hear. How about after breakfast?' Valerie clapped her hands together in excitement. Lauren watched the two women interacting and felt the warmth between them soften her. She hadn't realised how much tension she carried around her mother, but that seemed to be changing in the presence of Anna. Anyone who could get her mother to openly relax in this way had to be special.

*

'Morning Antoine.' Lauren spoke as she stepped into the office, noting the sudden change in his demeanour as she entered the room.

Pulling himself an inch or so taller as he stood to face her, she noticed sadness in his eyes, apparent through the glistening of recently shed tears. He stepped in to greet her with a hug. 'Good morning Lauren.' His voice trailed and his normally toned body had an uncharacteristically slumped feel to it.

'Are you okay?' Lauren ventured to ask. Their previous conversations had tended to be formal and business based, but over the last couple of weeks she had started to get to know the kind, gentle man who had worked so closely with her father over the years. The thought of him feeling sad touched her as if he were an older brother.

'Yes. I was just thinking of your father. I miss him,' he confessed. Lauren couldn't imagine what it must be like to lose someone who you had worked with day-in, day-out. They had been very good friends, discussed things together, made decisions jointly. They clearly had a unique connection. She hadn't really considered that Antoine would be grieving his loss - perhaps even more so than her and her mother. In fact, if she didn't know better, she could be forgiven for thinking that to her mother, her father had died years ago.

'Yes, I miss him too,' she reflected aloud for the first time. The last couple of weeks had been so busy she hadn't taken time to introspect. Perhaps she needed to give time to her grief. Allow the process to flow rather than distract herself in necessary work - work that would always be there. She needed her health in order to work. Last night had proven that, and yet here she was still pushing. Really, she should be resting, but with Anna tied up with her mother for the morning she had wanted to get out of the house. 'Do you want to talk about it?' she offered, feeling a deep sense of shared sorrow.

'What's to say?' The despairing tone signified the truth.

'Can we walk around the estate? Will you tell me what it was like working with him?' Lauren pleaded, suddenly feeling the need to connect with her father through this man. He must have many stories to tell, she reasoned to herself. *Sharing is good for the soul, don't they say?* 'I would love you to tell me more about him,' she reiterated. Since she had left home for London her contact with her father had been limited to brief visits and although they were close in personality, there was a great deal about him she didn't know. To some extent he had been a stranger to her, an absent father since her teens, though she never doubted he cared for her.

'Yes, it's a lovely day to wander the vines, and I'm sure there's a story or two that will come to mind,' he agreed, with a relieved smile and visible easing of sadness as his face, brightened by the idea. The vines seemed to do that to people, she thought.

*

'Hi,' Anna said, as she approached Lauren in the living room. Lauren visibly jumped, unaware of her entrance - deeply engrossed in the newspaper she was reading. Looking up, her breath caught at the sight - black fitted trousers, loose white shirt and that burgundy-red waistcoat. She looked hot. Lauren swallowed the air as she stared at the stunning fair-haired woman.

'Hi.' She fought the words out of her dry mouth. 'How was your day?'

'Good thanks. How are you feeling?' Anna moved towards the bar as she spoke and poured herself a Macallan over ice.

'Isn't that a criminal offence?' Lauren asked with a deep, full smile, nodding at the glass in Anna's hand. 'Ice with a single malt?' She confirmed to the confused look on her face.

'Ah, yes, some would say.' She laughed, clinking the ice around the glass to chill the whiskey. 'Never been one for tradition though,' she said, winking cheekily and moving to sit on the couch next to Lauren, who put down her paper and held her glass of neat whiskey in a toast. 'Feeling better then?' Anna looked Lauren up and down. She looked better, more refreshed after her day at the vineyard. She had a good colour in her cheeks and the dark bags had reduced slightly. Clearly the fresh air had done her good. 'You do look a bit better,' she said.

'Yes, I feel it. The air is good here and I didn't do much. Antoine is relaxing company,' she reflected aloud. She had spent the morning walking the vines as the softly spoken man had relayed stories about her father and the history of the vineyard. It had been interesting and his passion infectious. The grapes were ripe, and in the process of being harvested, but his manner had been calm, focused, and as if he had all the time in the world. It had been a lesson in patience for Lauren, whose standard day in London was always manic - too much to do with too little time in which to do it. With the exception of the couple of days of misty rain, the autumn weather had been warm and sunny, ripening the crop effortlessly. Getting the crop inside before the weather shifted too much, bringing the threat of grey rot, was of highest importance, taking Antoine's time from dawn till dusk. Lauren had learned about more than managing the vines from the wise sage.

'How was mother? Do you have a plan?' Lauren asked, keen to know more about Anna's day.

'I think we have a plan. I'm going to work mostly from photographs of you all. It will save anyone sitting for any length of time, although some sitting will be needed initially,' she confirmed.

'What does that mean?'

'Well. I started sketching your mother today and will finish the initial sketch for her tomorrow, before I leave...'

'Leave?' Lauren jumped to attention. 'I didn't realise you were leaving so soon.' The panic in her voice filled the room with palpable tension.

'We hadn't talked about it, but this was always a

preliminary visit. I need to get back to Paris. I can do most of the painting from my home, working from the photographs.' Anna spoke softly, her eyes searching the floor, her heart racing. The shocked look on Lauren's face, and eyes that filled with something close to despair, cut Anna. 'I need you to come to my place for me to sketch you at some point?' she said, looking up with a tentative smile, trying to recover the desperate situation.

Lauren groaned inwardly, slugged her drink mindlessly, walked to the bar and refilled her glass. Her hands were shaking. Her world was spinning on its axis at the thought of not seeing Anna. She hadn't anticipated her leaving so soon. In just a few days Lauren already felt they had known each other a lifetime - even though, technically, she knew very little about her, and vice-versa. Her eyes locked onto Anna's, sadness passing between them. She sighed. 'Yes, of course.' The thought of sitting for Anna brought some small comfort. She could arrange that soon enough. She too had unfinished business that she needed to address. She had to go to London. 'Perhaps I can come in a week or so?' She voiced the question, wishing she could go with Anna immediately.

'That will be perfect. I should have sketched your father by then.'

'Good evening darling… Anna.' Valerie's lively voice cut through the heavy air passing between the two women. 'Shall we have dinner?' she asked rhetorically as she poured her Kir Royale, looking firstly at Lauren then at Anna. 'Did I interrupt something?' she quizzed with genuine interest.

'No,' Lauren said, more firmly than intended, braving a smile at her mother that didn't deceive her. 'Anna was just telling me she is leaving us tomorrow and we were talking about me getting sketched at some point. I understand it went well today?' she asked, diverting the conversation to her mother as she greeted her.

'Fabulously darling. Anna is truly a brilliant talent. Thank heavens we found her. I am so looking forward to seeing the whole thing finished. I know just the space for it,' Valerie said excitedly as she pulled Anna in for a full-on hug. 'Such a talent,' she whispered into her ear. 'Now, do you both have a drink? It's time to eat,' she said, as she released Anna and marched authoritatively into the dining room - glass in hand - the two women following close to heel. Lauren looked perplexed. Anna smiled warmly.

*

'I was expecting your call two days ago,' the cold voice on the end of the line spoke sharply.

'Sorry, I haven't been well,' Lauren confessed.

'I assume you've come to your senses and I can put the last conversation we had down to your ailing state then?' Rachel's harsh tone and dismissal of Lauren's desire to discuss their relationship riled her.

'On the contrary,' Lauren retorted. 'I've had even more time to think. We need to talk, face-to-face. I'll come to London.'

'That's fucking gracious of you.'

'Don't be like that Rach,' Lauren pleaded softly.

'Don't be like what? Have you fucked her yet?'

'It's not like that.' Lauren sighed, having no desire to get into an argument with Rachel, but knowing that is where it would end up if she continued the conversation over the phone.

'Not like what? Do tell me Lauren.' Rachel pushed. The emotionally charged silence that followed tipped her over the edge. 'Oh don't tell me you're in love with her. For fuck's sake Lau, you're fucking married. Or had you conveniently forgotten that?' she barked belligerently.

'I don't want to talk about this over the phone Rach,' Lauren defended. 'I'm coming to London on Sunday and will be in town all week. Perhaps we can schedule some time?' she asked, awaiting the repercussion.

'Sure,' Rachel said in a softer tone, more accepting of defeat. 'I'll text you my schedule for next week. Do you want to meet in Brighton or do you want to meet in London? I have a manic week here so I'm not sure when I'll be in town.'

'Actually, I'd prefer a restaurant in town if you can do it. Dinner?' Lauren asked, wincing. 'I have work there too so we can text availability.' Lauren couldn't face going to their shared home in Brighton and didn't want to meet in her own house in St James's. She hoped that the neutral territory might help Rachel control her behaviour. Rachel wouldn't want to be spotted in the throes of a heated lover's tiff. That would be media fodder she could do without given her intention to push for a more senior position at Whitehall. She wouldn't want to jeopardise her *stable, dependable, married-lesbian* reputation - and her precious career. And... there was a side to Rachel that scared Lauren. Not that she had ever been physically violent towards her. But then Lauren had never pushed her before. Rachel had a vicious temper and Lauren didn't want to experience that alone together for fear that Rachel might lash out.

'Of course, I should have guessed you wouldn't want to come back to *our marital home*,' Rachel spat, in a disparaging tone to rekindle the animosity she felt towards her wife. 'Fuck you... Lauren. Fuck you.' Rachel's angry words were tinged with resignation... and sadness.

*

Lauren stood, staring out her bedroom window across the now dark lawns. *Be true to your heart Lauren and fear not the consequences. Life is too short.* The eucalyptus swayed in the starlit night as the words of her father ricocheted in her mind. What she felt for Rachel, this wasn't love. It might have been in the beginning, but not anymore. She cared about her, but when she dared to delve into a potential future, it wasn't her current wife's face she woke up next to. As she dared to dream, the reality dawned. She wanted, no needed, to feel loved, a connection. She had also wanted children and Rachel had promised she did too, in the early days. Whenever Lauren had raised the idea with her though, the timing always seemed to be wrong. Lauren had realised some time ago that Rachel's career was her highest priority, but she had never given up hope. Her frozen eggs would be there if needed... the thought made her shiver - excitement and terror combined. She hadn't even asked Anna about children. In fact, she didn't know much at all about the artist who had captured her heart - who had awoken her senses to love, to life. Her grey existence had transformed overnight into a rainbow of colour, in the presence of the gorgeous woman in the burgundy-red waistcoat. She missed everything about Anna, who had been gone just twenty-four hours now. After London, she would stop off in Paris for the sketching. The thought created a warm tingling sensation and the tension in her mind following the conversation with Rachel softened slightly. One step at a time, she reminded herself. She couldn't stop the smile that crept across her face as she slipped into the cool sheets with the image of Anna pressing every part of her mind and body. She ached to touch her, to kiss the soft lips that had tempted her - teased her with every word spoken, food eaten, drink sipped. Feeling Anna's warm breath against her face and breasts her fingers explored the pert nipples rubbing against the quilt. Lowering her other hand she pressed the hardened, supple, clitoris that was crying out for attention. Spreading herself, her fingers roamed frantically, spreading the wet silky fluid over the pulsing sensation - circling, pinching, and dipping briefly inside until the burning electric jolts shot through her, too quickly. She rode the shuddering, curling into the foetal position, wrapping her arms around herself. Far from satisfied, but welcoming the brief release, she slept.

12.

'Hey, you look great,' Rowena remarked as she looked up from her desk. 'Corsica obviously suits you. How'd it go?' she asked as she assessed the transformation in the artist standing before her. 'You look...' she mulled over her thoughts but couldn't find the words to describe. 'Radiant. That's it,' she said, satisfied to have found one word that seemed to fit.

'Hi Anna.' Eva looked up from the couch and the magazine that had been holding her attention. 'Wow, girlfriend! Something's gotten into you.' She stood to greet her friend with an overzealous squeeze. 'You look fab.' She ogled Anna unapologetically from top to toe.

'Hi,' Anna responded, as a smile took over her face. With a spring in her step she walked to the coffee machine and popped a pod in to brew, nudging Eva in the side as she passed. 'I'm good and Corsica is a beautiful place,' she said as her mind revisited key moments in the last few days. 'What's not to love about twenty-nine degrees of sunshine at this time of year?' she added, peeking out the expansive glass window over a misty, cold Paris morning. 'And...' she hesitated.

'Yes...' both women responded as their eyes sought to find out the real cause of the transformed woman before them.

'Remember that woman I met in London before I went?'

'The one you nearly canned the project over a couple of days ago you mean?' Rowena asked. 'Sorry, I haven't updated Eva.'

'The hot one you couldn't stop talking about?' Eva taunted, having sat through an entire evening with Anna as she had debated aloud the merits of the lawyer and whether she should have asked for her details. 'Did she text you then?' Eva asked, intrigued.

'No. Turns out she's the daughter of Valerie Vincenti. She was in Corsica for her father's funeral,' Anna explained.

'No shit,' Eva blurted, unperturbed by the funeral reference. 'And... you slept with her?' She asked, hopping up and down with excitement.

'Eva!' her mother admonished. 'That's personal. I'm sure Anna will let you know if and when she and...'

'Lauren,' Anna confirmed.

'When she and Lauren become... involved.' The older woman chose her words carefully as she looked at a love-sick Anna, whose smile seemed to come from a different place - a place of depth.

'Mum! Anna and I talk about stuff like that all the time,' Eva responded, with a *get with the programme* attitude.

'You may my darling. But I don't. So, you can talk sex over drinks, but not in my office,' she smiled. 'As long as I'm invited to the drinks,' she winked at Anna. 'In the meantime, how did it go with Mrs Vincenti?'

'Anna.' Eva interrupted before she could respond. 'Drinks. Tonight. My place at 7.' She commanded. 'I want to hear all about this woman who has done this to you.' She waved her hand up and down at Anna and moved in to hug her again. 'Gotta go,' she nodded towards Rowena and made for the door. 'See ya mum,' she said, closing the door behind her without waiting for a response. Rowena tutted and rolled her eyes.

*

'So, stranger, how have you been?' Carla gibed lightly with a beaming smile as she greeted her friend.

'Busy,' Lauren responded, returning the smile without it projecting the positive emotions it should have elicited in her.

'You look tired Lau, is everything okay?' she asked as they walked into the popular port restaurant. Lauren had taken the trip to Ajaccio specifically to see Carla before she headed for London and then Paris. She didn't know when she might see her again and felt a strong need for the woman's company. They had always been very close. Their intimate connection being so unique that they had both agreed never to muddy the waters by taking it to a physical level. It might make an insecure lover jealous, but their platonic love had clear boundaries.

'Ah… that's a loaded question,' the tired voice responded. 'Where do I start?' Lauren's eyes scanned the space above Carla's head as if searching for an answer. She looked at her best friend with as much lightness as she could muster, tears burning at the back of her eyes she scanned the horizon again. 'I feel a wreck,' she shared openly. Unaccustomed to feeling out of control, the last few weeks had thrown Lauren's world to the point that she didn't recognise herself - she felt more at sea than the luxurious private boats she could see gently rocking in their mooring, and her crew had deserted the ship, leaving her stranded.

Noticing the obvious distress in her friend, Carla reached out and took Lauren's hand searching for meaningful eye contact, knowing it would probably result in full-blown tears when they did connect. 'Hey,' she said softly. 'Want to talk?' she squeezed the unresponsive hand and Lauren's eyes landed on hers. 'This is about more than your father, isn't it?' the astute women observed.

'I'm divorcing Rachel,' the words came out slowly but leaving no doubt as to the certainty behind them. The tears flowed. Carla moved around the table, taking the seat next to her friend. She held her close, rubbing her back and squeezing her shoulder while she sobbed. As the waiter tentatively approached, Carla ordered a half carafe of house rosé, a bottle of St George, and the lunchtime specials for them both. Swaying the woman in her arms she remained silent, looking out to sea.

The wine and water arrived in an instant and Carla released Lauren to pour them a glass of each. Handing the water to her friend, she smiled weakly. Stroking the side of her face with a soft hand and brushing the drying tears with her thumbs, she lent in and kissed her softly on the forehead. 'Oh Lau, I'm so sorry. What happened? How can I help?' she asked, as she released her, holding her eyes with tenderness.

'The hug worked,' Lauren said, with a light laugh, recovering from the outburst, which she felt was an over-reaction to how she actually felt about the divorce. Yes, she felt sad their relationship had come to this, and even frustrated for not realising sooner that it was over. But she wasn't in any doubt that it was over and she should feel better for that fact.

'You're still grieving for your father remember. And now a divorce! Two of the highest scorers on measures of psychological stress are enough for anyone. No wonder you look like shit,' her friend expressed with concern. 'And I bet you were knackered before all this kicked off,' she said, knowing the working hours Lauren kept on a standard week. 'Are you going to rest?' She posed the question already knowing the answer would be no!

'I'm okay,' Lauren protested. 'I've just got to work through this with Rachel and hope she doesn't resist, so we can both move on. You're right about father though. I don't understand why he would commit suicide. It's just not him - at least not what I thought was him.' She reflected momentarily. 'I'm going to London on Sunday. I need to be in court on Wednesday and I'm meeting Rachel this week.' She sighed not relishing the week ahead.

'You need to look after yourself,' Carla said with sincerity. A deep smile filled Lauren's face as the memory of

Anna's face reflected back at her - those same words coming from her full, red lips as she had sat on the couch, deep-blue eyes full of concern appraising her every move, following her fainting episode. Heat rose through her body and coloured her cheeks. 'Penny for that thought?' Carla joked, picking up the shift in mood.

'I've met someone,' Lauren announced.

'Wow. Well she certainly has the right effect,' Carla remarked. 'I'm not sure what thought was in your head, but you lit up pretty damn quickly,' she laughed. 'You don't do things by halves, do you?'

Lauren blushed more deeply as she reflected on the thoughts she'd had about Anna and what she would like to do with her. 'She's special,' was all that Lauren could say, unable to remove the grin from her face. She felt lighter, freer, and happier. Just thinking about Anna gave her hope for a life she had long since given up on. The waiter quietly placed their food on the table, distracting the conversation. 'Anyway, enough about me already, how are you? How's Francesca?' Lauren enquired as she tucked into her lunch.

'She's great, we're great.' The introspective smile on Carla's face as she spoke was a clear demonstration of the love she felt for her partner of three-years. Carla and Francesca had met on-line and hit it off from their first contact. Francesca had been a neo-natal nurse working in London, although originally from Sardinia. Having hooked up online, Francesca had agreed to visit Corsica for a week's holiday and that had been that. She had returned to London to work her notice and moved in with Carla just before Christmas three-years ago. She now offered neo-natal support on a private basis, catering mainly for the rich and famous, some of whom harboured in the port over which they now surveyed. 'When you're next back here you should come stay with us for a bit.' Carla offered.

'Yes, that would be lovely,' Lauren committed.

'And do bring...'

'Anna's her name,' Lauren grinned, entranced.

'Anna. Right. Well, Anna who does this strange thing to my best friend is most welcome,' she laughed, raising her glass to toast the agreed future date.

'Deal,' Lauren's excitement didn't go unnoticed. The last three weeks had been the longest time she had spent on the island since leaving for law training some seventeen-years ago. Facebook had kept her in touch with her friend of course, but Lauren realised she had missed this... this real contact between real friends. Her brief visits home over the years had been marred by her mother, who had seemed intent on creating distance and formality between them - that only ever seemed to result in argument. Eventually she had stopped coming back on a regular basis. Her parents didn't use mobile technology so the brief catch up call, on an as-and-when basis, was the only contact they had, barring the odd flying visit. Lauren had been shocked at the impact of the last three-weeks on her. The peace and purposeful practice of managing the vineyard, Antoine and his passion, and even her mother's recent and unexplained shift in attitude towards her. And then Anna! *Anna...Anna...Anna.* Her presence had certainly transformed the energy in the house. She was very like Antoine in many respects - kind, warm, compassionate, loving. It felt good just being around these people. She briefly contrasted the feeling with her normal working day in London - the aggressive, harsh environment of legal practice. Egos, money, power. It felt ugly. The chase. The kill. She didn't feel drawn to it. Tired maybe? Had she lost her hunger? Possibly.

'Hey dreamer.' Carla nudged her out of her reverie. 'Coffee?' she asked.

'Sure.'

'*Hi*,' her phone beeped, raising her body temperature and glazing her eyes as the sender's name penetrated every cell of her being.

'That would be Anna then,' Carla grinned, shaking her head. 'You've got it bad my friend,' she teased.

'Do you mind?' Lauren asked as she lifted her phone to respond. Carla nodded as if to say, go ahead, whilst she watched with interest the transformation in the woman at the table.

13

Lauren stepped off the plane into the blustery London weather. The rain was heavy and the temperature noticeably colder than she had become accustomed to the last few weeks. In the summer, there might be no better place in the world, but heading into winter was a different matter altogether. She embraced the comfort of getting back to the work town so familiar to her - still curious as to the absence of drive that had been a part of her for so long - and fought the trepidation of meeting up with Rachel, who was understandably, baying for blood. Her blood.

Grabbing her suitcase from baggage reclaim, through passport control, she headed for the train service into the city. She grabbed a double espresso and added two sugars. Gulping the hot bittersweet liquid, provided instant gratification, she lingered on the instant feeling of mental clarity for a moment. With her suitcase and hand luggage she made her way quickly to the platform and boarded the waiting train. She would be home in an hour. The rain pounded the window as soon as the train moved out of the station. She sighed, sinking back into the chair, acquiescing to the gentle, rocking and clunking of wheels on track. Picking up her phone she knew she should call Rachel, instead she text Anna. They had texted regularly since her return to Paris, keeping the tone friendly and platonic, both closing with a single cross, neither revealing the depth of their bond and their true desires.

Lauren had shared her plans: the week in London for work, followed by the stop off in Paris for her sketching. She had been surprised to discover that Anna would be in London at the end of the week for a visit to her mums. She was flying over on the Friday and back to Paris on the Sunday. Lauren had desperately wanted to make arrangements for them to meet, but had refrained from suggesting anything until she knew for certain when she would be speaking to Rachel. She looked at her phone waiting for a response from Anna, then pressed a couple of buttons and made the call she needed to face. It went straight to answerphone. She breathed deeply in relief and didn't leave a message. Rachel would know she had called.

Lauren had tried to call several times before arriving at Victoria, the answerphone clicking in every time, and she hadn't had a text response from Anna either. As she stepped onto the platform, she felt unexpectedly gripped by loneliness. Stepping out of the station, the rain was still heavy. Even though her house was just a short walk from St James's, she opted for a cab. She would have been drenched just walking across the road, she figured.

Turning the key, the familiar click, slight dragging of the draft excluder, and the scent of freshly laundered clothes, tinged with dampness. Lauren breathed it all in and felt the stress drain from her shoulders. Li-Sze had been in to clean. Lauren smiled in thanks for her reliable, happy, smiley home help. Her phone beeped and she reached for it in anticipation - the tingling in her gut something between hope that it was Anna and anxiety that it might be Rachel. She didn't like the negative anchor she had developed towards her wife. Rachel didn't deserve to be treated badly. It wasn't as if she had done anything particularly wrong - neither of them had - they had just run their course, in Lauren's mind. *You back?* The text read. Lauren's heart sank as she dialled the familiar number.

'Hello Lauren.' The composed formality behind the tone was expected.

'Hi. Yes, I'm back. How are you?' Lauren posed the question for want of filling the space and not really knowing what else to say. 'When are you coming into town?' she followed up quickly, needing the security of a meeting date.

'I'm in town now.' Lauren visibly jerked, shocked that Rachel was, unexpectedly, in close proximity. 'Want to meet this evening? How about Sardo's? I know it's one of your favourites.' Lauren's stomach churned at the suggestion that seemed to violate her relationship with Anna.

'I don't fancy Sardo's. How about Quilon? It's close to me and you can come here first... if you want, that is?'

'Sure. I'll be there at six-thirty?'

'Okay, see you then.' Lauren ended the call feeling the tension and pain between them. They had been lovers, friends, and supporters of each other for more than ten-years now and yet they spoke as near strangers. It hurt like hell. But try as she might, she couldn't find the passion and love that had once existed between them. Yes, she cared, but that wasn't enough anymore. She wasn't being deliberately evasive or uncaring. She knew if she gave an ounce of hope that there might be a future, Rachel would grab at it. Grab her. Slowly destroy her soul. She couldn't allow that to happen. Not now.

*

The bell rang at exactly six-thirty. Lauren had already dressed for dinner, not wanting to expose herself in the presence of her soon to be ex-wife. The dark blue jeans and white crew-neck sweater - casually elegant - set off her tanned skin and dark brown eyes. She looked stunning, even though that hadn't been her intention.

'You had your hair cut?' Rachel observed, as her eyes travelled over Lauren's face with a forced smile. 'Looks cool! It suits you,' she complimented. She meant it.

'Thanks,' Lauren said, reaching up and fiddling with the brown waves that had become curls by the shorter cut. She stepped back to let Rachel through the door. 'Drink?' she offered, moving in for a formal embrace, edgily releasing Rachel with a brief peck on the cheek.

'Yeah. I'll have a Gin… large one.' She nodded her thanks, taking off the heavy coat to reveal a designer black straight-line dress, cut just above the knee. She looked hot Lauren couldn't help but note to herself. But then that was also the problem. Rachel was hot. That was never in question. Long straight dark hair, strong jaw line, dark, piercing eyes accentuated by long straight eye lashes, and legs that seemed to go on forever. Her slender build made her look even taller than her measured five-foot ten. In heels she stood just short of six-feet and her presence was imposing.

Lauren walked to the kitchen feeling under-dressed, and grabbed a glass. Two ice-cubes and a squeeze of lemon dressed the glass, before adding a large shot of Gin, and a tin of slim-line tonic from the fridge. She had made the drink many times before and knew exactly how Rachel preferred it. 'Here goes,' she handed the fizzing glass over, the quinine teasing her nostrils as she reached for her single malt over ice, which she had abandoned on the coffee table. She swirled her drink as if in deep thought, then took a sip and locked eyes with Rachel. Hurt, pain, sadness projected back at her and she looked away, diving for her phone to add some background music - hoping for a shift in mood. 'How's work?' she ventured.

'Work's good. Stable. Reliable.' Lauren couldn't help but note the comparative dig.

'I'm so sorry,' Lauren blurted. She hadn't intended to get to the point so quickly, but it was the elephant in the room and it needed acknowledging before the conversation deteriorated further. 'I didn't mean for this to happen.'

'You didn't mean it.' Rachel repeated slowly, emphasising each word as if the statement alone had been presented to her as sufficient justification for the imminent destruction of their marriage. 'I really don't know what to say Lau.' There was no hint of the earlier anger, for which Lauren was relieved. More disgust… It didn't feel much better, but it was at least different and she didn't feel quite so threatened by Rachel.

Lauren felt the essence of shame brush over her and had to work hard to back her own feelings over the commitment she had made all those years ago. In her own mind, she had never really wanted to get married. She didn't believe in the institutionalisation of something as fluid as relationships - and especially love. It had been a political necessity though, adding gravitas to the young councillor's profile. A statement of solidarity to the LBGT communities she served. Lauren would no longer be held to that commitment for the sake of Rachel's career.

'Is there actually anything for us to discuss, Lauren? You look as though your mind is already made up. Do I have any say in the matter?' Rachel asked, a look of resignation seemed to overcome her and her hands began to shake. She slugged heavily on the drink, holding the fizzy fluid in her mouth for longer, and pressed the empty glass onto the table. Lauren's eyes rose from the floor in apology. Tears streaming down her face, pupils dilated and cheeks blotchy. Rachel's eyes burned at the sight and she reached out, both arms pulling Lauren into her. She held the sobbing woman, her own tears releasing into the short curls. Lauren returned the hug, holding her ex-lover closely... for the last time. Naturally, Rachel pulled away gently. 'Let's go and eat,' she said.

*

'Is this about us not having children?' Rachel asked, as if seeking something tangible she could pin the demise of their relationship on. They had walked the short distance to the Indian restaurant arm in arm, in thoughtful silence, respecting their mutual grief, resigned to the truth. Their relationship was over. Rachel had considered fighting for her wife, but she too was aware that what they had wasn't really fulfilling. She loved Lauren deeply, but they had achieved a level of formality and distance inside the relationship that they might as well have been good friends. At least the expectations would be different now and she could pursue any of the many advances she had previously turned down. The thought of taking another lover appealed to her at some level. She had come close before now, but always restrained for the sake of their image - she could do without that sort of publicity, which would only damage her reputation. She sipped at the cold beer, seeking the answers lying behind Lauren's eyes, as she processed the question.

'I don't know. Maybe... unconsciously.' When they had got together Lauren had been determined in her desire for children at some point in the future. Rachel had casually agreed - if she were honest, hoping it was a phase she would pass through. Diagnosed with endometriosis in her early-thirties, Lauren had decided to have some of her eggs removed and frozen and Rachel had gone along with the plan. With appropriate hormone treatment, Lauren could carry at any point in the future, but when she had broached the subject of Rachel carrying her eggs, the politician had freaked out. That had never been on her agenda and her definitive no response had shocked Lauren. There had been no further discussion and Rachel had expected the notion to go away over time, but the distance that had been created then still remained.

'I'm sorry. I should've handled the pregnancy thing better,' Rachel confessed, taking Lauren's hand and brushing her thumb across her knuckles.

'It's a two-way thing. I was kind of obsessed. Perhaps I'm having a mid-life crisis,' she joked.

'You're only thirty-eight,' Rachel said dryly. 'That's a bit pre-emptive. Though who knows, with the treatment you've been through?' she recalled.

'Anyway...' she paused. 'How's Brighton's political landscape these days?' Lauren's upbeat tone and shift in demeanour signalled a much-needed change in subject. Asking the question affirmed the lack of conversation that had passed between them over recent months. 'Did you back Brexit?'

'It's great thanks, and yes... I did back leaving the EU.' *Right there, was another big difference between them*, Lauren thought. Rachel continued promoting her reasons for voting to leave, what her policies were regarding immigration, mental health issues, aging populations and the right to die. Lauren watched the enthusiasm grip her ex, as fluid and influential arguments effortlessly flowed from her lips. She reminded Lauren of her own time in court, preaching, theorising, and selling her version of the truth. People listened to the charismatic politician. Trusted her. Followed her. Lauren smiled in appreciation, asking questions here and there, honestly supportive of Rachel's success. Their relationship may be over, but she genuinely wished her well and would continue to support her, she vowed to herself.

They meandered back to Lauren's house arm in arm, like the best friends that they were. The rain had long since stopped but the air was still chilly. Thousands of stars reflected brightly in the clear, dark sky and a cold breeze had an awakening effect. 'Nightcap?' Lauren asked as she turned the key and entered the centrally heated room. The warmth felt hotter against her cold face and was comforting. 'I'm assuming you'll stay over?' Lauren offered.

'Thanks, that would be great. Cognac please.' Rachel confirmed, making no move to help herself to the drink, as she threw off her coat and heels. The energy between them had relaxed significantly. Rachel trying to respect the new position she held in Lauren's life as a friend, but also a guest in the house.

Lauren abandoned her coat and poured two large

shots handing one to her ex. 'Movie?'

'Why not? I feel quite wide awake,' Rachel smiled.

'You choose. I'll just go sort out the spare room,' Lauren remarked as she sprang out the living room door, returning moments later with a set of Rachel's cotton pyjamas, which she laid on top of the radiator. Rachel had always kept some items of clothing; books, videos and music at the house, but essentially it had always been Lauren's place. Their family home was in Brighton, which had been Rachel's, when Lauren and she got together. Whilst Lauren had some private things in their home, on reflection, they hadn't really shared much in each other's place at all. Both professional women had maintained their independence within their relationship. It certainly would make the split a lot easier and without the need to sell property to create the separation. The divorce was something they could sort out amicably in time, hopefully. 'Thank you,' Lauren touched Rachel's shoulder tenderly as she spoke.

'For what?'

'For being so agreeable.'

'I think you were just braver than me,' Rachel admitted. 'We weren't exactly lovers, were we?' She laughed. 'I'd like for us to remain friends,' she said, with a serious tone in her voice.

'Hell yes! I love you. I will always love you,' Lauren stated with absolute certainty. She stared at Rachel for some time as she selected and loaded the DVD, sipping, enjoying the warmth of the drink on the back of her throat. 'So, what did you choose?' she asked eventually.

'The Break Up,' Rachel remarked in all seriousness.

'Really!' Lauren burst into laughter as she looked searchingly at her ex who couldn't help herself. A smile escaped her and she started to laugh. Lauren thumped her jokingly on the arm. 'Get out of here. I'll choose,' she said, as she jumped out of the seat.

'I'm not watching some lesbian romance thing with you,' she huffed. 'That would be a step too far,' she winced as Lauren eyed her in humour.

14

Lauren entered her office building with butterflies bouncing around her stomach. It was a strange feeling, uncharacteristic, and unnerving. The familiar clean white walls - clinical - silver furnishings and highly polished wooden floor did nothing to abate her rising tension.

The evening with her ex had gone better than she had expected and she was relieved that they could remain on good terms - *cliché lesbian break up*, she smiled to herself. She had texted Anna as she had gone to bed. She hadn't expected the immediate response at 2am, but her heart fluttered in excitement when her phone lit up almost immediately. They hadn't chatted for long and Lauren hadn't mentioned anything about her evening with Rachel. That was a discussion she wanted to have face-to-face so that she could better gauge Anna's response. They had agreed to do supper together on the Friday evening after which Anna would be spending the weekend with her mums. They were scheduled on the same flight to Paris early on the Monday morning. She was excited and nervous about spending time with Anna, worried that their - her - feelings might have changed. In any event she needed to do the sitting for the portrait, she assured herself.

'Morning Arthur,' Lauren smiled at the long-serving receptionist as she flashed her identity card at the entrance barrier, striding out to stop the doors shutting on the lift.

Stepping into the empty space she breathed deeply to relax but the mix of heady aftershave and body odour hitting her senses had a claustrophobic effect. She wretched slightly and tried to concentrate on breathing slowly whilst ignoring the pungent smell, willing the floor numbers to pass quickly. She stepped out the moment the lift stopped, bumping past two employees entering the lift and tried to take a deep cleansing breath. Staggering into the corridor she realised she was sweating and her heart was thumping through her chest. She was on the wrong floor. *Fuck.* She stood for a few moments trying to compose herself.

Gaining some control over her breathing, she made her way slowly to the bathroom. Even the chemical smell irritated her senses, but the cooler air in the room helped her to overcome the feeling of sickness that had consumed her so suddenly. As the door opened behind her she dived into a cubicle and sat on the seat, lowering her head between her knees. *What the fuck is wrong with me?* she declared silently. The rattling of plastic tubes, clinking and clipping noises, zipping of a bag, clicking of heels and the door slamming indicated that the woman who had entered the room had completed her make-up application and now gone.

Lauren exited the cubicle and looked at herself in the mirror. The dark rings were still present and her eyes lacked the spark she had identified with over the years. The spark of influence - work, seduction, and compassion - that spark was missing. The dullness that remained, together with her lack of fire - the absence of hunger - was beginning to play on her mind. She always looked like she had colour in her cheeks courtesy of her heritage, but to her she lacked lustre. She splashed the cool water over her cheeks and rubbed, drawing redness to the surface. *Better*, she noted. Shaking her hands and placing them under the dryer, staring into her own eyes, she committed to taking better care of herself... starting now.

*

'What's this?' the grey-haired man in his early sixties motioned as he wafted the letter over his head before throwing it demonstratively onto his desk.

'As it says,' Lauren stated calmly. 'I'm resigning John.' John McDermott, senior partner at McDermott, Knight &

Davies, had been her boss and mentor since she started working at the prestigious law firm, eight years earlier. She was on track for partner now and this man had guided her, supported her, and vied for her when the other two owners had put forward alternative candidates for her current position. Now she was letting him down, and she felt dreadful. Her eyes averted his impassioned stare.

'You are kidding me, right?' he pleaded, rising from his seat and beginning to pace up and down his office. His face seemed to darken to the point of purple with every step he took. Lauren sat with her hands in her lap, squeezing the clammy palms, keeping the pressure at a point just short of pain in an effort to maintain her focus and commitment to herself. It would be easy to collapse under the emotional pressure, let alone her moral commitment to the cases on her books. It had taken an hour to write the short simple message, as she had toyed with all possible options. She felt torn. She would of course mentor a successor to take over her work, and she would give as much notice as she could. But her health was suffering and she needed some time to deal with the events of her father's untimely death, and her new role in her father's business.

'No. I'm sorry John. I need a break. I know...'

'Take a sabbatical for Christ sake,' he blurted, interrupting her impatiently with the suggestion. His fiery nature served him well in court, but not so well in matters of a delicate nature where he was often perceived as a bully. To stand up to him took immense courage... and persistence. He would be relentless in his efforts to persuade Lauren to stay - she had expected that. She hadn't expected him to suggest a sabbatical though. Already tired, she questioned whether she had the strength to resist the offer.

'I'll think about it,' was all she could say. He sighed heavily, thumping his overweight bottom into the strong, black leather director's chair, which huffed and squeaked in remonstration under the pressure. Adopting his best Victorian fatherly tone, he leaned his large frame back into the chair and rested his arms across his belly. The years of legal lunches, old boy's networks and social-political events had taken their toll, Lauren observed to herself. He was clinically obese, and doing a bad job of repressing the anger he clearly felt. *Candidate for a heart attack*, she mused, as the veteran lawyer continued his motivational speech.

Lauren hadn't heard a word he said. 'I'll think about it,' she repeated once he finished his spiel and she realised it was her turn to speak. He rose from his seat and presented his hand to shake, which she took as a sign that the meeting had been concluded. She shook the overly hot, sticky hand and walked out of the office, still in a daze. The more steps she took the lighter she felt, until a broad grin began to surface and she felt a slight skip in her step. *Had she really just resigned?* She felt like a small child who had just done something terribly wrong and gotten away with it - heady with relief and yet still slightly anxious at the possibility of getting caught.

She greeted colleagues with a new sense of self, entered her office, and got to work with energy she hadn't possessed when she entered the building. She had a court case on Wednesday and she never undertook a case without being fully prepared. She knew she would be burning the candle again, but at least in her mind there was an end in sight. By the New Year she would be free. The idea fuelled her and spurred her on.

It had been dark for a number of hours when Lauren left the office. She had been in text contact with Anna during the day, which always raised a smile. But she had given her undivided attention to preparations for court - a meeting with the victim to go over last-minute details and dealing with a final refusal of the defence team's proposal to settle out of court. She felt good.

The cool air brushed her face as she exited the revolving doors to the building, drawing attention to her body. She realised her stomach was complaining loudly. She hadn't eaten since grabbing a croissant on her way into the office. Eyeing the local pizzeria, she strode out, crossed the road, and dived into the restaurant.

'I'm sorry, but we're just about to close,' the waiter mumbled apologetically.

'Ahh!' she complained to herself. 'Any chance of a takeaway... please?' Putting on her influentially seductive look, she posed the question to the young, flustered, man.

'I'll check,' he said.

'Pepperoni with chillies,' she confirmed as he walked off to consult with the head chef. Returning he nodded in affirmation of the order and offered Lauren a seat at the bar.

'Would you like a drink?'

'Malt whiskey would be great, thanks.' Lauren smiled with gratitude as the man reached behind stacked bottles and pulled out the drink. 'On ice, please.' She smiled, remembering how she had teased Anna about adding ice to the single malt.

The drink arrived, together with the bill on a small silver tray. Lauren paid immediately not wanting to hold up the staff from leaving once her pizza arrived. The doorbell tinkled as the last of the seated customers left for the night. For a brief moment, there was a calm silence in the restaurant. Lauren swirled the drink, coating the ice, and swigged it back, enjoying the burning sensation as it eased down the back of her throat. Placing the empty glass on the doily, the man returned with the boxed pizza in a white carrier bag. 'Thank you so much,' she said, handing the young man a large tip as he opened the door for her to leave.

The walk home had taken long enough for the pizza to cool, but Lauren had enjoyed the fresh air, having been cooped up in her office for the best part of the day. She had texted Anna on her way home, but receiving no response, assumed she was now fast asleep. Stepping into her living room, throwing her bag and coat on the couch, flicking off her heels, she shoved a couple of slices of pizza into the microwave, poured a Macallan over ice and turned on the television for the late-night news. Taking the steaming hot pizza and drink in hand she collapsed into the soft, welcoming seat and enjoyed the feeling of being held by the large, yielding cushions. Resting the pizza on the arm, she sipped at the drink, luxuriating in the comfort and warmth. She felt relaxed - at peace - for the first time in a long time. The noises in the background faded as she drifted, first in thought and then into a deep sleep.

The beeping of her phone stirred her as she laid prone on the couch, unaware of how her glass had made it safely to the floor - the cold pizza still sitting on the plate on the arm of the couch. She moved slowly. The voices of the television coming into focus, she blinked at her mobile - Anna - it was 6.30. Laying on the couch staring at the name, she smiled. *Hi*, she responded as she raised herself to standing and headed to the kitchen. Coffee… filters… water. She reached for each item in turn and put the machine on to brew. The instantly reassuring, plopping and hissing sounds, followed by the aroma that filled the house accompanied Lauren as she undressed from the previous night and jumped into the steaming shower. It felt good. She felt good.

*

The court case had gone very well. The judge having little sympathy for poor management practice had levied the maximum award possible to her client, justifying Lauren's decision not to settle out of court. The excitement of the battle and the buzz of success had certainly lifted her spirits temporarily. She was pleased for her client - justice was always sweet in the context of malpractice. It was what had driven her in the first instance to do the job. As she stood at the bar, watching her colleagues celebrate their success, she found herself reflecting, briefly, on her decision to quit. The buzzing of her phone drew her attention away from the now intoxicated, and slightly raucous, executives.

I'm coming to London tomorrow, Ax

Lauren caught her breath as she read and re-read the message. She made her way past sweating, swaying bodies and stepped outside, as if to claim some level of privacy to her conversation. Anna wasn't due until Friday, she wondered.

Is everything ok? Your mum ok?

Lauren worried in response.

Yeah, all good. I finished work earlier than expected. Want to meet up? x

'Thank god,' Lauren spoke her thoughts out loud. The idea that Anna might have a problem, and the intensity of the fear that induced in her shocked her. She couldn't recall feeling so... protective over someone before. Relieved, she smiled, feeling the anxiety drain slowly away, she responded to the offer.

Love to. When do you arrive? x

Lauren began walking in the direction of her house, wrapping her arms around herself to brace against the chilled air, as she waited for the response. Nothing.

The microwave pinged its familiar ring and Lauren removed the enlivened pepperoni pizza, taking a bite of the hot food as she walked through to the living room. The leftovers didn't do anything for her appetite but Lauren had to eat something and her cupboards were technically empty. Milk, butter and cheese sat alone in the fridge. Bread had green-black dots forming on its crust, so had been thrown in the bin. Bananas, sitting alone on the side, were also a dark shade of black, which meant they assumed a horrid flowery taste that Lauren found quite unpalatable. They too were discarded. The cold, stiff looking pizza was the only edible option that remained. Heated, it had softened, but it was soggy. The chewy substance would have to suffice. Lauren threw a second slice of pizza into her mouth as she kicked off her heels and slung her black jacket onto the back of the chair. She glanced at her phone in expectation - still nothing. Stepping into the steaming shower she wallowed in the soap and heat as she cleansed her body, washing away the grime of city living. Her highly attuned ears caught the distinctive buzz above the rushing water and she quickly flicked the tap off and leapt out of the cubicle. Wrapping the large, fluffy towel around her body, her short hair still dripping down her cheeks and neck, she grabbed the phone.

I land at 5.30pm. Will be in London for 6.30ish? x

A rush of adrenaline pumped through Lauren as she fumbled a response.

Dinner? Fancy Sardo's?

The tingling sensation in her gut seemed to grow in anticipation.

Great. I'll meet you there. 7.30?

A hint of disappointment touched her. The idea of Anna being in town an hour before she would see her seemed like a lifetime. *It was ridiculous...*she chastised herself.

I'll book a table

I'm looking forward to it already

The response came immediately, together with an emoji big smiley face. Lauren smiled, feeling alive.

15.

'Hello, not so stranger, stranger,' Carla teased as she picked up the phone. Months, even years would go by without any contact from Lauren. It was the way their friendship worked. So she was surprised to receive the call, given they had seen each other only a week ago. She hoped her dearest friend wasn't in any trouble. 'Are you okay?'

'Hiya. I'm fine,' the coy response, so out of character, did nothing to reassure Carla. 'I just thought I'd catch up,' she muttered, evasively. She always felt safe around Carla, and she was the only person Lauren could think to call, but now she was on the phone she didn't quite know how to begin.

'Come on Lau, spill?' Carla's genuine attentiveness gave Lauren permission to share her thoughts, knowing she wouldn't be ridiculed.

'I'm meeting Anna tonight. In an hour actually,' she said, almost blurting out the words.

'And the problem with that is?' Carla gently teased, knowing full well there was no real problem. 'Don't tell me, you can't decide what to wear?

'Funny!' Lauren tittered in amusement, softening with the light heartedness injected by her friend. 'I'm really nervous,' she revealed. 'I mean really nervous. I haven't felt like this since my first date at school,' she confessed, looking at her own shaking hands and trying to control the butterflies in her stomach.

'Ahhh... that's sweet,' Carla responded, merging sympathy with a slight hint of sarcasm. 'You're really into her eh?'

'I guess,' Lauren mused. Just having her friend to share her feelings with was helping alleviate the pressure she had put on herself.

'Just be yourself Lau,' Carla offered. 'You're perfect, and you don't want someone falling in love with who they think you are, do you?' The psychiatrist justified.

'I know. I guess I'm worried that things will be different this time.' Even though deep-down Lauren trusted Anna's feelings hadn't changed that quickly, their text contact hadn't given anything away, being respectful and friendly.

'They'll be as they are sweetie. Just be you,' Carla reiterated.

'Thanks. Oh and… what shall I wear?' Lauren teased.

'Casual.' Carla confirmed, without hesitation. 'And, don't be a stranger…stranger. I like having you around again. Let me know how it goes.'

'You're right. I'll text. Thanks.'

Feeling more confident, Lauren ended the call and flicked through the clothes in her wardrobe. *Casual*, she mulled, as she hunted down the right thing for her date with Anna. *Date?* She pondered the idea and liked how it felt. She settled on a pair of dark blue fitted jeans, her brogues, and a brown-flecked caramel jumper, noting that the trousers hung a little more than they fitted. She had lost a few pounds over the last few weeks, but liked the feeling of not carrying any excess weight. She enjoyed the comfort loose fitting clothes afforded her. Appraising herself in the full-length mirror in her bedroom, she watched the dark brown curls bobbing above her shoulder. The dark bags under her eyes had softened a little, although her eyes still looked set back and her cheeks a little gaunt. Applying a touch of eyeliner and a splash of rouge she felt transformed and ready for the evening ahead. The thought caused her stomach to summersault and a warm sensation to spread across her chest. Checking her phone, she jumped at the two messages on the screen.

Just arrived x In town, see you shortly x

It was 7pm. Lauren grabbed her black Moschino coat, threw her bag over her shoulder and shut the door behind her. It was raining. Cursing the fact that she had left her brolly at work, she dashed down the street dodging raindrops as best she could, her bag raised above her head.

*

Walking into Sardo's brought a wry smile to Anna's face as she recalled the first and only time she had dined here, and how much had changed since that evening. She breathed in the familiar scent of fresh flowers coming from the tables. Observed the same subdued lighting, that delicately cast discreet patches of soft light, creating intimate spaces for each diner. She had just caught the start of the shower walking up from the tube station, so gently shook off the light spray as she removed her coat at the door, revealing skinny jeans, pearl white shirt and aubergine jacket. Grinning through steel-blue eyes as she embraced the calming ambience, she was greeted by the man she remembered. 'Hello, Naz isn't it?' she confirmed with a nod as she spoke.

'Ciao signorina,' the waiter greeted, with his languid smile and soft Italian tones. 'I remember a pretty lady.' His hazel eyes sparked as he nodded in response. 'You are here with Lorenza,' he confirmed. 'Please follow me.' Rarely had she heard Lauren called by her full name, but she liked the sound of it on his Italian tongue. It sounded *sensual*, she mused, feeling heat rise in her chest, as her mind lingered on a sensual image of her with Lauren. She followed the waiter as he led her to the familiar table tucked away in the back of the restaurant. 'Can I get you a drink while you wait?' he offered.

'I'll wait thanks,' Anna responded, gliding into the seat as directed. He placed two menus on the table, removed the reserved sign and retreated to the front of the restaurant.

Anna sat, reminiscing, immersed - the light classical background music, authentic décor and the smell of freshly cooked Italian food wafting from the kitchen. It felt homely, familiar. She sighed contentedly, allowing herself to be temporarily relaxed by the soporific atmosphere.

She heard the doorbell jingle, but it was the voice that made her insides jump - tumbling stars, sparkling and crashing - weakening the muscles in her legs, throwing her into emotional disarray. Although they had texted regularly, Anna hadn't phoned Lauren. They hadn't spoken since Corsica, but the effect of the slightly husky, soft tones, touched Anna deeply on every level. Quickly, she grabbed at the menu, opened it and tried to focus on its contents, anticipating the moment Lauren would appear in the alcove's small entrance. She didn't have to wait long.

'It's upside down,' the laughing voice came, pointing at the menu in Anna's hand. Blushing and laughing she stood and moved unashamedly into Lauren's open arms. Holding each other tightly, Lauren melted at the soft scent that tantalised all her senses. 'Hi,' she breathed into Anna's exposed ear. Anna groaned under her breath.

She pulled back reluctantly and looked Lauren over. 'Hi,' she beamed with such passion it took Lauren's breath away. 'Your hair,' she said, aloud as she pointed at the cropped cut.

'Ah yes. I forgot, you haven't seen it.' Lauren said a little embarrassed by her obvious omission.

'I love it,' Anna all but squealed, as she ran her fingers lightly through the short locks, inspecting the cut. The touch caused goose bumps to break out across Lauren.

Anna got lost in her fingers running through Lauren's hair, which had taken on a tenderness associated with something far more sensual than checking out a haircut. She pulled back sharply as she realised the effect on Lauren and cleared her throat before speaking. 'It really suits you.' She kissed Lauren more formally on the cheek, though lingering at the point of contact, before indicating for them both to sit.

'Can I get you ladies a drink?' Naz asked, gently reminding them of his presence.

'Wine?' Anna's eyes sought Lauren's for confirmation and received an approving nod.

'A bottle of Livon Friulano please Naz,' Anna requested, winking at the man who retreated professionally, with an affirming dip in his posture.

Both women sat simultaneously, sighed and locked eyes. 'You look… great.' Lauren was the first to break the connected silence, as she surveyed the woman in front of her.

'You look… tired,' Anna frowned, as she moved to stroke the side of Lauren's face. 'I mean you look lovely, but you do look tired too,' she qualified as her thumb gently moved under Lauren's eye, traced the dark rings, and moved down her jaw line. Lauren noted the sadness in the steel-blue eyes assessing her. Anna's concerned smile embraced Lauren with comfort. She felt cared about in a way that she had never experienced before. Not that she was one for being fussed over, but there was something about the way Anna treated her that felt different. Felt right.

The two women were drawn out of their captivation by the presentation of the chilled Friulano. 'You taste,' Anna insisted.

'Divine,' Lauren said, her eyes never wavering from the sight across the table. The double entendre duly noted, Anna continued to, unwittingly, unravel her with her deep steel-blue penetrating gaze.

An approving nod and Naz continued to pour the wine, housing the bottle in the cooler at the side of their table. Although they had been here before, the energy between them was different - even more electric… and terrifying.

'How's the portrait coming along?' Lauren nearly growled, as she shifted to a topic of conversation that might distract her from her seductive musings.

'Good, though I confess I haven't progressed your father in sketch yet,' she admitted. 'I'd like to talk to you about him when you're over next week. I need to get a better feel for his character,' Anna propositioned tentatively.

'Sure,' Lauren nodded. She could understand Anna's desire to know more about the man, her father, who had taken his own life, allegedly *better for all concerned,* or so the letter had read. Her thoughts presented themselves spontaneously and she could feel the anger rise up her body and fuel her mind. It hurt. *Did she really know him?* She thought she had known him well, but all she was left with was the unanswered question. *What could have caused him to take his own life?* Antoine had been somewhat evasive on the question when they had talked, understandably preferring to keep their conversation to the fond memories he had of her father and their work together. Momentarily struck by grief, Lauren coughed and looked into the space beyond Anna to release her throat before giving her attention to the menu in front of her.

'Sorry,' Anna apologised for the obvious pain she could see in Lauren's face. She wanted to reach out and hold her. Sweep her away. Comfort her. Remove the pain. But she knew that wasn't possible. She would be there for her though. That much she could, and would, do willingly. 'You are still coming?' she said, with a voice filled with hope and trepidation at the possibility of rejection.

'Of course!' Lauren said in a more determined voice, shaking off the momentary lapse into grief. 'Mother would have me disavowed if I didn't show up,' Lauren mocked, with a smile. The jovial tone lifted the mood in an instant. 'And...' She smiled cheekily, 'I can't wait to see your place.' Broadly grinning, Anna smiled with her and their alight faces homed in on each other, connecting them beyond the words that passed between them. They both looked down at their menus to break the excruciating sensation that drew them together. That feeling would need satisfying at some point... soon. 'What do you fancy?'

Anna looked up with a seductive smile, coughed roughly, and quickly reverted her gaze to the food options. 'Whatever you're having' she responded, temporarily unable to read the words, think, or make a decision. Her hands were shaking and her legs felt weak under the pressure of the lust she felt. There was only one hunger she could feel, lower in her body than her stomach. As she looked up, her eyes asking what Lauren was selecting for them, the stare that came back at her ripped deep into her heart.

'I need to tell you something,' Lauren said, the serious tone causing Anna's heart to stop dead.

'Uh ha.' she tried to sound casual, though feeling anything but.

Taking in a deep breath, 'Rachel and I are over,' Lauren said with a hint of sadness. She moved on quickly. 'It might take time to sort out the details, but we aren't together anymore.' Lauren's gaze wandered to the menu as a point of focus, not knowing how Anna might respond to the news and hoping not to see rejection in her face.

Anna leaned across the table and took the hand resting on the menu. Pressing her thumbs across the knuckles, lowering her head slightly to urge Lauren to look up. 'Are you okay?' she said with kindness and sincerity. 'How is Rachel?'

The compassion and consideration Anna showed for her ex almost made Lauren feel guilty for her own lack of remorse at the demise of their relationship. 'She's fine. It hurts of course, but we both know we need to move on,' Lauren said, as her eyes lingered on the tender hands holding hers. Smoothing her fingers across their surface, enjoying the soft pressure and warmth of the grip, she smiled weakly, the emotional pain evident in the watery eyes. 'I'm exhausted,' she sighed.

'Hey... if you'd rather go home, I'll understand?' Anna offered, very aware of the toll the last few weeks must have taken on her.

'No. I want to be with you Anna,' Lauren said unwaveringly, as she locked eyes with her. Anna involuntarily groaned at the intensity and depth she discovered in the dark brown gaze. Lauren was biting her bottom lip as if seeking an affirmation.

'I want to be with you too Lauren, but only when you're ready.' Anna pressed her fingers to the dry lips that were now bordering on a quiver, as she spoke. Anna knew she wanted to be with Lauren, but she didn't want to be a rebound affair. Recently out of her own break-up she needed the start of her relationship with Lauren to be based on secure footings. She couldn't cope with another heartbreak and as she looked into Lauren's eyes she knew that's where it would end for her if anything went wrong. Her heart ached at the thought.

Lauren trapped Anna's hand gently with her own, softly kissing her fingers, then tracing her fingers down into the palm to take the hand into her own. 'Thank you', she said in a deep sigh. There was that look of sincerity again. Pulling back slightly and taking a deep breath, she lifted her glass and raised a toast. 'To the future?' she posed as they clinked glasses. The tension that had been building had subsided and a calm poise had replaced the intensity. 'I'm hungry, how about you?' Lauren affirmed.

'Starving,' Anna responded. The cheeky, seductive, grin had reappeared - lighter, teasing, jovial.

Lauren could barely take her eyes away from the red, silky lips. She traced the gorgeous oval face, dwelling on the delicate lines that framed the intense, steel-blue piercing eyes.

Perhaps, this was the first time she had allowed herself to really take in the beautiful woman before her. *Exquisite*, she thought.

'How about a sharing plate?' Anna posed having studied the menu for a split second.

'Great,' Lauren said as she placed her menu on the side of the table. 'Anyway, how have you been? How's your mum?' she asked with genuine interest.

Anna held her gaze, studying the short locks that now framed the brown eyes and fine features. *Beautiful,* she thought.

*

'Where are you staying tonight?' Lauren ventured to ask as they wrapped coats around themselves and stepped out into the late-night chill. Winter was definitely just around the corner. Temperatures had dipped. Every breath was visible in the dark night. Linking arms with Anna, for warmth she told herself, they wandered down the cobbled side streets, heading nowhere in particular.

'Mum's expecting me,' Anna said, quietly averting eye contact. Lauren pulled her closer and slowed their walk to take as much time as she could grasp.

Reluctant to let go, she squeezed her arm and gave Anna a dejected look. 'Which station?'

'Don't give me that look,' Anna said poking her in the arm. 'I'll get a taxi when we're finished.' Lauren's face beamed.

Anna's eyes sparkled with the passing of each streetlight. Her heart thumped in her chest at the close contact, yet the anticipation of how the next few hours might play out caused anxiety to rise in her chest. Her breathing faltered and she felt suddenly weak. *What was she afraid of for Christ sake? Get a grip. You decide what happens next. Her relationship is over. What if she's rebounding?* The voice and questions consumed her thoughts, as concern swept through her body.

Sensing the change in Anna's posture, Lauren stopped walking and turned to face her. Taking her shoulders in her hands she tried to hold her shifty eyes with her own. 'Are you okay?' She looked the artist up and down intently, noting the pale colour that had replaced her previously pink cheeks and the dark, withdrawal expressed through her eyes. 'Hey. What's up?'

'Um… I think so. I'm not sure what just happened, but I feel a bit faint,' Anna responded, as she looked at her own shaking hands.

Lauren took the fragile hands warmly, squeezing them soothing the visible stress. The feeling of comfort and security surprised Anna but she bathed in it willingly. Moving closer, Lauren released one hand to pull Anna into a full body hug, rubbing the free hand up and down her back.

'Thank you.' Anna breathed the words close to Lauren's ear. The whisper that tickled her ear also raised the hairs on the back of her neck and caused her to visibly shiver. 'You're cold?' Anna noted.

'Umm… my place is just around the corner. Shall we go get a coffee and warm up before I throw you out onto the streets again?' Lauren said, trying to inject humour into the situation. Something had freaked Anna and she didn't want her to feel frightened off by her concerns. She hoped she would share her thoughts at some point, but didn't want to push her into talking.

'Yes.' Anna pulled out of the hug and instantly felt the absence of warmth and comfort of a moment ago. The depth of feeling caused her to want to cling on to Lauren even tighter. She resisted the urge, took a deep slow breath and met the concerned eyes of the woman who was clearly assessing her health status. 'I'm okay... honestly.'

Taking Anna by the arm, Lauren walked them both, slowly, the short distance to her house. She turned the key effortlessly in the lock, pushed open the solid white door of the Victorian town house and stepped into the centrally heated air - maintaining the comfortable silence they held together. Anna followed closely.

Stepping into the tall ceilinged hallway she couldn't help but notice the artwork that adorned the walls. 'You're a collector?' she quizzed, in a shocked tone. 'How did I not know that?' *I really know nothing about you!* She reflected on how little she knew about her, rising anxiety fluttering in her gut, as she admired the two original images. Both paintings were of Arabic women dressed in their Abaya cloak, offset by the vivid colours of the bustling market setting. One woman was admiring something unseen. The other was looking to sell the beads and other items of jewellery set out before her. Both sets of penetrating eyes looked out through their traditional headdress: their souls seeming to smile at the world. Contrary to the belief that the Khimar was a place for Muslim women to hide, where they could avoid connecting with the outside world, Anna felt instantly transported into their lives. She saw the pain in the hazel brown irises of the trader and a sense of loss in the darker eyes of the other woman. They revealed more in one look than she had seen in her ex at any point in their relationship, she reflected with irony. She knew the artist, before her eyes moved to the signature at the bottom of the canvas.

'I have a confession!' Lauren blushed and looked towards her feet, like a child about to be chastised. 'I checked you out after you gave me your card. I recognised your name, but stupidly hadn't made the link with your mum. She has an excellent reputation,' she confirmed. 'I hope you don't mind. I didn't want to say about being a collector, but I am a fan of her work… among others,' she added, hoping to be forgiven. 'I guess I wanted you to get to know me a bit better first, rather than think of me stalking you because I'm a fan of your mum!' Lauren said, shrugging her shoulders as if realising she might have made an error of judgement in this case.

'Stalker huh!' Anna appraised Lauren, eyebrows raised in jest as she tilted her head, with a questioning tone. 'I'm a fan of her work too,' she smiled. 'She has a real talent for capturing the emotional aspects of what she sees, adding depth that we can easily miss in real time,' Anna regaled as she looked back at the two women, whose eyes never seemed to leave her.

'Yes… I mean no. No to the stalker bit and yes to the talent,' Lauren started to laugh lightly. 'Would you like to come through?' She directed Anna into the front room of the house. The original fireplace was surrounded by, a two-seater and three-seater couch. A drinks cabinet, come bar, sat to the side with an archway leading into the expansive kitchen-diner containing a central island. It felt homely and yet spacious. Sophisticated yet cosy. *Lovely*. 'Please take a seat,' Lauren indicated with her hand to the cushion-backed three-seater couch. 'Would you like a drink?'

'Macallan, if you have it?' Anna requested, as she sunk into the deep cushions - the softness instantly relaxing some of the earlier tension and the anxiety seeming to fade. Her eyes hungrily perused the pleasant, warm surroundings - including the woman stood pouring a large whiskey… and over ice she noted with a wry smile. She watched the tall, athletic form with greater interest and a longing that was becoming familiar to her. 'So,' she said, as Lauren handed her the glass, their fingers contacting in the exchange. 'What else do I need to know about you?' she almost croaked out the words, as her nerves jumped, positively, at the light touch.

'Well… That's a long story. How long do you have?' Lauren teased as she sat on the other end of the couch, maintaining the space between them, kicking off her heels and wrapping her feet underneath her. Facing Anna, she studied her with passion, as the artist took the glass to her lips and sipped the amber liquid - the ice slipping around in the glass. 'Where shall we start?' she asked, looking to the distance, as if she were reviewing her past for the data she wanted to share. She sipped slowly, her lips teasing the glass. 'Okay. So, I know we don't know much about each other and we haven't known each other for that long, which is great as we have lots to find out. But I do know, I have never felt this way about anyone… and I would like to get to know you better. A lot better,' she said smiling seductively.

Anna nearly choked on her drink at Lauren's honest revelation, heat rising through her body - not from the burning liquid, but from the reciprocal feelings rushing through her. Attempting to recover herself her mouth opened and then closed again, with no words forthcoming. Coughing she cleared her throat. 'So, tell me about yourself?'

Lauren relaxed back into the couch swirling her drink - entranced at the way the alcohol glided and formed a delicate film across the glass. Staring into the past, she recounted the details of her early life to Anna: the loss of her sister; her move to London; her training as a lawyer and ambition for partnership; her distant relationship with her mother who had failed to accept her sexuality and her father's support of her lifestyle, and the demise of her relationship with Rachel.

As Lauren spoke, Anna felt emotionally drawn to her experiences. The sadness at the loss of Lauren's younger sister and the subsequent death of her father touched her deeply. Anna had not suffered by comparison. With supportive parents and no siblings, she reflected that she had never really known loss. Yes, she had been recently devastated at the end of her only really serious relationship, with Sophie, and her mum's recent diagnosis, but that paled by comparison with the experiences of the dark eyed woman sitting next to her.

As Lauren's eyes pulled away from the swirling drink and out of the trance, her gaze fixed to the steel-blue eyes that had been lightened, to near silver, by the tears pushing for release. The soft smile they shared, full of tenderness and unspoken understanding, reached their souls. Lauren leaned in and thumbed an errant tear from Anna's cheek. The artist captured the hand and pressed a light kiss on her palm. Maintaining the hold, squeezing tightly, she lowered the hand from her mouth. Raising her free hand to Lauren's face, she brushed her fingers through the short curly hair - trailing the high cheekbones and fine features with adoration. Reaching her mouth, her index finger tracked the curve of Lauren's lips, eliciting a painful groan as the wild brown eyes shut in ecstasy.

'Uh... I'm not sure I can take this,' Lauren said, her voice ragged and questioning. Anna pulled back sharply causing her to open her eyes. The penetrating, dark, stare caused Anna to gasp for breath as her heart thumped through her chest and her eyes tried to pull away. They failed. As the two women stared, unspeaking, dry lips wetted by revealing tongues, the gap between them closed. Slowly, but both knowing there was no going back, their mouths crashed together and they groaned in unison. Shifting so their bodies touched, their hands sought refuge in the other. Gently, purposefully, they explored each other. Hands moved under clothing to connect with warm soft skin, sending a high voltage charge through every nerve ending. Goose bumps revealed the inner earthquake that was about to shatter their worlds. Kisses deepened, tongues entwined, they danced in synchronous harmony - lost in a united inner world of desire, passion... and love. Neither wanted to stop, but the need to breathe resulted in a momentary break as Anna pulled back and held the near black eyes with her own.

'Mmmm,' Lauren murmured in acknowledgement of the unspoken message, before pulling Anna into her for a tender languid kiss. With less intensity, but no less desire, their touch softened.

Biting Lauren's lower lip, licking the swollen lips, Anna groaned and gently pulled back from the embrace. 'I... have... to... go,' she said in a voice that was groggy with lust and heavy with reluctance.

'Or else what?' Lauren teased, with a seductive smile, as she released her. 'I know. It's okay.' Lauren spoke the words as she stood to regain her composure. 'I'll call a taxi,' she offered.

'Thanks,' Anna said as she wobbled to a stand, only to be caught by Lauren, who pulled her closer, held her tightly and planted a soft kiss on her tender lips. 'Ummm... if you carry on with that...' she mumbled into the shoulder of the lawyer - the threat lacking any credibility or impetus as the warm breath teased her neck and caused a shiver to pass the length of her body.

'Argh,' Lauren grumbled as she pulled back, her body rebelling against the increasing space, and absence of heat. Her eyes searched the ceiling briefly as her hands dropped to the safety of her sides. Chuckling as their eyes met, Lauren turned away, reached for her phone and made the call.

16.

Anna turned the key quietly in the Chubb lock, stepped into the dark hallway and placed her bag quietly under the coatrack. A slither of light leaked from the bottom of the sitting room door. Her heart rate had settled, but she was still reeling from the aftershock of the kiss with Lauren. Her nerves felt on edge, her legs weak and her mind had already started running its familiar track. What ifs had circled and dominated her thoughts for the journey across town to her parents' house, in general talking herself out of a relationship with the woman she had just kissed. No. Not just kissed. The woman she had kissed with such passion and longing, she had never experienced before. It had taken all her strength, and some, to leave. But she had convinced herself on the ride home that that had been the right move. The floor squeaked as she stepped into the hall. It always squeaked, she noted. It reminded her that this was home, and she smiled. The smell of freshly aired linen wafted throughout the space, together with a spicy room scent that reminded Anna that Christmas was on its way. The familiarity was comforting and she breathed in the reassuring scents before opening the door to the living room.

'Oh my god,' Anna almost shrieked, as she jumped out of her skin. She hadn't expected anyone to be up at 2am, but the sight of her mother, pale and sweating, walking towards her, scared her in more ways than one. 'Mum,' she said as she reached out to take her in her arms. 'What the...' she stammered as her mum soaked up the hug.

'I'm alright.' Lisa tried to sound convincing, but failed.

'The hell you are.' Anna looked the grey skinned woman up and down. 'You look goddamn awful.'

'It's okay sweetie. It's just the end of a therapy day, so I'm not feeling so great. I'm glad you made it.' Her swollen face made her eyes look smaller and duller than normal. Anna's heart sunk as she held her mother, noticing the weakness in the reciprocal embrace. 'Let's get back to bed,' her mother urged, fatigued by the effort it had taken to get to the kitchen in the middle of the night.

'Where's mum?' Anna asked, wondering why Vivian hadn't helped Lisa.

'She's away until tomorrow, at a conference. And, before you start. She wanted to stay but I insisted she go. It's an annual event and it keeps her sane,' her mother humoured.

'Right, let's get you upstairs then,' Anna offered, shocked out of the happy bubble that had consumed her moments earlier.

The effort it had taken to get Lisa up the stairs exhausted Anna almost as much as it did her mum. They'd had to stop every two steps for her mum to catch her breath. No conversation had passed between them. Instead, Anna had simply held her mother to provide the support she needed and both had given the task their full concentration. It had taken ten-minutes to get her back into bed. She had breathed deeply, with relief as her body settled against the soft mattress. She was as white as the sheet she laid on. Tears had welled in Anna's eyes as she watched her mum drift off into sleep and she had checked three-times to make sure she was still breathing before she returned down the stairs, with a heavy heart.

As she walked into the living room, her phone pinged, distracting her from her negative thoughts.

Take care Anna. Sleep well. x.

Smiling she text back.

Arrived. Take care you. Chat tomorrow x.

A smiley came back at her and she put her phone back in her pocket. She didn't feel it. Sighing, a sense of solemnness overwhelmed her, her thoughts consumed with concern at the state of her mum in the bed upstairs.

She didn't sleep well. She tossed and turned, feeling tense and helpless. She watched the hours go by. When the clock finally ticked past 5.30 she threw the covers off and stepped into the shower. Her eyes swollen, her head fuzzy, she stood under the hot water. The pressure, just short of painful, served to enliven her a little - a coffee would finish the awakening, she thought. Stepping into her jeans, trainers, and a loose-fitting t-shirt, she descended to the kitchen and put on a pot of filter coffee. The smell instantly stimulating her senses, she clicked the radio on low. She needed the company, if only to get her mind away from the persistent negative thoughts that were beginning to possess her mind. She didn't do a lack of sleep very well. It made her feel more vulnerable, more susceptible to the sadness that lurked just below the surface, more anxious. And she knew she needed to be strong.

'Morning darling,' her mother's voice, stronger than just a few hours earlier, woke her from her daydream. 'Didn't expect to see you so early,' she smiled weakly as she hugged her daughter. Still in her dressing gown, she had a little more colour than she had done at 2am, Anna noted.

'Hi. How're you feeling?' Anna asked, fighting the anxiety that flared through her gut.

'Much better today,' Lisa nodded in affirmation as she spoke. 'Ready for some of that coffee,' she grinned as she looked towards the hissing, steaming pot. 'Sleep is a challenge these days,' she remarked, even though no question had been posed. Erratic sleep, coupled with exhaustion, weren't the only symptoms of the chemotherapy treatment, but they were the most impactful, preventing Lisa from throwing herself fully into her work and her life.

'I hadn't realised...' Anna started to speak, apologetically, as her eyes welled up.

'It's just the treatment darling. In a few months, we'll be through the worst of it,' her mum insisted. Whether she was being brave or convinced of a positive outcome wasn't clear to Anna, but she didn't feel quite as strong as her mum appeared and began sobbing.

'Sorry,' she spluttered, as Lisa moved to hug her. Her hold, noticeably stronger than it had been in the early hours, providing some reassurance easing the flow of Anna's tears. 'Sorry, I'm tired too,' she confessed as she wiped the tears from her face and hugged her mum closely. 'Coffee,' she said, pulling away and raising her spirits, if only for appearances.

'Great idea,' Lisa remarked, her eyes trying to smile, but still a little glassy from withheld emotion.

*

'Hey, you guys,' Vivian motioned with open arms and an excited tone, as she bounced through the door and grabbed Lisa and Anna in an all-encompassing hug. 'My two favourite girls,' she smiled infectiously. 'How have you been sweetheart,' she addressed her lover with tenderness, holding her away to appraise the tired, sunken eyes and swollen features. Anna watched as Vivian's hands caressed the sides of Lisa's face, her thumbs tracing the lines that had aged her mum through the treatment. All the while, her eyes holding Lisa's so she would know the real truth. Whilst the outside of the woman she had loved forever was changing, those changes were superficial to Vivian. Nothing could be changed that would result in her feeling anything less than undying love for her wife. Inner pain tainted the lively smile and the tender hug was warm and reassuringly confident. 'Anna, my darling, how are you?' Vivian turned to her daughter and gave her a gentle squeeze on the arm. Her eyes sparkled and a broad grin adorned her face as she spoke.

'Good,' both women responded simultaneously, then eyed each other and smiled softly.

Mum and daughter looked exhausted, even though they had spent the day effectively chilling out, going for a gentle walk in the park, arm-in-arm, kicking up leaves - reminiscing. It had been a strange day. They had chatted about the past a lot, things that people only talk about when time together is thought to be precious or limited - when death is a real possibility. Their relationship had always been close, but the day they had spent together had brought them even closer. The thought that her mum might die crucified her. A pain so deep it prised her heart in two. She had pushed the darkness to the back of her mind, trying to enjoy the day for what it was. Time together. Being present. Laughing. Crying. Loving.

'How about we dine out tonight? I want to hear all about your day,' Vivian proposed, raising the tone.

'Excellent idea,' Lisa confirmed, as she squeezed her daughter's hand and patted her wife on the arm. 'You're paying,' she directed at Vivian and winked towards Anna. 'I'm thinking Lobster...Rib of Beef...' Lisa pondered aloud, as she headed for the stairs to go and change. 'I've already booked the table by the way,' she said, with a cheeky laugh that filled the house as she climbed the stairs. Anna welcomed the new sense of normality for a Friday night in the Taylor-Cartwright household. Following her mum, she bounded the stairs two at a time and dived into her bedroom.

*

'Excellent choice,' Vivian remarked to Anna as the waiter took their order. 'The steak here is superb. Best in town,' she said, as she always did, even though they had all visited the restaurant on many occasions. 'I'll have the same please, medium rare and with fries on the side,' she instructed as she handed over her menu. The wine arrived just as the waiter took the remaining menus from the women and headed for the serving area. 'So, darling.' Vivian started with a wry smile. 'It's lovely to see you earlier than planned. How's Paris?'

'Paris is great. I've been busy. That portrait project... Corsica.' she recalled, her eyes glazing over as she remembered her brief visit to the Mediterranean island. 'The woman I met in London a few weeks back only happens to be the daughter of the woman who commissioned the work,' she tried to say in a casual tone.

'Why haven't you told us before now?' Vivian asked excitedly.

'Well I didn't think it was worth mentioning. But...'

'What? Come on Anna what's happening? I can see you're hiding something,' Lisa quizzed chirpily, as if wanting in on a secret with a best friend.

'But what?' her older mum chipped in impatiently. Both women staring at their daughter, hoping - praying - for good news. Like any parents they wanted her to be happy and when Anna had been devastated at the break up with Sophie they too had felt her pain.

'I stopped by to see her on the way here. We had supper,' Anna said, lost in her memory of the elongated, passionate kiss. Heat rose instantly to her face and her mouth went dry.

'Wow... must have been good,' Vivian teased, lightly, with a sparkle in her eyes, nudging her in the side, as Anna lowered her head in mild embarrassment. Whilst they had always been open and jokey about relationships, they were also respectful of the delicate balance where love - and the future - was concerned.

'Oh darling...' Lisa just watched her daughter with reserved optimism. She knew that coy look. She had looked at Vivian that way. She knew what it meant. Her heart leapt at the passion she spied beneath the embarrassment, but she also sensed reluctance in Anna, dampening the thrill. *She's holding back.* 'What's up sweetie?'

Anna sipped at the chilled wine. The subtle flavours reminding her of the evening she had shared at Sardo's with Lauren. She smiled at the memory of them laughing together, but her expression was tinged with something else. The depth of feeling in her heart destabilised her. 'I'm... scared,' she said honestly, as she looked from one mum to the other.

'Oh,' both older women exclaimed with a renewed seriousness to their tone. 'Sweetie, please try not to be scared. I know it's hard because you don't want it to go wrong, but you need to be free to love and be loved back,' Lisa said, holding Vivian's eyes and squeezing her hand across the table.

They were the perfect example of love, Anna thought as she watched her mums intently. 'I know,' she said, sighing, and taking another large glug of the wine at the thought of letting go of the fear that seemed to be taking a stronger hold as each day passed. *What's the worst thing that could happen?*

A couple more glasses of wine hitting the tiredness and she started to feel much more relaxed. The loss of inhibition that followed as the evening progressed enabled her to chat more freely about the gorgeous Corsican woman who had stolen her heart... and soul. As she spoke she smiled, an honest, deep founded smile. In a dream-like space Anna recounted the previous weeks in more detail than the clipped, *it was fine,* version they had been given over the phone previously. The two women asked questions, smiled, held hands and gave a knowing look at each other.

In some ways, they were vicariously reliving their early encounters. The lovers-dance. The push and pull as doubts warred with lust in the commitment battle. Courage overcoming fear as taking the plunge opens the heart to the deepest level of vulnerability that means, in and of itself, such love feels excruciatingly painful. But the rewards for exercising that courage and moving through the pain of love were always worth it. For a precious life spent with the love of a soul mate - priceless. Vivian squeezed Lisa's hand, reaffirming that love in the face of the only other woman in both their lives.

'When can we meet her?' Lisa asked softly. 'Since she has clearly stolen your heart, we would really love to meet her. Why don't you invite her for lunch on Sunday? She can even stay over and head to the airport with you in the morning,' her mother suggested matter of fact.

Anna's smile radiated towards her mum. 'I hadn't thought of that, but I can ask. I'm not sure what she's got planned. We haven't talked that much,' Anna confessed, before realising what her comment might have implied. Both mums raised their eyebrows and smiled. 'No,' Anna sniggered. 'What are you two like. We haven't slept together... yet,' Anna beamed with an uncontrolled wink at her parents. 'I'll ask her,' she confirmed.

'Ooo lovely...' Lisa cuddled into Vivian at the thought of her daughter finding what she had discovered with Vivian. 'Lovely,' she repeated to herself.

The women chatted their way through the sumptuous dinner, with Vivian adopting centre stage and recalling the key moments of her trip. There was something bizarre about a Doctor's mind set, Anna thought, as her mum spoke with humour about medical matters that the lay person would find most distressing.

'Well I don't know about you, but I'm stuffed. That hit the spot. The food at the conference was only one step up from hospital meals,' Vivian joked with sarcasm. Anna laughed heartily feeling quite inebriated after the best part of half a bottle of wine and a large cognac. Although she could take more, the tiredness had exacerbated the effect of the alcohol. Now she was feeling quite drowsy and couldn't wait for bed.

'Delicious,' her mum nodded in appreciation of the treat, as her hands held her full stomach. Vivian summoned the bill. Having paid they rose from the table and stepped out into the chilled Friday night air, and the humming buzz of central London.

The mums linked arms and nodded conspiratorially at each other, as Anna pulled out her phone.

Hi, how's your evening? x

Anna read the message that warmed her already flushed cheeks.

Great, dinner with mums. How about you? x

She waited, watching the phone as she walked a pace behind her parents. The buzz couldn't come quickly enough.

OK, working! Looking forward to seeing you Monday

The text finished with a smiley and a kiss.

Fancy coming to lunch on Sunday and going to the airport from mums?

Anna had asked the question before thinking too deeply about the consequences. The long silence that followed caused her to worry whether she should have asked at all. *Was she pushing Lauren too hard,* she wondered to herself? Waiting, she pocketed the phone, but kept hold of it so she would feel it vibrate when the response came through. By the time they arrived home she still hadn't heard from Lauren and was beginning to panic that she had frightened her away. Even with their undeniable connection, there was still a lot going on for them both. Perhaps it was too soon for Lauren? How long did it take to get over a ten-year-plus relationship? She knew she was still sore from her break-up with Sophie, so reasoned Lauren was probably also feeling raw. As they entered the warm, cosy living room, Anna felt sobered by the silence emanating from her phone.

'Everything okay darling?' Vivian quizzed gently, noting the change in her daughter's mood.

'Yeah fine. I'm just shattered,' Anna responded, forcing a smile that didn't light up her eyes. 'I'm going to bed.' She hugged both mums and headed up to her room as her parents slumped in the chair and switched on the television.

'Sweet dreams,' they said in unison.

'You too,' Anna responded wearily.

'She'll be fine,' Vivian whispered in her wife's ear as Anna closed the door behind her.

She began undressing as she entered her room. Dropping her clothes onto the bedroom chair she slipped, naked, under the quilt, phone still in hand. Even the gentle buzz of the phone didn't stir Anna though as alcohol and tiredness combined to drive her into a deep sleep. Waking to the smell of brewing coffee, she peered through sleepy, half-open eyes to read...

Sorry, battery died at work! Would love to come for lunch. Chat later x

She dived out of bed like a six-year old on Christmas Day - her early Christmas wish had been delivered.

17.

Anna rushed to the door at the sound of the bell. It was 12.30 on the dot and there was no questioning who stood on the other side of the barrier. She stopped on the mat, hand poised, and realised she wasn't ready to open the door to face Lauren. She could feel her heart thumping through her chest. Her breathing was hurried, her palms sweating and her hands were shaking. She needed to calm and compose herself. She felt weak, yet alive, and prayed her legs wouldn't give way when she caught sight of Lauren. It was only a couple of nights since they had kissed, the memory of which lingered in every cell of her body. That kiss had penetrated her soul like no other. She hoped Lauren felt the same way. She had definitely been affected and they had both needed to exert huge self-control to stop before they would have certainly ripped each other's clothes off. But was it just about sex? There was nothing Anna wanted to do more than make love to Lauren, but fear, and timing, had taken control of her brain and urged caution so she had over-ridden her basic desires and walked away. But, she wasn't sure she had the will or the strength to do so again.

Her mums were in their room getting changed for lunch. Anna had been ready for the last half-hour, and fidgeting ever since. She had changed outfit three times, not really sure what look she was going for, but searching nonetheless. In the end, she had opted for her light blue skinny jeans, white shirt and autumnal patterned silk jacket with matching scarf. The jacket had been designed for her curves and fit perfectly. She breathed deeply three times then turned the solid lock to open the door. Her heart skipped a beat then stopped as her eyes met Lauren's. A soft groan fell off her lips and she was sure she was about to faint, as she scanned the dark Corsican woman standing on the threshold. Her short

140

curly hair, soft chocolate-dark brown eyes and athletic build, stood in black jeans, baby blue shirt and a long black jacket. With a seductive smile planted across her face, Anna gasped for air. 'Wow...'

'Wow back at you,' Lauren said, as she gazed up and down, pausing at various points to admire the perfection standing before her. 'Mmm...' she growled. Anna felt naked, but not in an uncomfortable way. Warmth spread through her as lust consumed her body with Lauren's sensual gaze. 'Shall I come in?' Lauren asked at the frozen woman now blocking the doorway.

'Sure... come in... sorry... distracted!' Anna fumbled, regaining some composure before Lauren brushed past her to enter the hallway, leaning in to softly place a kiss on her cheek. A musky sweet scent floated into the space, as Lauren started to remove her coat, and assaulted Anna's senses. The brief but lingering contact caused tingling sensations to accompany the rising heat and increasing wetness in the blushing woman. She felt completely undone and wanted to bury herself in Lauren's arms, soak up that intoxicating scent and burn together - to take her here and now. If her parents hadn't been in the house, she probably would have followed her feelings and pressed her to the wall, planted the deepest, most urgent, kiss on her mouth and fucked her senseless. Her cheeks reddened even further at the flow of sexual images, and she looked away to gain some composure.

'Come through,' she said, her voice rugged, indicating to the living room. 'Aperitif?' She offered without needing a response. *God, she's so fucking hot*. The thought stayed with Anna as she poured two large Macallans, over ice. Her hands were still shaking, she noticed.

'Thanks.' Lauren smiled as she took the glass and immediately placed it on the low table.

She looked more composed than Anna felt. *Was it because she didn't feel the same way?* Anna wondered fleetingly.

Closing the space as if to answer the unspoken concern, Lauren held Anna's eyes. Lifting her hand, she brushed the hair from her face, gently looping it around her ear, cupped her hand around her neck and pulled her in for a soft, delicate kiss. As their lips touched Anna audibly moaned and wanted to take the kiss deeper, just as Lauren pulled away a few inches. 'In case you were wondering,' she said smiling softly as Anna adjusted to the space between them. She took Lauren's hand and squeezed it gently, soaking up the warmth and confidence she found in the hold.

'Hello,' Vivian interrupted, immediately noticing the electric energy between the two women. 'You must be Lauren? Lovely to meet you.' She smiled warmly and pulled their guest into a strong, welcoming, embrace.

'Thank you for inviting me,' Lauren addressed the older woman without releasing Anna's hand.

'Mum this is Lauren,' Anna blurted out as Lisa entered the room, just behind her wife. She released Lauren's hand to grab her mum and drag her into the space vacated by Vivian. 'Lauren is a huge fan of yours and has both *'Arabian Life'* prints,' Anna gushed.

'You didn't tell me that,' Lisa admonished her daughter, smiling and nudging her in the arm.

'It's really lovely to meet you Lauren. We've heard so much about you already... and you seem to have had a delightful effect on our daughter if you don't mind me saying,' Vivian said, in her characteristically direct manner.

'Mum!' Anna rebuked, light heartedly. Her mums would have them married off by the end of the day at this rate.

Lauren watched Anna with gentle amusement, thoroughly enjoying the approval she seemed to be getting from both her mums. A far cry from her own mother's response, she pondered briefly. 'It's really an honour to meet you Mrs Taylor...'

'Lisa.' Anna's mum interrupted. 'And Vivian of course,' she indicated to her wife who was now busy pouring them both a gin and tonic.

'Well, it's really an honour to meet you Lisa... and Vivian.' She nodded towards the woman at the bar, with a beaming smile. 'Really, I am... in awe.' Lauren spoke in candid admiration of the older artist. 'I love your work and would love to see more of it at some time, if that's possible?' she asked.

'Of course, darling,' Lisa offered, squeezing the arm of the lawyer with tender approval. 'Now, let's get that drink,' she stated, looking firmly in the direction of her wife and stepping towards the bar.

Anna's eyes met Lauren's, the force drawing them together physically, so that Anna's lips brushed hers lightly. 'Thank you,' she whispered. Lauren shivered at the warm breath across her cheek, smiled lovingly and put an arm around Anna's waist, taking the out held glass in her free hand. 'Cheers,' Anna raised her glass in salute. 'To the future.'

'To today, and to those we love,' Lisa added.

'To today,' they cheered together, sipping the chilled drinks.

*

'Snack anyone?' Lisa said as the women shook off their coats and headed into the living room, welcoming the warmth.

'Not for me thanks mum,' Anna responded, holding her belly as she collapsed onto the couch, 'I'm still stuffed,' she said as she and Lauren took the offered, rather large, Cognac from Vivian. Lauren shook her head in agreement and Vivian held her hand up in a stop sign. 'This is a bit excessive,' Anna remarked, almost to herself, as she sipped the burning liquid. *But what the hell... eh?* she thought, as the warmth spread across her mouth and tingled her throat. She was still feeling quite tipsy having shared two bottles of wine over lunch, and the aperitif beforehand. She was beginning to wonder if she was drinking too much. But the brief thought was banished to the back of her mind as the liquid warmed her throat and the side of Lauren's body against hers warmed other the sensitive parts of her body.

Lunch had been extravagant. Luxurious. She hadn't expected Lauren to pay for the meal, but she had insisted and paid before any of the other women could prevent her. They had chastised her lightly, secretly enjoying the unexpected generosity. They had sauntered leisurely, as two couples in love, back through the park for some fresh air before visiting a local art gallery. Lisa had talked through some of the exhibits, thoroughly entertaining Lauren who was hungry to understand the science behind the art. The two women were as thick as thieves as their conversation flowed. Anna linked arms with Vivian and followed closely behind, in wonder at her mother and Lauren. The feeling that coursed through her body was unfamiliar. There was tenderness... love even, but something less tangible beneath the surface that she could not name. It distracted her momentarily, until Vivian had pointed at a canvas and asked for her thoughts.

The darkening autumnal days brought in the cold quite quickly and so they had made their way home to the warmth of the centrally heated house, and now a large cognac rested in their hands. Lisa sat heavily into the large cushioned armchair, and with a deep sigh closed her eyes. She looked pale beneath the chill-induced red patches on her cheeks.

'You okay mum?' Anna asked with concern.

'Sure am,' she responded without opening her eyes. 'That was a beautiful afternoon,' she remarked, with a brief smile. 'Exhausting, but wonderful,' she clarified.

'I'm sapped too,' Vivian stated as she necked the remaining Cognac before looking toward her wife. 'Come on love, let me take you to bed?' She winked at the younger women before giving a hand to Lisa to help her up from the chair.

'It's still early,' Anna noted. 'It's only just after six,' she said. 'Don't feel you have to go because of us, please?'

'Wouldn't dream of it darling. I'm very happy to be lying down right now… and we have a TV and video in the room, among other forms of entertainment,' she nodded towards the younger women with a twinkle in her tired eyes.

'Okay, too much information mum.' Anna laughed, raising her hands in front of her face so as not to see the image her mum had tried to install. 'Rest well,' she said more seriously, blowing her a kiss. 'Give us a shout if you need anything,' she offered, knowing they wouldn't disturb her and Lauren for the rest of the evening.

'The spare room's made up… if you feel you need it?' Vivian commented softly as they exited the room and headed for the stairs.

Anna's eyes caught Lauren's as heat rose to her cheeks and they laughed together, bringing their faces within inches of each other. 'Mmm…' escaped Anna as her stomach flipped with the intensity of emotion that passed between them.

Lauren closed the short gap in an instant, capturing Anna's mouth with force and passion, making her intentions clear - eliciting a deep, guttural groan from Anna. As their tongues danced and lapped, Lauren's hands took Anna's head and pulled her back from the kiss. Holding her gently, looking into the deep blue pools, darkened with lust, she placed her forehead to Anna's. 'I've wanted to do that since I saw you,' she admitted. 'Since I first saw you,' she lifted her head, tilted it and smiled an honest smile.

'Me too,' Anna said as she traced the side of Lauren's face and pulled her into another deep, intense kiss. Anna's body crying out to be touched, her mind pulled her out of the kiss prematurely.

'Is everything okay?' Lauren questioned with worry.

'Yes, everything is wonderful,' Anna responded, biting her bottom lip in restraint, avoiding Lauren's dark eyes. She wanted Lauren in every way possible, but her mums' couch wasn't the place she had in mind for the intimacy she desired... no needed, from Lauren.

Standing, she held out her hand for Lauren to take. The message was clear and Lauren, standing to join her, was an acceptance of the unspoken request. Leaving their drinks, they walked in silence up the stairs and into Anna's bedroom. Leading Lauren into the room, Anna turned and leant back against the door. It clicked gently to a close and within a second Anna felt her back pressed against the warm wood as Lauren's mouth took hers, firmly, hungrily. She felt the soft, strong hands in her own, tightening their grip, owning her, confident in their actions. She groaned again as Lauren released her grip with one hand and found the boundary between shirt and jeans. Within seconds the firm pressure of her fingers on Anna's waist, moving up her back, caused goose bumps to course through her body. A second hand rode up the other side of her back, working together to unclip her bra, then moving to the front, seeking pert breasts and hardened nipples. Lauren groaned in pleasure as Anna's body responded to her touch. Their kissing intensified, increasing the sense of urgency and driving Anna's hand to Lauren's throbbing crotch. She could feel the hot, damp throbbing sex - akin to the feeling between her own legs. She pulled back swiftly. Black eyes met hers with an intensity that made her feel weak. Her legs were shaking.

'Bed. Now.' She grabbed at Lauren's shirt and began to quickly unbutton it, followed by her jeans. Lauren removed Anna's clothes at the same time as she pushed them both back towards the bed. Stepping out of her underwear Anna thrust Lauren onto the bed, covering her with her own body - legs, mouths and tongues intertwined, as one. They fit together. Lying still for a moment Anna savoured the feeling of the warm flesh pressing against every part of her. It felt so right it hurt.

Lauren became aware of the sudden stillness in the body pressing against her - driving her insane with desire - followed by the damp salty taste as their mouths pressed fervently, unrelenting in their desire. Opening her eyes and releasing Anna's soft lips, she looked intently at her.

'It's okay baby,' she spoke softly as she cupped her face in gentle hands and pressed her lips delicately on Anna's eyelids and around her face. Kissing the tears away and holding her tightly into her chest, she vowed. 'I'm not going anywhere. I love you Anna.'

Holding Lauren close, her face pressed into her neck, the comforting scent invaded her senses. The tears stopped almost as quickly as they had started. 'Sorry,' she whispered. 'I love you so much it scares me,' she breathed into her lover's ear as she kissed her face. Arousal shot through her instantly and with no ability to control the energy sparking within, she took Lauren's mouth in a long, intense kiss, whilst her hands slowly touched the soft, firm skin below her.

Lauren moaned under the soft caress, unable to still her body any longer, they effortlessly danced in sensual ecstasy - each knowing where the other needed them most. Anna's leg pressed against the throbbing centre, one hand around her waist pulling Lauren into the exquisite pressure, the other hand caressing her right breast, with her tongue teasing the lonely nipple. Under the unhurried, yet intense exploration, Lauren could barely breathe - parts of her body were exploding simultaneously like nothing she had ever experienced before. Uncontrollably, her head thrust back and fire filled her lower belly. It took all her strength of will not to scream out in pure pleasure. The earthquake that had been slowly building had taken hold and there was no preventing the exquisite orgasm that thrashed through her, rendering her insensible and then completely immobile. She was silent as the aftershocks filtered through her system and Anna continued kissing her softly.

'Mmm… you are so, so hot,' Anna spoke into the still shaking stomach of her lover.

'Fuck. I didn't expect that,' Lauren almost whimpered, as if talking to herself, as her hands fingered through Anna's hair. Pulling her up to eye level a sharp sensation pierced her heart. 'Oh my god,' she muttered in disbelief, as she pulled Anna in and claimed her mouth again.

The urgency building through passionate kisses, Lauren exerted all her strength to flip Anna onto her back and claim the nipples that were calling for attention. It was a weak effort, helped by Anna's willingness as she arched with the contact, pulling Lauren closer, begging for more pressure. But Lauren pulled away from the grip, revealing a devilish smile. 'Slowly,' she teased, blowing softly across the taut nipple. Anna gave a throaty growl and balled her fists, her head thrashing on the pillow. Lauren continued to tease the erect nipple with her thumb and fingers as she kissed her way down Anna's, now restless body. Trailing lower, Anna's scent intensifying Lauren's sense of urgency, she captured the swollen sex fully in her mouth. Releasing the nipple, an arm around Anna's waist, Lauren raised her lover's hips for better access. The subtle change in position caused Anna to gasp as the intensity of touch deepened instantly. Pressing her tongue deeply into her, she bucked and thrashed. Then, suddenly, she stopped, in tension.

Lauren stopped out of concern and looked up. 'Don't stop. I'm...' Anna's words were cut short as Lauren's mouth resumed with urgency. Her tongue swept across the throbbing clitoris, instantly followed by two fingers penetrating her slowly and deeply. Lauren could feel the soft centre contract and grip her as Anna was driven over the top. Shuddering shocks ripped through her body. Lauren kissed her sensitive parts gently, keeping her fingers in place until she could no longer feel the tension that had clamped them. Kissing her way back up, Lauren's whole body smiled at what had just transpired between them. Lauren placed a delicate kiss on Anna's lips before rolling onto her back and drawing the depleted woman into her arms. As their sparkling eyes met, a silent knowing passed between them. Lauren kissed the top of Anna's head as she rested it in her shoulder. Within seconds their breathing had slowed and they slept deeply.

18.

Anna woke at the soft heat that tickled her right ear, raising a smile that touched every part of her. She wanted to snuggle closer but Lauren seemed deeply asleep and she could hear the sound of pots and pans coming from the kitchen. It was already daylight outside. Taking a deep breath, she slowly extracted herself from the bed without disturbing Lauren, who just grumped at the movement, and threw on her dressing gown. Carefully opening the bedroom door, she tiptoed out of the room straight into her mum's path.

'Good night then?' The rhetorical question and beaming smile on her mum's face elicited the broadest of grins from Anna. 'She's lovely, darling,' Lisa said as she took her daughter's hand in her own and squeezed. 'Come on let's get some coffee? You guys have a flight to catch, remember?' she said, heading for the stairs.

'Morning gorgeous girls.' Vivian addressed her two favourite women as she set the coffee machine to filter the brew. 'I'm making eggs. Will Lauren have some?'

'I'm sure she will.' Anna smiled and shrugged at the same time, aware that she was hazarding a guess.

'You have a good night?' Vivian asked, with a wry smile and a wink. Not waiting for, or needing, a verbal response, she continued. 'She's adorable, Anna.' She soothingly rubbed her hand up and down Anna's arm. 'She is a good un,' she affirmed, nodding to herself, as she returned to whisking the eggs and pulling the bacon out of the fridge. 'Breakfast in ten,' she confirmed, with a look that said, *you'd better go get your girlfriend.*

Anna poured the coffees and took hers and Lauren's back up to the room. Stepping through the door, Lauren stirred awake and sat up on an elbow smiling profusely at the robe dressed woman as she handed her a mug.

'Hot,' she remarked, with sparkling eyes.

'It is,' Anna teased as she handed over the coffee. 'Don't burn your mouth,' she added with a head tilt.

'Mmm… now there's a thought,' Lauren gibed as she reached and took both coffees from Anna, put them on the side table and pulled her lover on top of her. Holding her, just staring into the sparkling steel-blue eyes, her breath caught in her throat. 'You are beautiful,' she said, before kissing Anna deeply, fingering lightly through her already tussled hair.

'Wooo there,' Anna said, pulling away as she struggled to gain her breath. 'We have a flight to catch, and breakfast will be ready in ten minutes. Actually, make that eight minutes now. And…' she continued. 'We stink of sex! Shower now.'

'I thought you'd never ask,' Lauren teased as she leapt out of bed, de-robed Anna and dragged her, playfully, into the walk-in shower.

*

'That's why I didn't start cooking,' Vivian remarked to a chuckling Lisa, as the two younger women entered the kitchen a half-hour later. Hair wet and heat darkening their faces, their feeble innocent smiles failed to convince the wiser women.

'We can get something at the airport, mum,' Anna said, perkily, as she approached Vivian and gave her a tight hug and peck on the cheek. 'We won't starve after yesterday… and we do need to get going,' she claimed, pointing to the clock in confirmation they needed to leave imminently to catch the train to Gatwick.

Lisa stepped towards her daughter and captured her in a full body embrace, squeezing tightly. 'You need to shoot,' she agreed. 'You know where we are,' she said, as her eyes glassed over a little. The sadness was perceptible. Anna's eyes glassed over too as she hugged her mum, not really wanting to let go.

'Thank you both for having me,' Lauren interjected as she approached both women, embracing them and planting a kiss on both cheeks, shifting the sadness that had passed between them. 'I'll look after her,' she affirmed, as a suitor might promise the bride's parents of their honourable intentions before being accepted into the family.

'We know you will,' Lisa said. She held Lauren as tightly as she had Anna. 'And you know you are always welcome here,' she offered, nodding, as Vivian put a comforting and supportive arm around her wife.

'Thanks mum.' Anna looked from one woman to the other as she spoke. Turning to Lauren she smiled, with just a hint of sadness still apparent behind her eyes. 'We'd better go.' Lauren nodded in response, turned slowly and followed Anna to the front door.

'She's in love,' Vivian remarked as the two women watched their daughter step into the waiting taxi.

'Yes she is,' Lisa sighed.

*

'You okay?' Lauren asked as she looked over at Anna. Everyone had taken their seats and the engine sound had elevated as they turned onto the runway. Anna had been decidedly quiet and detached since arriving at the airport. She looked pale.

'I'm not a fan of flying,' she said, gripping the armrests, the tension in her body palpable through white knuckles and taut skin.

'I guessed,' Lauren said with an easy smile, reaching for Anna's hand. Placing her hand over Anna's, she rubbed gently over the surface trying to calm her. 'How can I help?' she asked.

'It's easier with you here,' Anna grimaced then froze as the plane lurched forwards and picked up pace.

Lauren squeezed her hand and moved closer to provide some sense of protection. *Really!* she exclaimed to herself as Anna pinned herself to her seat. *And how often do you fly?* She pondered the question, suddenly aware of the stress that regular flights from Paris to London must cause Anna. Flying had never bothered Lauren. She liked the thrill of speed and the floating sensation - marvelled at the science that enabled such fluid mobility around the world. If it hadn't been for that mobility, their lives would never have crossed, she mused. As they rose above the clouds and the plane levelled off Anna relaxed into the seat slightly and her breathing slowed, though remained shallow. Her face still taut. Lauren took her hand into her lap and held it confidently. Putting the armrest back for comfort, she inched as close as physically possible and kissed Anna gently on the cheek. 'Does alcohol normally help?' She asked, partly in jest.

'Yes, I'll have a whiskey, please.' Anna allowed herself to look away from the window, momentarily. Turning to meet Lauren's compassionate brown eyes, she visibly softened and raised a weak smile.

'I suppose the mile-high club is out of the question then?' Lauren teased mercilessly. Anna just nudged her in the arm with her elbow and released a tense laugh.

'Thank god it's a short flight. I don't normally feel this bad.' Air turbulence caused the plane to drop suddenly and Anna gripped Lauren, who smiled serenely like being thirty-seven thousand feet above the earth was the most natural thing in the world.

'I've got you.'

'Not so reassuring right now,' Anna quipped. 'Just means we die together.'

I could think of worse things, Lauren thought to herself as she stared at Anna's distraught face. The realisation that losing her would break her heart hit her hard in the chest. She rubbed the spot to ease the compressed feeling that seemed to squeeze the life out of her as the sudden, unexpected awareness left a hole in its wake.

Within a short space of time the aircraft stilled and the cabin crew set about their work. Lauren ordered two whiskeys with ice and placed the plastic glasses, small packets of snacks, and miniature bottles on the pull-down table in front of her. She had already booked the Hotel Plaza Athenee Paris as a surprise, giving them the evening to wander the romantic City, followed by dinner together at the three-Michelin star restaurant, Epicure. She hoped the surprise would be well received rather than perceived as too extravagant, but given there was little she knew about Anna she was feeling concerned that she had taken too big a risk.

Anna had downed the whiskey within the first 5 minutes of the flight. Lauren smiled to herself as she watched the now sleeping woman. *God I love her. There is nothing I wouldn't do for her.* She pondered the intensity of her thoughts and took in a deep breath. But, instead of the anxiety of a moment ago she found something that was unfamiliar to her in her relationships - a strong protective streak. She breathed in the scent of the sleeping woman and immediately felt closer to her. The soft breathing, the gentle rise and fall of her chest, allowed Lauren to stand down from that protective mode and relax into the flight. Her body tingled as the mile-high club thought crossed her mind again. *Get a grip*, she admonished silently.

Anna began to stir as the plane started its descent. 'How are you with landings?' Lauren quizzed gently.

'Not as bad as taking off,' she responded as she smiled at the dark eyes appraising her. 'I'm okay... honestly.' She smiled, not wanting Lauren to think she was a complete wimp. Anna's shoulders dropped a couple of inches as the familiar bump and screeching of brakes indicated they had landed safely.

'I have a surprise for you,' Lauren beamed, as they wandered towards security. 'I've booked us a hotel for the night... in town...' She looked, almost apologetically, at the last-minute confession, hoping Anna would respond favourably. 'I hope you don't mind? ...I'

Anna leant in and pressed a kiss to Lauren's cheek, interrupting her flow. 'That's a lovely idea,' she said, smiling, feeling more relaxed at having her feet firmly on the ground.

*

'Oh my god, Lauren.' Anna gasped in awe as she entered, what appeared to be, a palatial suite. A fruit bowl and afternoon tea - selection of exquisite pastries, hot water, tea and Nespresso coffee options - sat on the table in the room. A tempting bottle of Dom Perignon sat in an ice bucket at the side of the table, with two tall, elegant glasses and a plate of prepared, ripe, strawberries. The sumptuous feast lured Anna, but not as much as the woman now stood at her side.

The hotel porter had quickly placed their bags in the adjoining bedroom suite, returned, and bid them a relaxing evening. Lauren handed him a tip that raised a smile to his face and he swiftly left the room.

Putting her arms around Anna, pressing her lips into the back of the soft neck that presented itself to her, Lauren hummed a deep, satisfying groan. Staring out over the Paris landscape together, alone in the luxurious surroundings, she felt more at peace than she had done in the previous, tormented, weeks.

'Mmm...' Anna responded to the soft lips on her skin. The tingling that emanated in her neck was pulsing down her spine and setting off sparks south of her stomach. 'Ahhh... fuck!' she couldn't help the groan escaping. Biting her bottom lip, almost drawing blood, awakened her momentarily. But the steady flow through her body was building and beyond her control - not that she wanted it to stop. The hands that had now eased their way under her blouse and released her bra were connecting the sensation between her nipples and lower belly. Slow, unhurried hands cupped her breasts, massaged gently, and softly pressed and tweaked the begging nipples. 'Don't stop...' Anna gasped in a whisper, as Lauren slowly traced a hand down her curvaceous body, slipped the button on her jeans and lowered the zip, whilst easing Anna gently against the full glass window, overlooking the Champs-Élysées and the Eiffel Tower. The City baring witness to the intimacy behind the thick panes on the top floor, privacy preserved by the Geranium clad balcony and tree-lined streets below, Lauren eased Anna's jeans and underwear to the floor. Pressing against Anna's back, one hand remained, continuing to tease her erect nipples. The second squeezed her right butt cheek, before seeking access to her hot, wet sex from behind. Anna shuddered at the deft touch that seemed to unhinge her instantly. Her palms pressed firmly against the window for balance and strength, she didn't see the stunning views from the window. Her legs struggled to hold her under the penetrating thrusts of Lauren's fingers as they moved deeply within her. Breasts neglected, Lauren moved to her knees for better access - thrusting deeply and rhythmically - as her second hand moved around Anna to deliver light circles to her swollen bud and provide necessary support to the buckling legs that were crumbling under the intensity. 'Oh fuck,' Anna screamed, her voice deeper and hoarse with arousal. She pounded at the glass as her body rode the waves.

'I've got you baby,' Lauren groaned, placing kisses on Anna's lower back whilst her fingers worked to ease Anna to a depth of orgasm she had never experienced before. Shaking weak legs could hold the weight no longer, as wave after wave of vibration passed through her. Jerking, she collapsed, into Lauren and took them both down to the floor. Her body reeling from the continuing orgasm, Lauren moved swiftly down the pulsing body to place delicate kisses on Anna's clit.

'No... Please!' Anna begged. 'I'm not sure I can take any more,' she voiced, unconvincingly, as Lauren persisted with delicate teasing strokes. Softly, gently, Lauren pressed her tongue as if to soothe the vulnerable parts. Easy caresses became subtly more insistent as Lauren's tongue followed a circuit - gently pressing inside Anna, then softly flicking - swiftly building the arousal again. Anna came so hard she involuntarily sat up with the force. Grabbing Lauren's head from between her legs, she pulled her vigorously up into a passionate, forceful kiss. They both fell back to the floor. Anna lost in her scent as it merged with Lauren's slightly floral perfume. 'Fuck... fuck... fuck...' she whispered as her swollen mouth pulled back to see the woman lying on top of her. Both smiled, falling into a whole-body embrace, with a connection that said... *I'm not letting you go.*

'Bath?' Lauren suggested as she pulled out of the long hold, still fully dressed and more than a little dishevelled.

'Mmm,' Anna nodded approvingly. Deep steel-blue eyes locked into Lauren. 'I need to touch you,' she growled, as Lauren rose and pulled her into her chest, placing kisses across her face.

'Later.' Lauren smiled as her hands cupped her lover's face. 'We have a whole evening and night together.'

'Now,' Anna looked wild with desire. Taking Lauren's hand urgently she led her through the bedroom and into the bathroom. Stopping, she turned towards the near black eyes and crashed her mouth against Lauren's. Two pairs of hands frantically removed Lauren's clothes. Flesh pressed against flesh and Lauren released a deep groan at the intimate contact. Anna pushed a knee between her legs as she pressed her to the white tiled wall. Lauren jumped at the slight chill on her back, adding to the pulsing and tingling, the sensory overload felt excruciatingly good. Immersing herself in the visceral experience - absent of thought - she thrust herself into Anna. Moving rhythmically, Anna pinned Lauren's hands to the wall while her mouth took pleasure in teasing the dark brown nipples, raising them to a peak - licking and flicking. Lauren could only beg at the sensations wracking her body.

'Oh god. I'm coming,' she let out the words and Anna stopped, instantly pulling away with a teasing look. She pressed Lauren's hands to the wall to affirm her authority in the moment.

'Oh no you don't... not yet,' she ordered. Pressing soft kisses on Lauren's mouth, Anna's free hand stroked down her taut, tanned belly, teased over her swollen clit and found her wet heat. Freeing her hand, she lowered it to rest in Lauren's back. Lowering to her knees, Anna pulled Lauren into her mouth as she plunged two fingers deep into her. Lauren bucked at the sensation. 'Now you can come for me,' she said, looking up briefly to see Lauren's head thrust backwards as her body tensed, and then began to shake.

'Fuck...' Lauren lingered on the word as she rode the orgasm that touched every part of her body. Shaking, she lowered herself to sit. Reaching out, she cupped Anna's face and kissed her lightly on the lips, whilst regaining her breath. 'How do you do that?' she quizzed with affection, trying to catch her breath.

Anna rose from the floor and turned the taps on to fill the bath, throwing in a large light-blue bath bomb and large glug of the complimentary bubble bath. Essence of lavender, clove and ylang ylang instantly filled the space.

Lauren watched her lover's body closely, admiring the curves that had brought her to climax so effortlessly. Anna's skin on hers... Anna's fingers deep... the obsessing thoughts and sight of Anna caused the tingling, throbbing response to rise in her lower body again. Averting her gaze, she cleared her throat. Quickly she stood and stepped, naked, out of the bathroom, fighting the weakness with determination. *Champagne*, she thought as she headed for the table to grab the bottle and glasses.

Returning, she placed the chilled bucket at the side of the bath, before popping the cork. Pressing kisses on Anna's shoulder and neck, she pulled her into her chest, writhing at the sensation of breast on breast, sex on sex - full body contact felt so... hot. She groaned. 'Do you have any idea what you do to me?' She whispered into Anna's ear, unable to stop kissing her neck as she spoke.

'Umm...' Anna teased. 'Let me guess,' she laughed as she kissed Lauren tenderly, before releasing her and stepping into the hot bubbly water. 'Bath.' She demanded Lauren join her. Lauren poured two glasses of champagne and stepped into the water, her whole body smiling as she lowered herself into the large oval tub.

*

Three-hours had passed as they had moved between bath and bed, before they finally got dressed and headed out for supper. Lauren had opted for her favourite attire: black fitted slacks, light grey shirt and long black jacket. Anna had decided on a sky-blue knee-length dress, with a darker blue jacket and two-inch heels, bringing her equal in height to Lauren. As their eyes wandered over the other, raised eyebrows signified mutual appreciation. 'Wow!' Lauren said, and smiled seductively as she took Anna's hand firmly in her own.

'Wow you.' Anna reached for Lauren's face and swept an errant hair to the side.

The dark, cold evening biting their faces was in stark contrast with the warmth and comfort of the hotel suite. Linking arms and pulling each other closer they took the short walk to Epicure, taking in the early Christmas lights and street buskers serenading passers-by. The Eiffel Tower was a splendid sight, lit up like a giant Christmas tree. A variety of aromas from freshly prepared street food, potpourri and other scented gifts, and roasting chestnuts, wafted across their path with the light wintery breeze. The maître d' greeted them warmly, recognising Lauren instantly, and escorted them to their table.

'Do you know everybody?' Anna whispered as they took their seats, surprised at Lauren's apparent connection with the man.

'Nearly,' she responded casually, not giving anything away but holding Anna's eyes tenderly across the space between them. 'Did I tell you?' The words came out softly as Lauren's eyes seemed to drill into Anna's soul.

'Not in the last five-minutes,' Anna teased, returning a gentle smile.

'I love you,' Lauren said. 'Just in case you had forgotten in the last five-minutes.' She looked over the top of the menu as she spoke. Only the dark eyes and curly locks were visible to Anna. But, boy did those eyes speak volumes, catching Anna's breath as she looked up.

'Mmm,' emanated quietly from Anna's lips as she lowered her menu to the table, her tongue running across her bottom lip. 'Keep looking at me like that and we won't get past the starter,' she remarked. Reaching across the short space between them, she took Lauren's hand and pressed her thumb across the knuckles.

'Mmm... there's a thought,' Lauren flirted in response, as she admired the soft hand in her own and reacted to the pressing thumb.

'I'll have whatever you're having,' Anna propositioned.

'That would be you then,' Lauren responded, at the same point her stomach growled. 'However, I need to eat first,' she said, wincing. She didn't want to take her gaze off the steel-blue eyes that matched perfectly the attire Anna had selected, but her stomach had other ideas so she returned her gaze to the menu.

Having placed their order, Lauren looked intently at Anna. 'How do you want me?'

'Umm...' Anna stuttered.

'For the portrait?' Lauren clarified with a cheeky, knowing smile, whilst Anna recovered from the rushing heat that had plunged through her.

'Ha ha. Funny lady,' she flicked Lauren's hand with her fingers. 'Tease!' Appraising Lauren through artist's eyes she tried to process the legitimate question. 'Good question,' she pondered, her eyes still searching, taking in the inner Lauren that she felt privileged to have experienced with the outer Lauren, the one presented to the world. *How to capture the contrast?* 'Mmmm...' She grinned seductively unable to reconcile her thoughts in that moment.

Lauren could see the passion rising in Anna's eyes, seduction written across her face, and it took her breath away as colour darkened her naturally tanned cheeks. She wished she hadn't asked. 'When you get your head out of the gutter,' Lauren admonished, jokingly as Anna's body clearly reacted to the images she was constructing, unconsciously brushing across her bottom lip with her tongue.

'I think I have a good idea,' Anna continued ignoring their banter for a moment. In her mind, she knew she would enjoy every second of transforming the beautiful woman before her onto the canvas and couldn't wait to get started. 'I'm going to take some photos when we get to the barn,' she answered. 'And... you need to tell me about your father,' she reminded, leaning back in the chair - still assessing Lauren - as the wine was presented to their table.

Lauren's eyes searched no particular space in front of her as she pulled memories of her father to the front of her mind. Briefly, his sudden death struck her, but she drifted further back in time - seeking childhood memories. 'He was a very quiet, personal man. I didn't see much of him, especially after the death of Corry and my Grandfather, and I guess he was more in love with the vines than his family - in some ways. I know he loved me though. It's kind of strange because he never said it, as far as I can remember, but it's just as if we knew we loved each other.' Lauren reflected, with a hint of sadness. Anna watched every flicker of emotion as Lauren continued to recount her memories. 'I think he was most animated when showing me anything to do with the vineyard. When I said I wanted to study law, at one level I think it broke his heart. But he always had Antoine there to take over the running of the business, so I never felt pressured. I just think he would have loved for me to follow in his footsteps.'

'And will you?' Anna asked, innocently.

'I don't know,' Lauren looked into Anna's eyes. 'A lot has changed for me in the last few weeks. A lot...' she mused. 'I even resigned from work last week,' she snorted as she reflected on the hideous meeting with her boss.

'Wow, I hadn't realised,' Anna sat up in her seat, genuinely surprised. 'I suppose we haven't really talked much,' she said, reflectively.

'Sorry. I should have said. You're right we haven't talked much and I realise that at some level we hardly know each other... but I know how I feel.' Lauren held Anna's eyes to make the point. Breathing deeply and bringing her attention back to her thoughts, she continued. 'So, I need to take some time to work out what I do next.' The words hit Anna, as the question of whether she would be a significant part of *that future* worried her. 'Though I do have to take care of Corsica... and handover in London... so I'm not free of anything just yet,' she voiced pragmatically. 'What about you?'

'What about me?' Anna looked confused.

'What plans do you have for the future?' Lauren looked on edge as she asked.

'No plans... well not really.' Anna struggled to regroup emotionally as her mind addressed the question. She hadn't spoken to Lauren about anything, let alone her plans for, and struggles with, conception, and her desire for a life out of the city. She wasn't sure now was the time to bring up the topic. Sipping the chilled wine and losing herself in thought she was saved by the arrival of their starter, but her hesitation to answer the question hadn't gone unnoticed and a tangible distance seemed to have appeared between them.

Lauren smiled softly as she sampled the delightful cuisine and bathed in the atmosphere. 'I love this place,' she said, bringing them both back from their reverie. 'Good?' she asked, after a few moments of watching Anna savour every mouthful of the sumptuous meal.

'Awesome. Thank you.' Anna smiled, lost in the taste extravaganza as sensation after sensation tantalised her tongue.

Meandering back to the hotel, the long route, they effortlessly synchronised both step and pace. Stopping suddenly, on the edge of the Seine, looking out across the water, Lauren turned to face Anna. Taking her hands, she pulled them to her mouth and kissed across the chilled knuckles. 'Thank you for sharing the day with me,' she almost whispered. 'It has been the best birthday present I could have wished for,' she confessed, as she put her arms around Anna and pulled her in for a tender kiss.

Anna stepped back, in shock. 'It's your birthday? You never said anything,' she admonished, with a hint of frustration.

'Sorry... again,' Lauren murmured, as her eyes scanned the ground. 'I wanted it to be a special day for us, rather than...'

Anna cut her off as her mouth took Lauren's in a passionate kiss, eliciting a deep groan as Lauren's tongue explored and danced with her own. Lauren's hands firmly planted around Anna's hips joined them as one, their bodies fitting perfectly together. Slowly easing away from the kiss, Lauren took Anna by the hand and walked them silently back to the hotel.

*

Anna turned over and bumped into the soft warm body next to her. Opening her eyes slowly, the dark brown gaze penetrating her, shot straight into her womb and her breath stalled. Paralysed by the intensity, heat flooded her body as Lauren's mouth closed the gap and planted a kiss on the end of her nose.

'Morning,' she said in a husky, low voice, adding to the sensual tension that had begun to pulse through Anna's body.

Releasing the air she hadn't realised she had been holding in, Anna's hand tingled as she delicately brushed the warm dark skin, down to firm breasts. Stroking across erect nipples, taking in the deep chocolate, lust-filled eyes. 'Morning,' she croaked.

'God you are so sexy.' Lauren whimpered at the touch as her eyes perused the flushing face. Her fingers started their own exploration of the pink nipples that had raised their heads, teasing her mercilessly.

'Ahhh,' Anna moaned at the touch, aware that the rising heat needed releasing. Her hips bucked and she pulled Lauren's mouth to her own, fiercely delving her tongue into the wet space to confirm her intentions. Lauren responded by taking control. Her hand immediately sought the swollen bud and wet heat, while her tongue flicked and brushed across Anna's erect nipples. Anna thrashed and groaned as ecstasy filled every nerve ending in her body. The orgasm came quickly, but it touched Anna deeply. Sobbing uncontrollably, Lauren held her tenderly in her arms and pressed light kisses on her lips, eyes and cheeks.

'Shower?' Lauren said, after Anna had calmed. Rubbing her hands through the fair wavy hair, delicately allowing her fingers to caress her soft cheeks - tracing the light lines, slightly upturned nose and full lips, she smiled lovingly. Anna tried to smile, but something in her eyes held a different message. 'Come on,' Lauren said jumping them both out of bed, like a puppy excited about going for a walk, dragging Anna at pace into the shower.

19.

'Wow, this is absolutely gorgeous,' Lauren exclaimed. Standing in front of the converted barn, her eyes surveying every aspect, she studied, in awe of the beautifully transformed ex-cow shed. The vast expanse of glass - contrary to traditional French design - enabling spectacular views across the valley from inside the building and highlighting the open foyer, stairs and mezzanine from the outside, was an exceptional feature.

Anna smiled as she took Lauren's hand and tried to see her design afresh. 'Yes, it is quite spectacular,' she agreed.

The fifty-minute taxi journey had been undertaken in a semi-comfortable silence, with brief commentary about the traffic, weather and other inane topics. Lauren had been desperate to find out what had upset Anna. The emotional residue following their earlier lovemaking was still sitting between them, preventing the intimacy they both seemed to desire and had previously experienced. She squeezed Anna's hand and gave her attention to the beautiful building as they stepped over the threshold, not wanting to push her into a conversation before she was ready to talk.

Lauren was immediately struck by the lightness inside the converted barn, especially since much of the traditional brickwork had been retained. Even down to the old feeding stations that had been made into a significant piece of decoration. Lauren was taken aback as Anna walked her around the considerately designed space, introducing the living room, kitchen, dining room, downstairs bathroom and separate toilet. Familiarised, Anna put the coffee machine on to brew. Lauren noticed the absence of Anna's work.

'Where do you work? She asked.

'In the loft,' she answered, with a nod towards the spot lit kitchen ceiling. 'I'll take you up there later. Please,

166

make yourself at home,' she indicated with waving arms at the space. 'Want to take the bags up while I sort the coffee?' She asked. 'First room on the right is mine,' she pointed in the relevant direction above them, as Lauren headed towards the front of the house to collect the two cases that sat just inside the front door.

Lauren paused on the stairs as she ascended, taking in the expansive view across the rich green fields. The trees were well on their way to losing their leaves - gold, orange and yellow leaves stirred across the sky as the breeze swept them into the air, and the remains of the early morning frost sat in the shadows, untouched by the low sun. Lauren's breath caught at the sight, humbled by the simplicity and magnificence of the nature that surrounded her. The vines were special, of course, but Anna's barn - here - in the middle of nowhere. There was something captivating about it. About her, Lauren reflected. Taking the door to the right as instructed, Lauren stepped into Anna's bedroom and put the bags on the floor next to the dressing table, noticing the key feature: a double king-size bed and the classically Parisian rugs adorning it. Feeling uneasy about delving further into the room she turned, left the room and quietly closed the door. The smell of coffee wafted up the stairs and Lauren could hear music coming from the living room. *Anna likes music. I didn't know that.* She sighed at the thought and carried the pensive look into the kitchen.

'Everything okay?' Anna questioned as she approached with the coffee in hand.

'This is lovely Anna,' Lauren remarked. 'Stunning in fact.'

'Yes, I love it too.' She smiled, filtering through her memories, her eyes never leaving Lauren's. 'Come on, sit.' She pointed to the bar stools around the central island. 'Let's drink

167

this then I'll show you around the studio and we can get to work.'

Lauren nodded in agreement even though the thought of getting to work couldn't be further from her mind. She wanted to savour this place and her short time alone with Anna. And, she wanted to know what was bugging her, such that she had closed off.

With the coffee consumed and Lauren more informed about the renovation of the barn, which had taken place over the five-years that Anna had been working in Marketing for a large corporate, the two women headed to the loft. As soon as Anna opened the door they were flooded in sunlight and Lauren noted the surprising warmth. The roof structure had been designed to capture natural heat and light to ensure a constant temperature and ambiance - ideal for Anna's work. Stepping into the room, Lauren's eyes feasted on the array of canvases stacked around the room and various forms of art materials that lay on shelves and tables. The heady scent of acrylic and oil hung in the air and a subtle smell of cleaning fluids effused from the small sink in the far corner. It smelt like home to Anna who associated the smells with her birth mother. The artist breathed in deeply as she waved her arms to indicate the space. 'This is where I do most of my work,' she said with a more relaxed smile. Lauren followed her hands.

'You are amazing,' Lauren said in a serious tone as she appraised the image of a new-born child lying naked on its stomach, fast asleep. The angelic look had been captured perfectly.

'Thank you.' Anna fidgeted with the compliment as she watched Lauren step from one piece to another, holding each with genuine admiration, totally engrossed.

'I knew your mum was good... but...'

'Mum's awesome and has taught me everything I know. I'm not sure I could ever be compared...'

'You underestimate yourself,' Lauren interrupted. The seriousness in her tone broke as she looked up from the canvas, her eyes radiating approval and affection. Anna mused as she held the dark, intensifying gaze. Lauren stepped closer and kissed her tenderly.

Anna moved to deepen the kiss and Lauren groaned into the warm touch. The buzz of a phone pulled them apart.

I'm in Paris and thought I'd stop by. I really need to talk to you. Be with you in ten. Love Soph x

As Anna read and re-read the text message her heart sunk. Her stomach churned, her shoulders dropped. She felt sick. Their last communication had been brief and one-directional and she hadn't expected to hear from her ex again. Thumping pounded in her chest and unpleasant sensations hit her in the gut. She paled.

'You okay? Lauren took her by the arms and looked with concern into the vacant, watering eyes.

'No. Sophie is on her way.' Anna looked shocked.

'Oh,' was all that Lauren could say as she released Anna and took a step away from her. 'What do you want me to do?' she asked, reverting to a formal tone.

Anna jolted herself out of the painful trance and held Lauren's eyes. 'Stay here, please. She wants to talk, but I have nothing to say. So it will be a brief visit.' She stepped towards Lauren taking her hand and rubbing her thumb across the knuckles, indignant over Sophie's unsolicited invasion of her... their... privacy. Lauren pulled her in and held her close, pressing a kiss on her head, hoping to ease the stress from her now tense body. Even Lauren's body had instantly tightened, with a surge of anger, at the news of the impromptu visit. 'I'd better go downstairs. She still has a key and I don't want her just walking in,' Anna said as she looked into the worried face. 'I'll be fine,' she reassured, cupping Lauren's cheeks and pressing a tender kiss on her lips.

*

Standing in the foyer, staring out through the glazed frontage, Anna twitched at the sight of the dark blue BMW approaching. She could feel the anger invade her body as she spied Sophie confidently bouncing out of the driver's side and springing her way to the front door. Searching her handbag, she pulled out a key, just as Anna opened the solid oak barn door.

'What do you want, Sophie?' Anna greeted defensively, suppressing the rage that was burning in her chest. They had never spoken about the doubles-partner incident and Anna hadn't realised how hurt she had been by it, until now. Seeing Sophie for the first time since then, in the flesh, bouncing around as if she was returning to her lover following a tournament win, riled her. 'So?'

Lowering her eyes to the ground, fidgeting her hands and kicking at the stones on the path, Sophie mumbled. 'Sorry Bella.' Looking up to Anna, with watery doe eyes, the dark green rim highlighting her blue green irises, and a pained smile, she hoped for forgiveness. 'Please, Bella. I really am so sorry. I behaved like a spoilt fucking brat in need of approval. Sex was that approval. I didn't think about what was important to me... that you are important to me.' The well-rehearsed lines tripped off the tennis player's tongue and the tears welled in her eyes.

'So you've been to therapy then? Or have you just been coached by your fucking PR people?' Anna spat the words fuelled by the rising anger hitting her throat. Sophie shook her head in denial of the accusation. 'Don't tell me... she ditched you? Is that what this is about?' Anna accused, holding on firmly to the door that sat only partly opened. The chilled air sucked out the warmth from the barn as Sophie seemed to penetrate Anna with her words and sap her, leaving her feeling cold and weakened under her spell. Sophie was addictive. She was dangerous. Anna averted her gaze and breathed deeply.

'Can I come in? Can we talk? Please?' Sophie begged.

'Why the fuck should I let you...'

'I know you're angry, and you have every right to be...' Sophie interrupted. 'I'm really sorry...'

'Don't you come here and fucking tell me what I have the right to feel, not feel, say or do. You lost that privilege the day you fucked your doubles partner. Remember? Though I dare say there were others.' Anna was shouting.

'No Bella. There weren't others.' Sophie lowered her gaze, her posture uncharacteristically slouched, her head shaking. 'And I made a huge fucking mistake. Can you forgive me? Can you give me another chance? Please?' Sophie dropped to her knees and raised her hands pleading for a second chance. Her hands dived into her pocket and she pulled out a small wrapped box. 'It's not what you think,' she blurted. 'But I want you to have this gift as a sincere apology. I want us to be together Bella. I know that now. I really am so sorry. I was a complete prick, stuck up my own arse. Please?'

Lauren stood at the top of the stairs, invisible to both women. The shouting had stirred her protective response and she had positioned herself somewhere she could interject should Anna need her support. But by all accounts, Anna seemed to be standing her ground more than adequately.

'What about our children Bella?' Sophie asked tentatively, knowing it would touch a cord.

Lauren felt struck in the chest and she froze at the words emanating from the front door. Her stomach flipped. Her legs weakened and she slumped to the ground. *No. No. Their children? They have children?* The sudden reality ricocheted around her mind, spinning her thoughts out of control, as her heart thumped through her chest. *What the fuck!* Was that why Anna had suddenly gone cold on her? Had she really finished with her ex... or did she... did she still love her? Lauren couldn't conceive of the idea that Anna might still be in love with Sophie after all they had shared together, yet there was still a great deal she didn't know about her. Maybe she had misread the signals. Certainly, Sophie seemed to think they had unfinished business. Lauren's heart sunk, a black hole opened and sucked her into its depths. She didn't have the strength to stand. Tears flowed down her cheeks as emptiness filled her. With shaking hands, she picked up her phone.

'We've planned it for years Bella. I thought that's what you wanted... what we wanted. Jesus, it's cost enough already.' Sophie continued with flailing hands, pacing on the spot, her eyes searching for a way through. 'Surely, we can do this together,' she continued.

Lauren watched silently as Anna's body drooped in apparent submission. Her heart stopped at the sight.

Resigned to the truth in Sophie's words Anna sighed, any fight she thought she had had deserted her. Sophie had a way of causing her to concede, most often willingly. She seemed to tap something inside Anna that the artist couldn't resist, even when deep down she knew she should. Sophie recognised the submission the instant it happened and smiled contritely. The predator had entranced its prey, created the opportunity to pounce. The victim lay bare, ripe for the taking, and Sophie knew how to take - how to levy the final blow.

For a moment Anna held the door firmly in its half-closed position, still processing the barrage that had just consumed her like a tidal wave. She breathed deeply, raising her height by an inch, and allowed her eyes to dwell on the beautiful countryside. Standing taller, she zeroed in on the woman she once thought she loved. For the first time, she could see her clearly and she didn't like what she saw. She didn't like the sensations she felt when Sophie dominated her, overpowered her, and then bathed in smug victory. She didn't like the fact that she had turned up, without warning, and on the back of her sordid affair, only to declare that she wanted what they had been planning all along. Anna wasn't convinced by the act, but she was intrigued as to the change of heart. *Why now?* Presenting an aura that maintained her distance she opened the door fully. Sophie stepped confidently into the foyer with open arms, moving towards her stunned prey, enveloping her in a stiff embrace. The victor.

'Drink?' Anna offered modestly, as she paced into the kitchen.

'Wine would be great,' Sophie beamed, tilting her head with a wink and a weak attempt at a seduction.

'White or red?' Anna said with indifference.

'White please.'

Anna couldn't help but notice that Sophie's confidence seemed unaffected by her inability to touch Anna as she might have done previously. Perhaps she didn't even notice. The egocentricity of the woman seemed alive and well Anna thought, as she opened the fridge door and pulled out a bottle of Sauvignon. 'So, what do you want to talk about?'

'This place looks amazing Bella,' Sophie remarked as her eyes scanned the kitchen. She hadn't been to the barn in quite some time. She had always been travelling and unable to visit - at least that had been the excuse and Anna had accepted her reasoning without challenge. Most of their time together had been spent at Sophie's London house, close to Wimbledon, also with easy access to the fertility clinic. But even that had been infrequent. 'You've done a great job.' Sophie stood and wandered, without invitation, out of the kitchen to appraise the other ground floor rooms before returning to the kitchen, a glass of wine waiting for her. 'I love this,' she waved her arms to indicate the whole space as she sat at the central island.

'What do you want to talk about Sophie?' Anna refused to be dragged away from the topic as she patiently posed the question for a third time.

Sophie sipped from the glass. 'Nice,' she said, placing the glass on the surface and twirling the stem as she gathered her next lines. Anna watched. Sophie looked up, her wet eyes holding Anna's momentarily before she lowered them again to focus on the swirling wine. 'I really am sorry Bella. I fucked up. I know that. Truth be told, I knew it at the time. But...'

'But what?'

'But I was too fucking arrogant to admit it. I never thought you would leave me. I thought we had something really special.'

'Really?'

'Yes.'

'Special? So fucking special you go and fuck someone else. How in your mind did you justify that Sophie? How the fuck did you screw someone else while thinking I'm the special one. Help me here please, because I just can't see how that works?'

'I know. It's screwed up. I'm screwed up. She meant nothing.'

'Oh, I see. She meant nothing so that's okay. You can fuck all night because every fucking orgasm she gives you means fucking nothing. What planet are you living on? You can't have that with someone and not feel anything. But right now, you know what? That's not what sickens me. It's your fucking lying. You can't even be honest with me.'

'I am being honest Bella. Really. I wasn't thinking and it was never going anywhere with Tamsin. It was just a spur of the moment thing. We had just won...'

'Priceless. You'd just won so you decide it's appropriate to take that success to the fucking bedroom. With her?'

'No… yes… no. It wasn't thought through. I'm sorry.'

'Damn fucking right it wasn't thought through.' Anna breathed deeply and moved away from the table to create much needed space. 'Fucking incredible,' she said, her body in tension, shaking her head as she spoke.

'I know you're not expecting this. Me. Coming here. I just… I just hoped we might be able to start again.' Anna sniggered as she continued shaking her head at Sophie's ridiculous suggestion. 'Maybe with time… we could?'

'Not even with all the time in the world Sophie. You lost that privilege when you shagged your doubles partner whilst I was planning for our family. I may be able to forgive you in time. But I'm not going to be able to forget what you did to me… to us.'

The sound of heels on the tiled floor drew Sophie's attention, as Lauren walked elegantly into the room and into her space. Holding out her hand she introduced herself. 'Hello. You must be Sophie,' she smiled confidently. 'Anna's told me a lot about you.' She took Sophie's hand firmly and ignored the tennis player's stunned look. 'Mmm… wine? Great idea.' Lauren continued, unaffected by the thickness in the air. Moving around the central island she strode towards Anna, swept her into her arms, and kissed her passionately. At the corner of her eye she could see Sophie's mouth drop open. She hadn't expected that. Lauren held the kiss a few moments longer, feeling Anna's receptivity to the explicit show of affection.

'Oh shit.' Sophie gasped as she watched the passionate embrace. 'You moved on fucking quickly,' she sneered, through tightening lips and wide eyes as rage fuelled her.

Pulling out of the reassuring embrace, Anna looked in the direction of the comment.

'Sorry. Did you say something?'

'Fuck you Anna,' Sophie spat. 'Enjoy your fucking wine

with your girlfriend. And I thought you really cared... about us... about having children... Fuck, was I so fucking suckered,' she ranted viciously. 'Take note,' she directed at Lauren, pointing. 'Suck you in then fucking spit you out. You'll be the next sucker,' she threatened. Turning sharply, she stomped out of the kitchen, slammed the front door and ran to her car, wheels spinning on the gravel path, she was gone.

Lauren turned to face Anna, whose eyes were wet with the tears now tumbling down her cheeks. She was sobbing and shaking. Locking eyes, Lauren's full of compassion, she gently brushed the tears away with a tender touch and pulled her close. Falling into the strong arms, their bodies fitting together perfectly, she allowed the tears to fall and clung to the embrace.

As Anna's sniffles abated, she pulled away from Lauren and looked into her brown eyes - eyes that were seeking answers. 'I'm really sorry about that,' she sniffled looking towards the driveway. 'Are you okay?' She studied Lauren, hoping not to see rejection.

Lauren frowned, her eyes felt distant. 'I'll survive. I had no idea...'

'I know. I'm sorry. I didn't expect to see her again, let alone have her turn up here unannounced. Please tell me you don't believe what she said about me.' Anna's vulnerability caused Lauren's heart to ache.

'Hey...' She pulled Anna into her arms. 'I may not know you well, but I have a highly attuned sense of character and I don't believe a word of what she said. Though I will admit I did call for a taxi initially.' She squeezed Anna tightly as she confessed.

Anna slumped in her arms. 'I wouldn't blame you if you had walked out,' she said, as tears streamed down her face again. 'Sorry, I'm...'

'There's nothing to be sorry for. I love you. That's why I

cancelled the taxi and came downstairs instead. Her arrogance was annoying me.'

'Thank you for rescuing me.' Anna snivelled and wiped her hands across her face. Grabbing a tissue from the box she blew her nose and then moved back into Lauren's arms where she felt safe.

Lauren kissed the top of her head and sighed, creating a comforting warm spot on Anna's scalp. 'Want to talk?' she asked softly, running her hand through Anna's wavy locks, tucking the hair around her ears and placing light kisses on her cheeks. Anna nodded. Pulling her in, she squeezed the artist tightly, pressing their bodies together, before releasing her and reaching for the wine glasses. 'Wine?' she offered in a lighter tone.

'Whiskey. I need something stronger and right now my association with white wine isn't a positive one,' She tried to smile. Failed. 'Let's go through to the living room.'

Lauren pulled two tumbler glasses from the kitchen cupboard and threw in two cubes of ice from the freezer. Holding them up in question. 'Where's the whiskey?' she asked.

'In the cabinet in the living room.' They walked in tense silence. Lauren poured two large shots and handed a glass to Anna as she lowered herself into the deep soft lounger. She sighed as her body landed and was caressed by the large cushions, throwing her head back into the soft material. She looked drained and beaten. Lauren sat next to her, put her arm around her and pulled her into her shoulder, Anna curled into the comforting and familiar scent.

Taking a deep breath, she began to talk. Lauren held her close and remained quiet throughout. Occasionally, she rubbed her hand gently up and down Anna's arm or kissed the top of her head, reassuringly.

Anna had met Sophie in a work context as the company she worked for had been commissioned to deliver a marketing campaign for the pro tennis player. She had been seduced by Sophie's confidence and charm and Sophie had wooed her fearlessly. They had decided to keep their relationship out of the public eye, in the early days, to protect Anna from media invasion. They had maintained that privacy over time, out of habit and because it suited them both. Sophie always liked the freedom to be sociable *allegedly with boundaries* and Anna preferred a more reclusive lifestyle.

They had planned for a family and Anna made a number of visits to the London Women's Clinic. Two attempts at AI had failed. Following the last failure, Sophie had become more distant: rarely calling, staying away from Paris, always busy, and leaving Anna to deal with her sense of loss and despair alone. Anna had felt deserted and confused, but put Sophie's withdrawal down to the pressure of needing to be totally focused and dedicated to competing successfully. With hindsight Sophie had never been that attentive. With the constant travelling for tournaments, their relationship had been played out over a long distance for the most part. Though in the early days they used to Skype daily, that had stopped after a time, because it had been too difficult to coordinate their schedules Sophie had maintained. The signs had been there all along, she just hadn't seen them. Hadn't wanted to see them. As she talked about it now, she realised how naïve she had been. Had she hoped that having a child would bring them together? She had even attended the fertility clinic alone because Sophie had been in Australia and then the United States, for the Grand Slams.

When Anna discovered the front-page spread - Sophie with her tongue down her doubles partner's throat - she had been devastated and deeply hurt. Betrayed. She had immediately stopped the third planned insemination and tried to wrap her head around her work.

Just three-months later, Anna's mum had been diagnosed with breast cancer and she had found herself walking into the quaintest Italian restaurant. The rest was history, so to speak.

Anna's revelation - her desire to have children and her struggle with conception to date - stirred something deeply embedded in Lauren. *Anna had already tried to conceive, with another woman... and failed. Did it matter who that other woman was? Did it make a difference? Did she still want children?* Questions poured into Lauren's mind, overflowing, creating a sense of unease, jabbing at her earlier confidence in their potential future. She felt herself stiffening at times, as new doubts pounded through her mind. Even knowing some of her concerns were unfounded, her personal experience with Rachel had surfaced in her mind and now needed attention.

'I can't have children,' Lauren said matter of fact, in a moment of comfortable silence between them. 'I wanted them.' Anna noticed the use of past tense.

'Wanted?' she questioned. Pulling gently out of Lauren's shoulder, she sat to face her, seeking her dark eyes. She needed to see into her soul - beyond past hurts, beyond mental conditioning.

'Wanted, as in had planned to have children with Rachel. It was early in our relationship. We discussed it and Rachel was in agreement... until her career took off... *If she ever was really in agreement?*' Lauren shared the question that had haunted her over the years, as to her ex's true intentions. 'I can't have children, but I have my eggs on ice just in case something changes. I was sick a while ago and there were no guarantees for the future, so took the decision,' she confessed, her eyes seeking Anna's to know what she felt about her revelation.

'What about now?' Anna asked, biting her bottom lip pensively.

'Honestly? I haven't thought about it for such a long time.' Anna's eyes dropped to her hands. 'But since meeting you... as I said, my life has changed dramatically in the last few weeks. I've been re-evaluating everything. Maybe even hoping... hoping that we might make a go of it,' she was beginning to waffle.

'It?'

'Us. A relationship. Children maybe? I know we haven't talked about it. We haven't talked about much. But I have thought about not a lot else since meeting you again,' she confessed. Anna's watery eyes rose up and locked onto Lauren's. The deep, steel blue seemed to pierce through her heart and cause her neurological system to fire off in all directions. The tingling released into goose bumps as Anna's fingers traced the side of her face, across her high cheekbones, down to her chin, down her neck and across her collarbone.

'I'd like that with you too.' Anna left no room for doubt as she moved in quickly and claimed Lauren's mouth. Her tongue brushing against soft lips, teeth biting down gently to elicit a groan. Their tongues danced synchronously, as arousal built and the kiss deepened. The two women closed the physical space between them, breast on breast, thighs intertwined. They groaned in unison as Anna pressed firmly against Lauren, her hand reaching under the open shirt and capturing her breast.

'I want you,' Lauren growled with increasing sense of urgency. Grabbing Anna's buttock with one hand, the other massaging her head through her hair, she lowered her kisses to Anna's neck and bit down, causing Anna to flinch and squeal as the stimulation awakened a new level of connection between them.

'Oh my god.' She screamed as Lauren flipped her onto her back on the couch, ripped the shirt apart popping the buttons, and bit down hard on her erect nipple. Grazing her teeth across the tender flesh, ripples of excitement coursed through Anna and her hips bucked against the toned thigh pressing hard against her. 'Ahhh,' the guttural groan, fuelled Lauren's arousal uncontrollably as her hand desperately searched for... and unbuttoned Anna's jeans. Anna moved to help and Lauren pulled them down, lowering her mouth to Anna's belly as she kissed her way to the musky scent that was drawing her in. More deeply than she had imagined possible, she was consumed by the sexual odour filling her nostrils as she took Anna into her mouth, her fingers working the tense nipples senseless. Anna bucked beneath the rasping tongue as it swept across and delved into her sex. Sensation after sensation, wave after wave, coursed Anna's body and mind as she gave herself completely to Lauren. Incapable of stopping the process, her heart pounded and electric shocks chased through every cell when Lauren pressed two fingers deep into her centre. Penetrating her hard and fast, yet deep and all consuming. Quivering turned to shuddering as the intense orgasm swamped her system. Holding onto the edges of the couch she immersed herself in the pleasure that seemed to never end. Her breathing was still heavy and the aftershocks still jumping through her as Lauren moved up and kissed her lovingly.

'I love you so much.' Lauren's eyes smiled as she spoke. 'I love the feel of you coming in my hands. I want you to have my baby.' The words were out before conscious thought could prevent them, jolting Anna to alertness.

'Sex talking,' she said, trying to laugh off Lauren's words, aware of the pang of anxiety that had just hit her.

Feeling hurt, Lauren pulled away a fraction and presented a serious look to Anna. 'No,' she said. 'I mean it. I want you to have my baby.' She pulled Anna into her and kissed her in affirmation of her intention. Anna's initial resistance to the touch softened as she responded with her own affirming kiss.

Stopping to breathe. 'Are you serious? I mean really sure?' Anna probed gently, not wanting to be rejected but needing to be clear.

'Never been surer in my life. I love you Anna. I'm in love with you. I have loved you since the first time I saw you... when you poured wine all over yourself,' she smiled with the memory.

'Don't remind me,' Anna sniggered, brows furrowed.

'I will remind you to the day I die... I... love... you.' She pointed at Anna as she spoke each word.

'Okay.'

'Okay what? You'll have my baby? Or okay that I remind you?' Lauren teased.

'I think I would like to have your baby. And keep reminding me,' she smiled, placing a tender kiss on Lauren's beaming mouth.

20

Anna spent the next two days photographing Lauren at every hand's turn - as they walked, in the house, in bed. Capturing the essence of the woman as she occupied herself, mostly unaware of the intrusive lens. With each and every shot her connection had deepened, to the point that she was ready to present her perspective on the blank canvas she now faced. Two exquisite days spent in perfect harmony, before Lauren had left for London - back to her work as a lawyer. Anna stared at the white dimpled canvas until the trance took her over and unconsciously she started to paint. Slept. Painted some more. Even missing meals hadn't affected the quality or intensity of her work. This was the high that she loved. The feeling that time stood still whilst the creation was evolving in front of her eyes. She always felt as if she were channelling her impression, as if the art was working through her rather than coming from her. It was such a fine distinction and she had never been able to explain it to anyone. Her mum understood of course. She stepped back with the end of the brush held between her teeth as she assessed the canvas, jumping out of trance and nearly dropped the brush as her phone buzzed furiously to get her attention.

'Hi.' The deliciously husky voice on the end of the line sent Anna's body into spasms. Even from a distance the woman affected her like no other.

'Hi you,' she responded, her body caressing the phone as if it were the person on the end of it.

'I've missed you,' Lauren admitted, the sadness evident in the pauses and subtle change in the tone of her voice. It had only been three-days since she had taken the flight back to London, but with her work it was the earliest opportunity they had had to speak. She had texted regularly but it wasn't the same as hearing Anna's voice. She could never say what she wanted to say by text, it was harder to really chat, and as soon as they ended a session Lauren was left feeling lonelier than ever.

'I've been painting,' she said, attempting to lift the energy between them, knowing she wouldn't be able to see Lauren for at least another week, maybe two.

'I bet it's awesome already.' Anna could feel Lauren's dark eyes on her work; sense the smile on her face, as she appraised the canvas in progress.

'Well, it's a start,' Anna laughed, knowing she was a long way from her desired end result. 'How's your work going?'

'Good. I've managed to hand over a couple of cases that were at an early stage, so just a handful I need to deal with directly.' She paused and hesitated as if there was something unsaid between them.

'And?' Anna quizzed, becoming familiar with Lauren's natural quirks.

'I was wondering...'

'Yes,' Anna spoke softly, urging Lauren to speak her mind.

'Would you like to come to London next week? I've been thinking a lot about...' Lauren blurted out the words before Anna cut her short.

'Yes. I would,' she said instantly. She could hear Lauren release a deeply held breath on the end of the line and sensed her physically relaxing.

'Great. I love you.'

'I love you too Lauren.' Her heart pounded as she spoke the words that meant so much.

'I've got to go. I've got an evening meeting. I'll text you when I'm done.' Lauren lingered on the phone - silence filling the space between them - until the line went dead.

*

184

'Hey Anna,' Eva shouted as she pressed the phone to her ear, a spiky redheaded, athletically built woman attached to her other ear, whispering sweet nothings, her tongue searching the sensitive cavity.

'Sorry, am I disturbing you?' Anna asked as the thumping background music invaded her living room via the handset. About to end the call with her friend, the sound muffled before Eva responded.

'No, you're good. What's up? You coming out?' Eva asked, having shaken off the attachment and moved into a quieter space near the toilets.

'Where are you?'

'In town. Fancy coming out later?'

'Umm...' Anna felt resistance sweep through her. The idea of dressing up and going to a nightclub didn't really appeal, but her need for company on a Saturday night, and a distraction from her loneliness, felt overpowering. 'Okay. You heading to *Le So-What*?' She asked.

'Yeah. I'll be there about ten.' Eva glanced at her watch, showing the time at 8.30. She had started at the local bar after finishing work at 7.30 and was already bored with the clientele hitting on her. 'You can stay over at mine if you like?'

'Maybe,' Anna responded, unable to commit to the sleepover. She could spend a couple of hours dancing and maybe chatting, she tried to convince herself. 'I'll see you at the club.'

'Awesome,' Eva sounded genuinely pleased. 'Promise you'll protect me from the wolves out here,' she joked.

'Honey, you need protecting from yourself,' she retorted with a laugh. 'Now, go have fun and I'll see you later.'

Eva returned to the bar, sipping her beer as her eyes scanned the environment. *Fun!* Fortunately, the leech was now hanging off another victim. She perched on a red faux-leather stool at the bar and ordered another beer, now just biding her time before heading off to *Le So-What*. She felt warmly excited about seeing Anna. There was something more genuine about their relationship. It made her feel like a real person rather than a piece of meat. The ash blonde, with lipstick that was too red for her complexion, and with eye shadow that didn't go with the green-blue of her eyes, passed the chilled bottle of Budweiser across the bar with as much seduction as she could muster, trying to catch Eva's eye. Eva smiled superficially. 'Thanks.'

'Anytime gorgeous,' the woman flirted. 'I'm Sylvia by the way... in case you're interested.' She blinked her eyes too quickly and Eva watched in mild fascination as the heavy mascara seemed to delay the parting of the top and bottom of her eye-lids.

'Thanks... Sylvia.' Eva lifted the bottle and tilted it towards the bar woman in a toasting gesture. Hoping not to encourage any further advances she turned on her seat and allowed her eyes to survey the room, the sight and realisation of her situation, sobering her momentarily. Was she getting too old for this? Sipping at the beer, she picked up her phone. Her fingers carved out a text. *Do you fancy supper instead?*

Two drunken women began fawning over each other. Unsteady on their feet, they seemed to bounce around a small space knocking into other drinkers. They grabbed at each other and began to dance. At least it looked as if it should have been a dance but seemed to quickly turn into a display of openly sexual behaviour, encouraged by the whooping and chanting of the voyeurs who were taking full advantage of the early evening free show. Eva watched the display feeling quite detached and her eyes continued to scan the room. She had seen the tall Italian-looking woman earlier in the evening and got the feeling that the woman seemed to have been staring at her. But when Eva caught sight of her standing by one of the tall tables she seemed to quickly avert her gaze back to the scene on the impromptu dance floor.

Eva watched the elegant woman with renewed interest. She seemed out of place, she thought, in her designer slacks, shirt and jacket. *Was she also out of place here?* Realising the judgement she had made, which could easily have been about herself, she smiled sardonically. The woman was two, maybe three, inches taller than her, with long dark-brown waves of hair that looked nearly black in the subdued bar lighting. She couldn't tell the colour of her eyes, but her skin was tanned and young looking with high cheekbones. Maybe mid-twenties, hard to call, as she seemed more mature in the way that she carried herself, she wondered, just as the woman turned and caught Eva staring at her. She smiled as Eva raised her bottle in mock toast and even from a distance Eva thought her eyes sparkled. *Wow.* The woman raised her glass in response before turning away. Someone had approached her, distracted her, Eva noted. *Damn.* The dark crew cut that spoke to her was significantly shorter in height and of a stocky build. She looked towards Eva. She didn't look happy and seemed to say something to the Italian, who just shrugged and then followed her into a booth at the back of the bar. Eva turned back towards the bar, looked at her phone for the time, and sighed. Sylvia's eyes were on her and she seemed to be scowling. *Oops, clearly not taking a hint!*

Eva hadn't realised she had a response from Anna, but the sight of it cheered her. *Would love to. Why don't you come here? I'll cook!* Two praying Emoji symbols and a kiss ended the text. Anna felt quietly relieved at the idea of not going out, and comforted at the thought of being able to chat with her best friend.

She smiled at the relief of being able to extricate herself from her sorry Saturday evening. She was tired of being tagged as a player and the idea of partying till dawn didn't appeal. It was just habit, a bad habit. Maybe she really *was* getting too old, different women, different beds every weekend. She sent a smiley with a wink in response. *See you in an hour* the text read.

*

The smell of garlic, onions, tomato and herbs hit Eva's olfactory sense as Anna opened the door. Diving into a hug, Anna held Eva tightly, rocking her back and forth, before kissing her on the cheek and dragging her excitedly through to the source of the delightful aromas. She hadn't realised quite how happy she was at not having to go into town, until now, and how desperately she had craved the company. Eva returned the show of affection, equally pleased to be out of the Saturday-night, Parisian, cattle market.

'Drink?' Anna held up a bottle of Merlot that had been corked after their messaging an hour ago.

'Please,' Eva nodded and Anna poured them both a glass, hers being a small one. 'Not like you,' Eva noted the short drink. 'You on some diet or something?' she quizzed, teasingly.

'Ha, ha,' Anna retorted. 'Not exactly,' she tried to hold the truth from her eyes. Failed. The smile was written across her face like a beacon.

'Ah, ha. Come on Anna, spill?' Eva lowered her eyes to draw Anna to look at her. 'You've hibernated for the last few weeks. Hardly spoken to mum - who happens to be your agent, and then I get a random call on a Saturday night, when you don't really want to party.' Eva accurately summed up the situation matter of fact.

'I know. I've been busy. Preoccupied.' Anna's eyes glazed over as she spoke. 'We can chat later. I assume you'll stay over, so drink up and get me up to speed with life on the scene,' Anna said, regaining her composure.

*

'Mother!' Lauren said more firmly than she intended, as she succumbed to answering her phone after blocking the call twice already. The last thing she needed was a lecture about a lack of contact, or questions about when was she coming back to take care of *her* business in Corsica. She didn't have answers to any questions her mother might pose and could do without feeling pressured into making any rash decisions. *She sniggered to herself at the thought of not making rash decisions... and the situation with Anna!* Her life had been turned upside down in a short space of time and she needed some time to adjust to her feelings and her new relationship before giving her full attention to the situation in Corsica.

'Hello darling.' The softness in Valerie's tone knocked Lauren off guard. 'I was wondering how you are? Last time I saw you, your head was on the floor having challenged the fireplace, and lost,' Valerie quipped. Guilt swept through Lauren. She hadn't considered that her mother might be worried about her health. Historically they hadn't talked much, but with the death of her father and her subsequent role in the family business, Lauren supposed she should have made contact. She owed her mother that at least.

'Sorry, I've been really busy. But I'm fine. How are you?' Still Lauren couldn't shake the formality she felt between them.

'I'm very good thank you. I'm phoning because I have an invitation?' Lauren's attention peaked at the obvious lure.

'Invitation to what? When?'

'To my wedding darling,' her mother gleefully announced.

Lauren nearly choked as she forgot to breathe. 'Wedding?' she repeated the word slowly. 'What?'

'Yes darling. I know it's all rather quick, what with your father,' she prattled. 'But I'm in love and time's ticking, as it is for Henri.'

'Who?' Lauren interrupted, feeling irrational fury rising rapidly in her chest.

'Henri. You remember darling. The man who saved your life when you threw yourself into the fireplace.' The slight gibe grated and Lauren couldn't tell if the humour had been intended or it had been a sarcastic dig.

'He didn't save my life. He sutured a cut. There's a big difference.'

'Oh don't be a spoilsport. At my age I need my illusions. It helps me to think of him as a hero. He's my hero,' she gushed.

Lauren winced at the end of the phone. She hadn't seen this coming and was stumped for words. 'Right,' she mumbled.

'Anyway, we're getting married darling and I want you to be there - at the house, 17th December. And, yes, I know that's only three-weeks away, but at my age darling it doesn't pay to wait, and especially when you know it's right...' She wandered into a lover's reverie as she spoke, leaving Lauren shell-shocked and confused.

'Right,' Lauren mumbled again. 'Great.' She tried to sound enthusiastic as Valerie continued to regale her with her plans for the event. Lauren nodded into the phone hoping she had placed her 'um's and 'ah's in all the right places, not that Valerie would have noticed, she thought after the call had ended.

*

'What? Carla exclaimed as Lauren recalled the conversation that she had just had with her mother.

'Yes, getting married… to a man it seems she barely knows. I don't get it,' Lauren queried, more to herself than to her friend. 'How can she do this? Father's not been in his grave three-months for Christ sake and she's moving on like she's…'

'Hey Lou,' Carla interrupted in a calming voice, though unsure as to what to say about the surprisingly short-notice love affair. It was certainly uncharacteristic of the older woman, who had prided herself on propriety for as many years as she had existed. Even Carla was confused. 'It's quick…' she hesitated before continuing. 'It's unexpected. A real surprise actually,' she admitted. 'How did she sound?' She asked with interest.

'Deranged. She must be deranged,' Lauren responded instinctively, before giving it some thought. 'Happy actually! Fuck, Carla. I don't believe it.'

'Hey, look… it's perfectly natural for you to feel… strange, even confused?' She searched for the right word. 'I mean… no one would expect that of your mother.' Carla waited for a response.

'I know.' Lauren huffed, then silence.

'And let's face it, it's not like you've had a close, communicative, relationship with her. You guys don't normally talk about stuff like that.'

'Isn't that the truth,' Lauren huffed, again.

'I bet she doesn't even know about you and Anna, does she?' Carla pointed out.

'Err… no! I know I'm over reacting. It's just that she seemed… I don't know, like we were best friends or something. She talked as if we have always been open about stuff, when the reality is that we haven't, and she has just thrown it at me. I can't help but think of father and how she's moved on so quickly.'

'As she said, at her age she can't afford to wait and it seems that she is in love with...Henri.'

'Seems so.'

'And you also know these things can happen quickly, right?'

Lauren smiled to herself as she thought about her and Anna. 'All right Missy Freud, I get it.'

'Are you okay?' Carla asked, unsure as to whether to end the call.

'Not really,' Lauren confessed, her voice breaking suddenly as the tears that had been building behind her eyes burned their way through closed lids.

'Oh sweetie,' Carla said softly, wanting to hold her friend and absorb her sadness. 'Give yourself time.'

'It's okay. I'll work it through. I know this is my stuff. It was just such a shock. I didn't see it coming.' Lauren paused. 'Anyway, I'll be over soon for a catch up. I'll grab a hug then,' she tried to make light of the distress she was feeling.

'Take care Lou. It'll all work out in the end,' Carla tried to reassure her before the phone clicked dead. Shaking her head, she turned to Francesca, 'You won't believe this...' she said.

*

'So, she's the real deal then?' Eva asked as she and Anna slumped onto the rug on the floor, Eva with a large Cognac in her hand, Anna with a camomile tea. The log fire blazed a strong heat into the centre of the room, crackling, popping and with an occasional hiss as it took hold of the wooden logs that Anna and Lauren had chopped earlier in the week.

The quickly knocked-together meal had been more than sumptuous and Eva had chatted endlessly about work and her mother's latest ventures. Anna felt comforted by her presence and youthful exuberance, but now into the early hours of the morning, tiredness was catching up with her. She had hoped to hear from Lauren before now, but not even a text had materialised. *Must be an intense meeting* she mused, trying not to allow her mind to worry that Lauren was doing anything other than official business.

'Yes, she is.' The thoughtful tone and intensity of eye contact left her in no doubt that Anna was serious about Lauren. Eva only hoped that Lauren was as serious about Anna. Given Anna's recent experience of her ex walking out on her she worried that she couldn't cope with another significant betrayal. The thought created an unfamiliar tension in Eva. Protective of her friend she put her arm around her shoulder and pulled her into a hug.

'I noticed you're not drinking tonight.' Eva remarked as they stared into the orange-red flames.

'Uh hum,' Anna tensed a fraction in the hold.

'Got anything to do with the chat you said we'd have later?' Eva probed lightly, thinking about Anna's previous periods of abstinence, when she was trying to conceive with Sophie.

'We are going to have a baby,' she said and involuntarily tensed as she felt the words being processed by Eva.

'Wow. That's... quick. You hardly know her. Are you sure...' Anna cut her off pressing her fingers gently to Eva's lips. The touch caused an unexpected response in Eva's gut as the feel of Anna's soft warm fingers lingered on her lips. *Stop.* She battled against the sensations rapidly lighting up parts of her body no friend should be able to ignite. She stared at Anna, lost in the sensual feelings that pulsed through her, despite all her metal effort to contain them.

'Sshh… Yes, it is quick. Yes, part of me wonders if it's the right thing to do so soon. But then… I just know I'm in love with her… and I believe she's in love with me too, and we're getting older.'

A cold shower descended heavily on Eva as the words, *I'm in love with her,* drove the reality home.

'When I'm with her I feel like I've known her forever,' Anna continued, but Eva had delved into a pit of self-realisation. How long had she felt this way about Anna? Did she really love her too or had her love life reached the lowest of all lows?

'It's just the details. I don't know much about her, but I guess that gives us something to talk about,' she joked and looked up at Eva. The beep of a text jolted them both out of their independent thoughts, and the loud crack of a burning log drew Eva's eyes away as Anna reached for her phone.

Hey! Sorry it's so late. I guess you're asleep already. Busy and then mum called, nothing to worry about. Chat tomorrow. I love you x

Anna's eyes reflected the flames flicking in the fireplace as she read the message. Her cheeks flushed pink radiating heat. But more than that… Eva noticed the change in her mood as the two women connected remotely. She was pleased for Anna, so why did she have a sinking feeling in her gut? Why did her world feel even emptier all of a sudden? Why was she here rather than out on the town? Answering her own questions, she was sick of the club scene. The same, drunken, one-night stands… week in week out - nothing of meaning coming out of it. Watching her friend bathe in lust for someone she loved and wanted to be with - create a family with - felt like the wakeup call she needed. Looking at Anna as she texted, Eva vowed to change her life. An image of the tall Italian looking woman spontaneously appeared. *Was that a missed opportunity? Maybe the mysterious woman would be at the bar again. Eva had never been that struck by anyone before and would like to find out more about her. But what about Anna? Why had she reacted as she had? This Lauren had better not let her down,* Eva thought protectively as she wrestled with her own confused feelings.

Just going to bed. I miss you. Eva's here though keeping me company. Sleep well. I love you x

Pressing send and catching Eva's gaze, Anna nodded. 'Ready for bed?' she asked, as she stood and stretched, immediately feeling a slight chill on those parts of her body that had been snuggled under the heat of the now dying fire. She shivered.

'I was just thinking the same,' Eva stood and mirrored Anna's stretch before turning towards the foyer. Heading up the stairs, they exchanged a brief hug before Anna scurried into her bedroom as her phone bleeped again. 'Thanks for supper.'

'You're very welcome. And thanks for listening. Sleep well.' She blew a kiss as she shut the door. Beaming, she gave her attention to the message.

Are you tired? Want to chat? x

Sure, Skype in 5 x

Anna had just finished brushing her teeth, spitting into the sink and rinsing when her phone started to ring. Hastily she dived out of the en-suite and onto her bed, grabbing the phone. She lay on her back waiting for the signal to connect them, smiling inanely at the black screen.

'Hi,' Lauren said, casually. Her deep smile causing a surge of adrenaline to course through Anna as her heart raced and her breathing became unsteady. 'I missed you. I'm sorry it's so late, but it's lovely to be able to talk to you. I thought you'd be asleep by now. It's been an... interesting evening.' Lauren's eyes wandered off-screen as she recounted the last sentence.

'I missed you too,' Anna responded with equal measure of longing in her eyes, as she stared at the slightly pixelated face on the screen. 'Is everything okay?' she probed gently, sensing something was amiss.

'I think so,' Lauren said reflectively. Fleetingly Anna's heart sunk as doubt fought its way into the front of her mind, casting a shadow over her dreams. 'Mother called to say she's getting married,' Lauren revealed.

'Wow. Really. To who? When? But your father...' The surprise was evident in Anna's voice. Lauren breathed a deep sigh and her head dropped as she released the air. Anna could see the pain in her lover's face, knowing the deep brown eyes would reveal a lot more if they were physically occupying the same space. She had an overwhelming urge to hold her and take the pain away. Frustration hit her at the physical distance between them.

'I know. It's out of the blue. I didn't expect it. I'm sure I just need some time to adjust.' Lauren dismissed the conversation. 'Anyway, it got me thinking and...' she hesitated before continuing. 'I wanted to ask you if you'd like to visit the clinic next week when you're here?' She looked hopefully into the screen with a hesitant smile. 'Something mother said... about not waiting when you know you are in love. Well, it resonated with me. What do you think?' The words were loaded with passion.

'Ermm...' Anna froze for a moment, even though she had just started to prepare her body for pregnancy by easing back on the drinking and taking vitamins, she hadn't expected them to start the process for a few months at least.

'Sorry, I shouldn't have asked.' Lauren homed in on the look on Anna's face, reading reluctance. 'Too soo...'

'Yes.' Anna stopped her and grinned like a cat with the cream. 'Yes, of course! I want to have your baby Lauren. I want us to be a family. Together. I hate that you have to go away to work. I want you here. Why wait? Yes... Yes... Yes... I'm sorry I hesitated. I didn't mean to. I just hadn't thought about...' Both women beamed at each other, the phone freezing Lauren's pixelated face as the signal slowed. Anna waited. Her heart raced.

'You still there?' Lauren's voice preceded her image appearing on the screen.

'Yes. And it's still a yes,' Anna beamed at the camera. 'Shall I call the clinic and arrange something?' Anna offered. She had been thinking about the process of carrying Lauren's child a lot. Anxiety mixed with excitement as adrenaline coursed through her body at the idea of giving birth to her lover's child. More importantly, it connected them in a way that no other ritual or ceremony could.

'Sure. Now I need to let you sleep,' Lauren studied the screen, not really wanting to end the call. 'It's late for you.'

'You expect me to sleep now?' Anna teased. 'Okay my love. Sleep well and chat tomorrow. I love you.'

'Love you too.' They lingered whilst time stood still, before the phone clicked. Neither would be sure who pressed the button to end the call.

21.

Lauren's smile radiated across the arrivals hall as she bounced on her feet, head bobbing, to see through to the customs exit, excitement pulsing through her as Anna appeared through customs. They locked eyes instantly and nothing else in the world existed in that moment. Anna closed the gap in several speedy paces, never averting her gaze, and threw her arms around her lover.

'Oh God, am I so glad to see you.' Anna gripped Lauren, out of relief at having her feet on firm ground as much as her delight at holding her close.

'Mmm...' Lauren groaned into the hold, as she took in Anna's scent and the heat of her contact. Releasing her sufficiently to look into her face, she planted a long tender kiss on her lips. 'I've missed you so much,' she said as she gently moved out of the kiss, locking onto Anna's steel-blue eyes. Her body was on fire, but the arrivals hall wasn't the place to allow her feelings to direct her behaviour. That would get them arrested, she jested to herself.

'I love you,' Anna said, running her hands through Lauren's brown curls and cupping her face, placing a tender kiss on her lips before moving away and picking up the bag she had abandoned. 'Let's get out of here,' she said, heading towards the railway station exit.

Lauren took her hand and squeezed tightly, unable to stop the grin on her face as her heart leapt with the joy of having Anna close to her. They comfortably occupied their own bubble of calm on the platform edge, as other passengers milled around, tourists seeking information to confirm their reading of the maps they had just acquired. Hurriedly scurrying to another platform when they realised their train headed in the opposite direction. Even the station announcements, barely comprehensible because the quality of sound, merging the words into an incomprehensible soup of noise, couldn't disturb their world. Lauren looked up instinctively as their train approached and they speedily navigated their way to claim two unoccupied seats before a family of large, but slow moving, European tourists descended upon them. They laughed as they made themselves comfortable for the short journey into town.

'How do you feel? About the clinic I mean.' Lauren asked, squeezing Anna's hand. Their appointment was scheduled for 3pm. Anna turned to face a pensive stare and brushed her fingers tenderly down the line of Lauren's face.

'Anxious. Excited. Different.'

'Different?' Lauren quizzed, seeking clarification.

'Different compared to the last time I did this. It feels very different. Doing this with you... feels... so right. I feel like we really are in it together and I'm not sure I felt that last time. I wanted to feel it and I think I deluded myself because I wanted it so much. If I'm honest, I never felt as if I was with my soul mate then.' Lauren's dark eyes sparkled even though the weather was dull and the lighting in the train subdued.

'I'm scared,' Lauren revealed after sitting quietly for a short time. 'I've never done this before and it's a really big thing for me,' she said with sincerity. 'The idea of being responsible for another life scares the shit out of me.' She locked eyes with Anna. 'And then I look at you and I know there's no one else I'd want to do this with. I'm not sure it makes me feel any less scared though.' She winced, before smiling and planting a kiss on her lover's cheek.

*

'Oh my God. Did we just commit to starting IVF on my next cycle?' Anna's dazed look filled Lauren with something she couldn't describe. Pride... love... lust... longing... caring? They all merged into a wonderful cocktail of emotional belonging that nothing could destroy. Clinging to a bag containing signed contractual paperwork, leaflets, and hormone drugs, Anna had slipped her arm into Lauren's for support as they made their way back to the lawyer's house. The two-hour appointment had been extended as they had convinced the consultant of their desire to begin the process at the earliest opportunity. Conveniently, Anna already had a history with them and Lauren's eggs had been stored with them for the last seven-years, so the process had been more procedural in nature than medical. The unfreezing and fertilisation process would take about five-days, so all Anna needed to do was take the hormones that had been provided and keep in touch with the clinic. They had agreed to select a different donor than the one Anna had previously sourced through the clinic - a fresh start, unique to them. They had both agreed.

'I know. How do you feel? You're the one who's got to go through all the crappy stuff,' Lauren grimaced with genuine concern.

'I've done it before. I know what I'm letting myself in for. At least this time, the embryos will have a better chance than AI ever had,' she remarked, stopping Lauren and pulling her in for a chaste kiss, before resuming their walk. 'It's exciting though. To think we could be pregnant by Christmas... or at least, well on the way, eh?'

'Scary thought,' Lauren flinched.

Anna stopped walking. 'Are you okay?' she said with a more serious tone to her voice.

Lauren turned faced her lover. 'Yes, I'm very okay. Scared, but very, very okay.' She turned and lengthened their stride with a skip in her step.

*

Settling into the house, Lauren went to pour herself a glass of wine. Looking towards Anna, raising the bottle, she asked. 'Do you want a drink?'

'I've been off it pretty much since you left,' Anna smirked. 'Just in case. But I think I might make an exception tonight, to celebrate. Just one glass though,' she confirmed. Lauren poured a small glass for them both and, kissing her lover tenderly, handed her the glass. Anna missed Lauren's lips on hers the moment they parted.

'I was planning to cook for us tonight,' Lauren said as they slumped into the couch, kicking off shoes and putting their feet up on the coffee table. 'Fancy Sea Bass or rib of beef?' Lauren asked.

'Umm…' Anna toyed with the flavours her imagination conjured. 'Sea Bass,' she nodded. 'Perhaps we can have the beef tomorrow.'

'Sorted.' Lauren jumped out of the chair with renewed vigour and strode into the kitchen.

Anna followed languidly behind and perched on the edge of the stool, watching as Lauren's deft hands worked their magic. *Hot.* The wine eased away any residual tension from the flight, leaving just the excitement of the day and a warm feeling deep in her chest.

'Mmm,' escaped Anna as her thoughts drifted to the lean body moving effortlessly around the kitchen. Sharp knives made light work of the vegetables, and a lemon-based sauce had been constructed with the attention of a professional chef. Seeing Lauren absorbed in this way was having an erotic effect on Anna. Heat rising, goose bumps and tingling sensations interrupted her musings, and with only one thing on her mind she stepped off the stool and pressed against Lauren's back, kissing the back of her neck. Lauren's breath caught and she jumped nearly slicing her finger with the sharp blade. She placed the knife carefully on the board and made a move to turn into Anna's arms. She was forcefully stopped.

'No you don't...' Anna demanded, as her teeth bit down on Lauren's right ear lobe. Restricting Lauren's movement with the pressure of her body, her hand moved under her shirt, fingers lightly tracing the twitching body from waist to breast. Moving under the cup of the bra, Anna took Lauren's pert breast in her hand and flicked across her erect nipple with her thumb. Lauren groaned and convulsed with the surge of arousal. Her hand reached up and around Anna's head, pulling her deeper into the side of her neck. Anna's left hand traced down Lauren's stomach, seductively carving out circles around her belly she slipped her hand lower. Under the waistband of Lauren's fitted jeans, she flicked the button with thumb and finger as she descended. The zip eased its own way down as Anna's hand reached for the shaved flesh and then lower. She delved into the hot wet sex and groaned at her pleasure. Lauren shuddered and her legs gave way suddenly. Anna held her firmly as she fingered the pulsing clit and slipped teasingly inside Lauren. Releasing her breast to free her hand, Anna swiftly pulled the impeding jeans to the floor and flipped Lauren to face her, two-fingers still firmly embedded inside Lauren, the movement serving to increase the erotic sensation taking her lover over the edge.

'F...u...c...k!' Lauren screamed as her body jerked involuntarily. Vibrations raced and rocked through her and her hands gripped the kitchen surface to support her powerless legs. 'Fuck... Anna. Fuck.' The mantra enlivened Anna to continue fucking her. Just as Lauren thought she had recovered, Anna pressed deeper. Deeper...slower... she took Lauren over the edge again. Lauren's dark eyes never left the steel-blue eyes penetrating her with every thrust of her fingers. She collapsed into her Anna's arms and Anna placed a tender kiss on her lips before releasing her. Casually walking back to the seat she had vacated, she perched on the stool again. With a wide grin and head tilt, she assessed the dishevelled woman still leaning on the kitchen side regaining her breath.

'I love you,' she said.

'You are in deep trouble later,' Lauren growled. Her dark eyes traced Anna, noting the swollen lips that Lauren would die for, and the heaving chest with alert nipples shouting for attention. 'Big trouble,' she flirted as she pulled up her jeans and straightened her shirt. Returning to her chef duties with a shake of her head and shaking hands, she groaned as she twitched with residual shuddering sensations continuing to overwhelm her body.

'Mmm. Promises, promises,' Anna teased as she sipped her wine and feasted on the tousled hair and creased shirt in front of her.

*

'Are you going to see your mums?' Lauren asked as she poured the freshly brewed coffee. Anna put her arms around Lauren's waist from behind and snuggled into her neck. 'Don't start that again,' Lauren flipped around quickly and pulled her lover into her robe-clad body, kissing her lightly on the nose. Anna pulled tighter and claimed Lauren's mouth with a deep impassioned kiss that took Lauren's breath away. 'You're insatiable,' she remarked, as they came up for air.

'Mmm. I'm getting ready for you to make me pregnant remember,' Lauren's eyes flared with lust and longing. 'I love feeling close to you.' She kissed Lauren again, more tenderly this time, as if savouring every part of her mouth and lips. Lauren fell into the kiss and responded with her own exploration.

'Well?' Lauren asked as they pulled away.

'Well what?'

'Mums?' Lauren sniggered. 'Good job memory isn't required for IVF,' she teased.

'Yes... I'll pop in for a bit today while you're at work.'

'You sure you don't want me to come with you?' Lauren asked.

'No, it's fine. If you're not there they can quiz me about you,' she said with a fond smile.

'Are you going to tell them about us having a baby?'

'Yes. They were aware last time and I hope it will help mum. Give her something to look forward to.' Anna reflected solemnly as she spoke.

'Good,' Lauren said, more authoritatively than she had intended. Anna had always had a very open relationship with her mums, unlike Lauren's relationship with her mother. She felt closer to Vivian and Lisa, having met them only once, than she had done to her own parents at any time in her life. 'I think they'll be great,' she said smiling, nodding her approval. 'I've got to get going,' she grumped, pulling away from Anna and heading for the shower. 'I'm going to try and finish early so I can go with you to the airport later,' she called from the stairs.

'Great,' Anna responded, inaudible to Lauren, as a wave of sadness passed through her. She hated the idea of leaving, but she too had work to do - a portrait that needed to be finished. She planned to have it done for the 17th December, for the wedding. Lauren had insisted that Anna accompany her to the event, so at least taking the canvas would legitimise her presence, she reasoned. She worried what Valerie would make of her and Lauren's plans for a family, and felt more than a little uneasy.

*

Shit. I'm stuck at work and not going to be able to make it to the airport. Fuck. I'm so sorry. I miss you already x

Anna felt her heart sink as she read the message, having missed two calls from Lauren and been unable to reach her when she tried.

Hey. No worries. Speak later. Mums all good x

She responded with a big smiley, which was a long way from the sadness she was really feeling. But she didn't want Lauren to be distracted by something she couldn't do anything about.

She had spent the best part of the morning listening to her mum complain bitterly about the chemo, though she wore the hair loss well, Anna had noted, she looked closer to trendy than sick. Except for her sunken dark eyes, which looked weary and sometimes vacant. It was the vacant and distant look that hurt the most. It was as though her mum withdrew into a different time and space, and Anna wasn't a part of it. In those moments, she had felt so isolated and disconnected from her and the fear that followed hit her like a steam train. Worse still, she felt powerless to do anything about it. Vulnerable. It was as if her mum was fading into the distance and no matter how hard she chased she could never catch up with her. Then she would return from her internal journey and Anna would take a deep breath. With raised hope, she would try to steer the conversation to keep her mum close. But the to-ing and fro-ing was distressing, and exhausting.

The one highlight of her day had been when her mum's eyes had sparked up at Anna's news. A dull winters day had been turned into a brighter future for a short time as they reminisced together. Lisa had reflected on her experience of conceiving Anna and even though Anna had heard the story many times they had laughed until their sides hurt. Lisa had tried AI and failed to conceive on three occasions. At her wits end, highly stressed and anxious, she had pushed Vivian to agree to them finding a donor privately. They had quickly excluded their personal friends who had all declined, primarily because they had never considered having children and didn't want the responsibility of knowing they had a child out there. There was also a strong fear that the child would turn up at age eighteen with a big chip on its shoulder and claim financial recompense from their 'father' for creating an allegedly dysfunctional situation.

They had contacted the eventual donor through a medical colleague of Vivian's, and having chatted for a couple of months they agreed to give it a go. It had been a little disconcerting having a strange man turn up to their house, let himself in, and entertain himself in their bedroom with a video and box of tissues, but he had produced a vial of sperm that Vivian then syringed into Lisa. Within two months of trying they had a positive result, and so Anna came into being.

Now, sitting on the train, watching the rain trickle sideways down the opaque and scratched window and the grey, slow moving landscape beyond, Anna shuddered. Her eyes locked onto her case, and she envisioned the hormone drugs it contained. Her gut tightened in an unpleasant way and she felt as if she were struggling to breathe. Was she doing the right thing? What if Lauren left her? She fought the stream of rising doubts to the point of mental and emotional exhaustion, until the train pulled to a stop and she entered the terminal building, becoming preoccupied with checking in for her flight. She felt sick with worry, and this time it wasn't just about the need to fly back to Paris.

*

The flight had been relatively smooth and Anna had worked hard to prevent the sick feeling escalating. She hadn't even started taking the drugs yet so she knew it couldn't be a side effect, and she definitely wasn't pregnant. Breathing deeply, she savoured the cool winter Paris air, taking the edge off of the nausea. As she exited the airport building and hailed a taxi, her fingers tapped nervously at the keys and pressed the send button before she could re-think the message.

Lauren pocketed her phone off the table and excused herself to take a toilet break, a surge of adrenaline filling her veins at being back in contact with Anna, albeit briefly. She had fielded back-to-back meetings all day and this last one had been going for three-hours already, with no sign of an end in the next hour. Her body had stiffened and her mind protested through sluggish processing. Drained and exhausted she was ready to call it a day, but knew that was an unlikely possibility for the next couple of hours at least. The one light in her day was being able to read and respond to the text from Anna. Professional standards had dictated that she refrain from looking at her phone whilst in the meeting, but she knew that she would have messages waiting. Anna would be in Paris now, Lauren reflected, and immediately wished she were there with her. Stepping into the bathroom she switched on her phone. Her stomach heaved and dropped at the same time, as she read the last message received. It had arrived half an hour ago.

I'm sorry. I'm not sure I can do this x

With shaking hands, she tried to call Anna, but the phone diverted to answer phone. She didn't leave a message. Beside herself with worry, she paced the ladies room, possessed. She had to compose herself before returning to the meeting, but her heart and mind were far from being on the job now. She wanted to run immediately to Anna. Anger and frustration ripped through her. Baffled. Confused. She tried to work out what had caused Anna to send the text. Had she pushed her too hard about pregnancy? She didn't think so, but then again, she didn't really know Anna that well. Everything seemed fine this morning. Was it about her mum? She clawed through her mind to find any signs that would warrant Anna's withdrawal. And... withdrawal from what? Their relationship?

Family? *Fuck*. Moving to the sink she splashed the cool water on her face and looked at herself in the mirror. Her eyes were dull, her jaw tight. The door opened and a woman she didn't know entered.

'You okay,' the tall blonde woman asked, leaning towards her. Her stunning blue eyes caught Lauren's breath and stabbed at her heart. The resemblance to Anna's eyes was striking... and disconcerting in that moment. The woman seemed genuinely concerned.

'I'll be fine thanks.' Lauren responded more sharply than she intended. She moved quickly to dry her hands and face with a white linen towel. Holding the soft cotton to her face for a fraction longer than she would do normally, she breathed deeply to regain her composure and threw it into the wicker basket. Picking up her phone, she exited the room and paced back to the meeting room without sending a response.

'You okay,' John McDermott asked, looking her up and down quizzically. 'You look like your cat's just died... and I know you don't have one,' he tried to jest, before realising that Lauren wasn't in a good place. 'Sorry,' he apologised for his insensitivity, recalling that her father had recently died.

Lauren, glared at the man, and moved to take her seat at the table. She was in no mood for procrastination. She needed to get the meeting wrapped up and get home. 'Can we get this finalised. I need to get out of here ASAP.' The intensity behind her request left no place for discussion. Sitting, her cough indicated a resumption of the meeting to the other participants who immediately broke away from their conversations and resumed their places at the table.

Two hours later Lauren stepped into the street-lamp lit darkness. It was raining, but that wasn't the cause of the pain deep in her chest. There hadn't been any text following the last one from Anna and it would be 10.30 in Paris now. Lauren took the short walk home in record speed. Diving through her front door, she threw off her wet coat and shoes before pouring a large Macallan... straight. Staring at her phone, her hands were still shaking and she felt restless. Pressing the call button, she waited. The answerphone kicked in. Moments after the bleep Lauren found her words.

Please call me Anna. Anytime you get this. Please. I love you.

Lauren didn't end the call, the answerphone clicked off. She took a long swig of the burning fluid in an attempt to shock her body out of the depression it had slipped into. The fire in her throat grabbed her attention, providing brief relief from her spiralling thoughts. Wide-awake, she paced the room.

*

Anna sat back from the canvas, assessing her work. She hadn't even taken the time to unpack since arriving home around 9pm. During the hour-long taxi ride, she had chased her distressing thoughts away by committing to getting stuck into her work. Her work was her safe haven and always inspired her. From the moment she started mixing the paints, something deep inside her had spurred her on. Absorbed, she had only stopped to fill her mug of herbal tea. She was pleased with her progress - her work was taking shape and she hoped that Valerie and, particularly Lauren, liked it. As she had worked on her representation of Lauren, the earlier anxiety and fear had dissipated and a new excitement about the future had developed. She had forgotten the earlier message she had sent. Picking up her phone she was surprised not to have received a text, before realising she had had a missed call from Lauren.

The sadness in Lauren's voice, asking her to call, caused her chest to thump and her heart to race. *Oh shit, the message.* Anna jumped out of her stool in panic. It was

2.30am. She did say call anytime, Anna recalled, her finger pressing the call button before the thought had even registered. Come on, she said to herself, as the phone rang and rang.

A groggy, somewhat reticent, voice hit Anna's ear just before she expected the answerphone to click in. 'Hi.'

'Hey baby,' Anna spoke softly, apologetically. 'You okay?' she asked tentatively.

'That depends.' Lauren felt distant. Having paced for hours, her head in a tailspin, she felt like a wounded animal, cowering, unwilling to subject itself to such deep hurt again at the hands of an abusive owner. Anna felt her pain as if it were her own.

Sobbing she broke down. 'I'm so sorry. I was confused and feeling so lonely. And... worried. I hate being apart from you.' She blurted as the tears streamed down her cheeks.

'I'm scared too Anna. But I'm not in any doubt about us, or what we're doing. If you are then you need to let me know before we take this too far.' Lauren's tone was formal and the distance between them stabbed at Anna's heart. A painful silence passed between them. 'Please don't cry. It kills me I can't hold you right now. I want you in my bed, not frigging 250 miles away every night.' She breathed deeply into her constricted chest trying to release the tension created by the earlier message, adjusting to the relief she felt that Anna wasn't about to desert her. The strength of her reaction to the possibility of Anna leaving her surprised... and threatened her. She loved her more deeply than she had anyone in her life... ever.

'I'm sorry... I...'

'Don't be sorry sweetheart. There's nothing to be sorry about okay.' Lauren spoke with a softness in her tone as their pain dissolved through mutual reassurance.

'Okay.' Anna snivelled, thankful she hadn't lost Lauren completely through her sudden rush of insecurity, and with hindsight, irrational message. 'I love you,' she said.

'I need to be in Corsica for a few days next week.' Lauren said, changing the subject. 'Why don't you join me? We can fly out there on Sunday. Spend some time together, just the two of us.'

Sighing, Anna felt immediately at ease with the idea of a trip to Corsica. Time alone with Lauren would be fabulous, and she actually looked forward to seeing Antoine and Valerie again. 'Okay?' she said, wearily. The weight of concern alleviated, tiredness hit her suddenly and she stifled a yawn.

'I need to let you get some sleep.'

'Okay,' Anna said eventually, feeling reluctant to end the call, battling her body's desire for sleep.

22.

'Hi Lauren... Anna.' Antoine smiled warmly as he took each woman into his arms and kissed them on both cheeks.

'Hi Antoine,' Anna spoke first, as Lauren nodded and then patted the man firmly on his back during their embrace.

'How lovely to see you both.' He looked into the brown eyes with a glint in his own, before holding the steel-blue eyes with an engaging smile.

'I know you've already met, but Anna and I are...'

'A couple,' Antoine interrupted, as they exited the building. 'Love is unmistakable to the seeing eye,' he stated matter of fact. Lauren locked eyes with Anna, smiled, and then both women coughed lightly clearing their throats.

'How's mother?' Lauren asked. Antoine tutted and shook his head as they walked.

'Mon dieu,' he mumbled. 'That woman!' he declared. His overt display of desperation tempered by his smile and obvious affection for Valerie. Acceptance of Valerie had never been a problem for Antoine. They had shared a special relationship. One of mutual understanding - an agreement to which they were both, equally, bound. With the death of her husband, she was free to follow her heart. 'She causes me many problems,' he jested, his arms raised in protestation.

Lauren laughed, oblivious to the intricacies surrounding her parents' relationship, or those of her father and Antoine. 'I'm surprised you haven't throttled her by now,' she teased.

'Ahhh... many a time I might have considered that an option,' he laughed. 'Your mother is a good woman, Lauren. Never let outside appearances determine your judgement of her. She loves you.' The profound statement surprised Lauren into pensive silence.

'Umm,' Lauren mumbled. Antoine winked at her as they stepped into the Outlander. Anna reached across and took Lauren's hand, squeezing it firmly. Lauren squeezed back, but her eyes were on the horizon and her look brooding.

'Darling. How lovely to see you. And you brought my favourite artist with you too. How splendid.' She rubbed her hands together, bubbling with joy at the sight of the two women. Lauren stared open mouthed at the transformation in her mother. Turning up with an unannounced guest previously would have rubbed her mother up the wrong way, even if that guest had been her partner of ten-years. She had certainly expected a bit more of a reaction turning up with Anna, who her mother barely knew.

'Hi Mrs...' Anna started.

'Valerie, please. You are family after all.' Valerie smiled warmly at the artist, who beamed a smile back at her. 'Come on Lauren... get with the pace,' Valerie teased as she wrapped an arm around Anna, leaving Lauren aghast at the open front door.

'See you in the morning.' Antoine nodded. He smiled perceptively at Lauren and waved, as he shoved the car into gear and drove off.

'Sure,' Lauren whispered, vacantly. Still entranced by what had just transpired, she stepped into the house and trailed the chirpy pair of women into the living room.

'Drink?' Valerie asked, waving an arm sweepingly towards the bar.

'Macallan please,' Lauren responded.

'Water please,' Anna said, her eyes catching Lauren's. The look didn't go unnoticed, but Valerie simply cleared her throat and poured the drinks.

'You must be starving,' Valerie surmised, sipping her Champagne. I've asked Henri to join us for supper. I hope you don't mind. I thought it might be good for you to meet him properly before we get married.' She laughed lightly.

'Has she been on the Champagne all day?' Lauren mouthed to Anna.

'No, I haven't,' Valerie responded, stopping both women in their tracks. 'Love changes everything, don't you think?' She eyed Lauren, then Anna, knowingly. 'To love,' Valerie toasted.

'To love,' both women returned, raising their glasses. Tapping their glasses together, holding each other's gaze, Anna tilted her head in admiration of the changed woman.

'Now! How about you both freshen up? I assume you'll be staying in the same room,' she confirmed with a wry smile, as the two women headed up the winding stairs. Lauren's jaw dropped. 'Now go. Henri will be here shortly.' She chased them off with a wave of her hand and marched through to the kitchen, mock barking orders to the chef.

Bemused, Lauren turned to face Anna as she closed the door to the bedroom and shrugged. 'What the fuck?' Bordering on anger, her mood flipped the instant Anna pressed her fingers softly to her mouth, stopping time momentarily, sparks firing from the lightest of touch on her lips to her lower regions. She groaned as the intensity threw her off balance.

'Love changes everything, remember.' Anna recalled Valerie's words as she pressed the full length of her body against Lauren's, pulling her into the hold by her buttocks. 'Remember...' she reiterated as she took Lauren's mouth with a depth of passion that nearly floored the bemused woman. Groaning, Lauren succumbed effortlessly and took Anna's head in her hands, deepening the kiss.

Eventually releasing the hold, 'We've got about ten-minutes,' Lauren said, just on cue as the front door bell rang throughout the house.

*

'Lauren… Anna… this is my wonderful Henri.' Valerie introduced the handsome man stood at her side as the two women entered the living room, looking flushed and more alive than they had when they arrived.

Anna noticed the rouge cheeks of the older woman too and a light bead of sweat lingered in the hairline of the Doctor, whose eyes sparkled. She smiled. It seems they had a lot in common, in spite of the difference in age between the two couples, she thought, as the sensation of Lauren's fingers inside her just moments ago, still throbbed between her legs.

'You remember Henri, Anna?' Valerie affirmed. 'He attended to Lauren when she accosted that fireplace,' she jested, pointing at the offending spot.

'Hi Henri. Yes, I remember.' Anna laughed and moved in to air kiss the Doctor, giving him a full-on hug.

'Hi,' Lauren said, greeting the man more formally, with a stiffer embrace.

'Hello… hello.' The Doctor's sparkling eyes darted from Anna to Lauren. 'What did I do to be surrounded by so many beautiful women,' he charmed, his arms outstretched, holding the space around them both.

Oh my God, Lauren said to herself and smiled ineffectually at the charmed response. She had never warmed to such over-zealous adoration from men… or women come to that, finding it very old school and somewhat patronising. This didn't feel like a good start, she decided.

'Be nice,' Anna whispered, delicately nipping the ear she breathed into and poking Lauren in the ribs. Lauren choked as the sensation charged her already sensitive body. The speedy shower they had shared had done nothing to relieve the sexual tension the kiss had started. Adding to it was purgatory. Lauren huffed as she acquiesced to Anna's instruction.

'It's lovely to meet you, thankfully under different circumstances,' Lauren charmed, as she moved in to link arms with the Doctor and escorted him through to the dining room. 'Come on mother, or I'll steal him all night,' she quipped. Looking back over her shoulder at Anna, she smiled. The older man had quite a spring in his step, Lauren noted, as he moved light of foot and held her arm confidently, with masculine strength.

The meal had been a surprisingly relaxing experience for Lauren as the Doctor held court and regaled stories of his humorous clinical experiences. Anna was minded of Vivian and had come to the conclusion that the medical profession's sense of humour was a universal one. They had laughed a lot, more than Lauren could ever remember laughing whilst in her mother's company. And, whether she liked it or not, her mother looked very happy. Anna also looked more content and relaxed. She looked at home here, Lauren mused. Breathing deeply, she surveyed the three-people around the table and realised she hadn't missed her father's absence. Replete from the meal, she casually swirled the Cognac in her glass, entranced by the way the alcohol held the sides as it moved, savouring the soothing effect the evening had had on her mind and body.

Looking up from the glass her eyes connected with Anna's who was laughing with her mother and Henri. The sensation that filled her was like no other she had ever experienced. It petrified her that this woman could affect her the way she did. Then, as she reminded herself of the commitment they were about to embark on, she knew there was no one else in the world she would rather have a baby with - no one she would rather have carry *her* baby. It was surreal. It had happened so quickly, and at the same time nothing had ever felt more right or more certain. Three-pairs of eyes stared at her. 'What? Did I miss something?' Lauren pulled herself into the room. Henri laughed haughtily and they began to rise from the table and make their way through to the living room. Lauren followed, a million miles behind.

Yawning and shaking off the tiredness Anna nodded at Lauren and towards the ceiling. The silent request was clearly understood.

'I'm going to call it a night,' Lauren said, excusing them both as she finished the last of her drink and placed the empty glass on the low table.

'It was really lovely to meet you Henri.' Anna hugged the man and planted a kiss on his cheek, then hugged Valerie before Lauren took her hand and led her to the door.

'Night Henri... Mother.' Lauren smiled warmly. 'Thank you both for a delightful evening.'

'Sleep well,' they responded in unison.

*

'I still don't get it?' Lauren continued, in between brushing her teeth, toothpaste foaming at the sides of her mouth as she tried to speak and brush at the same time.

'What's not to get?'

'It's so quick,' she said, her head nodding with the confusion.

'Uh huh.' Anna looked at the bemused woman, gesticulating between them both. 'Quick can work, right?' She screwed up her face to make the point.

'But that's different,' Lauren defended.

'You bigot,' Anna teased as she poked Lauren in the side for the second time that evening. The tickle caused shocks to run through Lauren. 'They're happy. That's what matters... surely?' Anna continued. 'And, I know he's not your father - no one can replace him - but you don't know what their relationship was really like. Some people move on really quickly.' Anna's words made sense.

'You're right. I need to...what is it - *get with the pace*, wasn't it?' she sniggered as she mumbled, still in disbelief.

'So... you want to make a baby?' Anna's hands moved around her lover's waist and pressed her tight into her body. The fresh taste of mint passed between them. 'Mmm... did I tell you?' Anna whispered as she pressed delicate kisses down Lauren's neck, noting the goose bumps that appeared at her touch. 'Come... to... bed... with... me.' Kissing between each word, she pressed Lauren towards the bed. As Lauren's legs found the frame she fell back onto the mattress, pulling Anna down on top of her. They groaned as they landed. Pulling back, she held Lauren's dark gaze. 'I love you.' The sincerity in her voice burnt through Lauren's heart.

*

'How was your evening?' Antoine asked with a wry smile as Lauren poured a coffee from the pot in the office. 'The Doctor... he is a fine man, no? I am happy for Valerie,' he said squeezing Lauren on the arm as an affirmation of his support for her mother.

'Yes, it seems he is very popular,' Lauren confessed, through a sigh. 'And, it also seems mother is besotted with him.' She noticed the sparkle in Antoine's eyes as she spoke.

'Ah... you worry it is too soon?'

'Umm... maybe?' Lauren mulled. 'But who am I to say that... eh?' she admonished herself for still harbouring concerns.

'They have known each other a long time, you know...' his eyes carried the compassion of his voice. 'And now,' he sighed. 'Circumstances have conspired for them to be together. Love changes everything, don't you think?' He turned to stare out the window and across the vineyard, as he spoke of love.

'I didn't know they had a history,' Lauren confessed. How much had she missed over the years? What would her father think? she wondered.

'Your father would have wanted Valerie to be as happy as he was,' Antoine remarked, as if reading her mind. He spoke with authority. Lauren couldn't decide what it was she had sensed in his voice. Passion... Love maybe. In any event he had an uncanny way of knowing her thoughts.

'If he was that happy, why did he take his own life?' Lauren asked. Antoine turned back to face her. His eyes had darkened and showed signs of watering.

'Maybe you need to speak to your mother,' was all he said, as he stepped into his office. Lauren followed, in the uncomfortable silence that had forged a gap between them.

*

'So, my darling Anna, how is my portrait coming along?' Valerie chewed into a piece of toast that she had dunked into a milky coffee as she eyed the artist with kindness.

'Well... I think I'm capturing the spirit of what you are looking for. I've bought some photos of the work in progress.'

'I look forward to seeing them,' she responded, almost immediately dismissive of the conversation. 'How is your mother?' she asked with genuine interest.

Anna was surprised at the level of concern in her voice and the fact that she was even aware of her mum's illness. 'Oh, err... she's coping thank you. Chemo is horrid, but the prognosis is good,' Anna added.

'Yes, I can imagine.' Valerie seemed to wander into thought as she spoke. Pulling herself out of the reverie she continued. 'Well... she and her partner are more than welcome to stay here if they would like some recuperation time. We have plenty of space and a great climate of course,' she said, smiling warmly at Anna.

'Thank you. That's very kind and I'll let them know - Lisa and Vivian,' she said, confirming their names.

Valerie smiled and nodded. 'Good. That's settled then. Please invite them to my wedding,' she stated, as if that had been the discussion point all along. Rising from the table, she touched Anna softly on the shoulder as she passed her. 'Enjoy your time in Ajaccio today. It's a gorgeous time of year. Fewer tourists,' she added derisively.

'Ah… okay.' Anna sat momentarily in stunned silence, but squeezed the hand resting briefly on her shoulder by way of thanks.

*

Anna's stomach fizzed with butterflies as she entered the traditional Corsican restaurant. Lauren had hold of her slightly sweaty hand, but the inexplicable nerves, made her feel light headed and slightly weak.

'There's nothing to feel nervous about,' Lauren said, squeezing her hand. 'They're my friends and they're really looking forward to meeting you.' She bounced light-footed as her eyes sought out the Psychiatrist and her wife. Lauren spied Francesca first, who nodded towards them. Carla turned her head and waved them over.

'Hi stranger,' Carla directed at Lauren. 'And you must be the mysterious Anna,' she said, rising from her seat and taking her into a warm embrace.

'Hi,' Francesca added, standing and kissing both cheeks of the women in a more formal greeting. Carla held Lauren for longer, swaying her back and forth before releasing her.

'Hi,' Lauren and Anna responded. Anna's nerves had dissipated immediately they had hugged.

'Come and sit down.' Carla tapped the bench seat next to her. Francesca copied the move and slid into the unoccupied space on her side of the bench. Lauren took the seat next to Francesca and Anna sat next to Carla, who immediately grabbed the hand nearest her and squeezed it. 'It really is lovely to meet you. And, I'm hoping you will bring this one home more often. We've missed her,' she said, motioning at Lauren, who bowed her head at the gentle admonition.

'I hope so too. I love it here,' Anna said honestly. Lauren raised her eyebrows. They had never discussed Corsica but she had sensed Anna's natural comfort with the place.

'So... how's your mum?' Carla asked Lauren, with some concern and a little humour.

'Strange as it seems, she's the best she's ever been. Love changes everything apparently,' she joked, more able to see the funny side, but still with some unanswered questions. 'I'm happy for her.'

Looking from Lauren to Anna, Carla smiled. 'So, you both look... radiant,' she said. 'In love in fact.' She reached across and stroked a thumb across her wife's knuckles, acknowledging her own feelings.

Lauren looked into the steel-blue eyes that had stolen her heart. 'Yes,' she laughed.

'Are we invited to the wedding then?' Carla joked.

'Whose?' Anna teased back. Lauren's jaw hit the floor. She hadn't given marriage a second thought. She still had a divorce to process and the idea of getting married again filled her with horror.

'You've gone pale my friend.' Francesca turned to face Lauren and laughed. Anna winked at Lauren seductively, receiving a perplexed glare in response. Lauren winced. Anna sniggered as she watched Lauren squirm in her seat.

'We...' Lauren started.

'We're not getting married,' Anna confirmed, smiling towards a relieved Lauren. 'We are having a baby though. Well at least we're planning to.' Lauren sprayed the drink she had just revived herself with. They hadn't agreed to reveal their plan, but she couldn't take back what had been said.

Francesca passed a napkin to Lauren. 'Well, you know where I am when the time comes,' she said, in seriousness.

'Francesca is a maternity nurse,' Lauren clarified for a confused looking Anna.

'Oh, awesome,' Anna clapped her hands together in excitement. Maybe we can give birth over here after all then, she thought, whilst nodding in Francesca's direction. 'That would be brilliant,' she said, looking towards Lauren for approval, before covering her lover's hands with her own.

23.

'God, I feel like death today,' Anna remarked, stepping out of the shower. She buried her head into the warm, deep pile towel and plonked herself on the toilet.

'You look pale,' Lauren noted as her eyes lovingly caressed the tired looking woman. Their few days in Corsica had been full on. Lauren had spent the days with Antoine talking strategy for the coming year. Anna had spent a lot of her daytime with Valerie, who entertained her with a shopping trip and a visit to the local tortoise park. The older woman's capacity for activity and talking had impressed Anna and surprisingly she had enjoyed her company, seeing a lot of Lauren in her.

'Urgh... period... that explains it.' Anna looked at the bloody tissue before dropping it between her legs. Holding her head in her hands she yawned. 'Why are periods so exhausting?' she commented reflectively.

'We need to let the clinic know.' Lauren said, bounding out of the shower, wrapping a towel around her waist, and kneeling in front of Anna. Holding her cheeks, she pressed a kiss on the top of her head.

Pulling herself from the borders of sleep Anna raised her head and a slow smile stretched across her face. 'Yes, we do.' The thought suppressed the tiredness momentarily as she pondered the future. She would need to stay in London for a week or so around mid-cycle for the IVF process to be administered. A buzz of excitement energised her and she pulled herself up from the toilet and into the arms of her lover. Shaking, she pressed her lips to Lauren's who opened willingly to her request. Holding each other, wet eyes met wet eyes as their emotions soared.

'Coffee?' Anna proposed to the still semi-naked woman.

'Great idea.' Lauren wrapped her arms around Anna and pulled her head to her chest for a few moments longer, before letting her go.

*

Descending to the wafting scent of coffee, Lauren felt a sense of exhilaration she had never experience before. This significant moment was a transition point in their short time together. They really were about to embark on creating a family. Standing in the doorway, quietly watching her lover pour their coffee, she couldn't stop the sense of awe rising in her chest. Behind it a wave of anxiety pressed, at the enormity of their decision, but she pushed that feeling to the back of her mind. Anna jumped out of her skin as she realised Lauren's presence.

'Jesus! You scared the shit out of me,' she snapped, holding her chest to recover herself. Breathing deeply to slow her heart rate, she began to giggle.

'Sorry...' Lauren held her hands up in submission whilst sniggering. 'I was admiring the amazing view,' she explained. Walking over, she kissed the recovering woman tenderly on the mouth. Lauren's scent caused a shiver to pass over Anna as she reached across the counter to grab her coffee.

'God you smell good,' Anna groaned, grabbing her cup. Lauren kissed her again.

'And we've got work to do,' she remarked, heading for the living room where her laptop sat on the table, squeezing Anna's bottom as she pressed past her.

'That's not fair,' Anna flirted back, but took her coffee, and the stairs, and made her way to her loft-studio. 'Text me,' she shouted back down the stairs, with a laugh in her voice, but Lauren was already engrossed in her emails.

*

'How are you feeling?' Lauren asked, as she held Anna's eyes intently. The nurse had left them alone in the treatment room. Lauren's face was full of concern, but her eyes radiated the deep love that she felt... and more. After an edgy two-weeks Anna seemed to have become accustomed to the emotional ups and downs elicited by the hormone treatment. Now the outcome was down to nature alone. She had just received three-embryos, the question was simply: would the IVF take or not? Lauren felt an overwhelming urge to wrap Anna in cotton wool for the next few weeks and hope. She would even have vowed to go to church if she believed it might do some good. She laughed inwardly at her desperate thought.

'Strange. I feel strange. I know this is going to sound really weird, but I had a really odd feeling almost immediately.' Lauren noticed she looked stunned and slightly flushed, though the heat in the room could explain the latter. 'Only time will tell.' She shrugged her shoulders. A wave of something filtered through her and she caught Lauren's eyes. 'Will you hold me please?' she murmured, struck by an overwhelming surge of indefinable emotion.

Lauren dived across the short gap between the chair and couch to enclose Anna in her arms. Anna breathed in the familiar scent and felt immediately comforted. The warm breath and soft kisses started to drive her sex into spasm. She groaned.

'Do you think we should?' Lauren nodded at Anna's state of undress with a wry smile. 'Orgasm is supposed to help, isn't it?' she stated in semi-seriousness.

'I think you'll find that's the case for AI,' she said, slapping Lauren on the arm. 'Nice try though, Ms Vincenti,' she laughed.

'Damn it... maybe later?' she propositioned with a wink. Though if she were honest she felt a little petrified at the prospect of doing any damage to the fallible process. The thought was a sobering one and she pulled away a fraction, placing a tender kiss on Anna's soft mouth. They were interrupted by the soft click of the opening door as the nurse entered the room.

*

'How are you feeling?' Lauren asked, looking pensively at Anna as she pulled on her coat and heels.

'You don't need to ask me that every day,' Anna teased lovingly, as she stroked Lauren's concerned face, tracing her features seductively with her index finger. 'I'm fine.' It was just over a week since the implantation and only seven days until Valerie's wedding. Anna's mums had declined the offer on this occasion, due to the treatment commitments Lisa had in her diary. But they had promised to visit in the near future. Valerie had jumped at the opportunity and invited them for Christmas, which they had tentatively accepted.

'Okay, but call me if anything changes...promise?'

'Of course.'

Lauren pointed a determined finger at Anna, feigning seriousness, as she hurried out the door. Work had been exhausting, working long hours to catch up for the time spent with Anna through the IVF process. She didn't feel as well prepared for Court as she would have liked, but backed herself to find a way to get her result. The buzz of working a courtroom kept her alert and stimulated. Although she planned to finish with McDermott, Knight and Davies early in the New Year, her boss had been hounding her to reconsider - to at least take a sabbatical. In spite of all that was going on between her and Anna, and the fact that they had now spent quality time together at her London house, she had found herself pondering the idea to the point of it becoming a serious proposition in her mind. They could comfortably live in London, and it would be close to Anna's mums. A sabbatical would give her the time she craved without throwing away a career she had worked so hard to achieve, she had reasoned. Being in Corsica with Anna also felt so right... so relaxing and easy. But, at times, an unsettled feeling that came over her seemed to revolve around not having her work to go to. Was she addicted to it? Whilst she enjoyed her time with Antoine at the vineyard, she couldn't see herself there on a permanent basis. Corsica still felt claustrophobic to her, compared to London, and even Paris. Maybe she should look for something in Paris, she pondered, as she took the short walk to her office. The cold misty morning penetrated her thick coat and she shivered.

'Morning,' John McDermott said, bounding towards her with a pile of case-files in hand. 'Ready for court? Can't wait to bring those bastards down. Five mill... that's what I'm gonna take them for. Try and fuck with me,' he said, with a sadistic grin plastered across his face. His passion for his job seemed to border on aggressive, vengeful even. Lauren retracted at the blast of negative energy. 'What's up with you?' he bemoaned. 'Where's your fight Vincenti?' The greying man spat the implied accusation as he passed her and entered his office, slamming the door shut with his foot.

'God!' Lauren cursed at the closed door. Striding to her office she closed the door behind her and leant heavily against it, breathing deeply to steady her shaking hands. Did she really have the fight, or was she losing her edge and just trying to convince herself she needed her work? A sudden rush of heat and butterflies coursed through her gut and she felt her heart pounding through her chest. She bent over to avoid fainting and cursed to herself. Lightheaded and physically shaking, she moved slowly to sit on the black couch, normally reserved for her clients. Resting her head back against the cool leather, her eyes closed and she realised just how tired she felt. Her stomach flipped and her anxiety level flew through the roof.

A knock at the door jolted her to her feet, making her head swim violently and immediately her legs gave way, throwing her back onto the couch. Looking up at her clerk, Jason Lavery entered the room carrying another batch of chunky files. He walked smartly in and dropped the files onto her desk. 'You okay Lou?' He studied her. 'You look rough,' he said, matter of fact.

Lauren could feel cold beads of sweat forming on her face and a chill trailed down her back and chest. 'You're shivering. Are you sure you're okay? Can I get you something?' he asked, hands by his side awaiting instruction from his boss, with a look of concern.

'Thanks Jason.' Lauren forced a smile onto her pale face and the young man frowned in response. 'I'll just stay here for a bit. Some water would be great,' she conceded realising the need to stay in one place for a while. Jason filled a glass from the water cooler in the room and placed it on the low table in front of her. 'Thanks.' She leaned back into the seat again and raised her eyes to the young man, in disgust with herself. The door clicked behind him. In the silence, Lauren became acutely aware of the ringing in her ears and closed her eyes once more.

'You ready?' The voice boomed at her throbbing head, as the door crashed open and John McDermott bounded into the room. Lauren jumped out of the seat, her heart pounding through her chest at the rude awakening. 'What the fuck?' he threatened, arms flailing in her direction. 'We're in court in half an hour. What the fuck are you doing Lauren?'

'I'm sorry. I wasn't feeling well and just needed to rest for a minute,' she muttered, not wanting to admit she had fallen asleep. 'My head is killing me.' She squinted into the artificial lighting.

'We don't have time for this.' The rotund man spat as he paced the room, as if seeking a solution that involved firing her. 'What's wrong with you? Do you need a Doctor?'

'No, I'm sure I'll be fine.' Lauren stood, her head pounding even louder, her vision blurred. She staggered towards her desk. 'Shit,' she moaned, at her own weakness. 'I think I need to go home,' she almost whispered. 'And please stop shouting at me,' she added.

'You have to be fucking kidding me.' Lauren watched as spittle sprayed with his words. Turning swiftly, he took the files from Lauren's desk and marched out the door. 'Fucking women,' he mumbled. Lauren picked up her phone and called for a taxi.

*

Hearing the click of the front door opening, Anna jumped. She wasn't expecting anyone and her heart raced as fear hit her in an instant. Facing the living room door, she watched not knowing whether she should investigate or hide. The groaning sound that followed the opening of the living room door caused her to instantly relax as she recognised the voice. But the sound emanating from Lauren, and the uncharacteristically pale face that emerged through the doorway caught Anna's breath.

'No. What happened?' Rushing towards the collapsing woman she took the weight of her in her arms and pressed a hand to her face to check her temperature. 'You look awful. I'll get a Doctor,' she said as she moved Lauren to the couch and laid her down. Removing her shoes, she grabbed the beige throw and placed it over the shaking woman before heading to the phone. Lauren didn't have the energy to protest and collapsed into the couch.

'We need to take you to the out of hours clinic,' Anna said as she pocketed her phone. 'I've called a taxi. It'll be here in ten-minutes.' Moving towards the couch she slipped the shoes back onto Lauren's feet and waited, staring. Lauren fought to keep her eyes open, until the doorbell made her jump and she tried to stand up too quickly. 'Easy does it,' Anna said, jumping to her feet to help Lauren to the door.

They walked slowly into the clinic. Anna helped Lauren to a seat before attending the registration desk. By the time she returned to sit next to her, Lauren's eyes were closed again and her head rested against the cold, painted brick wall. Several people were called before the sound of Lauren's name caused her to stir. Groggily she staggered into the side room.

'Well you don't have a particularly high temperature,' the attending nurse remarked. 'Lungs are fine. There's no infection that I can tell. Have you had anything like this happen before?' she asked. Lauren shook her head as she processed her medical history.

'Something similar, when you passed out at your mother's a couple of months ago,' Anna reminded her.

'I'd forgotten that,' Lauren sighed with the effort of speaking. She felt drained and needed to sleep.

'Okay. Well I'd like you to get some bloods done. There may be something viral going on, but my guess is that you are also anaemic. It would be best to be sure.' She spoke as she completed the blood-forms and handed them to Lauren. Both women exited the room and headed to haematology.

It had taken them close to three-hours for the hospital visit and Lauren looked pale and vulnerable. Sitting on the couch next to her, Anna felt helpless and she didn't like the feeling. The embryo, she was sure was growing inside her, changed a lot of things for her... for them both. The balance between life and death seemed more visible. Tangible. The impact of loss heightened. She didn't want to lose her family.

The fact that her thoughts of losing Lauren in this moment were clearly irrational - she wasn't dying - didn't prevent the emotional response she now found herself rallying with.

Brushing the loose curls from Lauren's face she studied the beautiful woman and it occurred to her what their baby might look like. The dark penetrating eyes, long eyelashes, and high cheekbones, narrowing chin and curved lips, sat in perfect symmetry upon the normally tanned skin. Highlighted by the dark brown curling locks, Lauren could have been a goddess in another life. Anna leaned in and kissed the dry lips softly. Lauren moaned in her drowsy state, twitched at the absence of touch, and sighed as Anna helped her up the stairs to bed.

*

Seriously anaemic, the blood results had confirmed. Lauren had been ordered to rest and iron tablets prescribed. Two days into treatment and she was, against Anna's better judgement, back at work. John McDermott had taken on a couple of Lauren's bigger cases, complaining bitterly at her apparent loss of interest - and capability - accusations that were unjust and unfounded in Lauren's eyes. He had won the court case when Lauren had been incapacitated and made no bones about reminding her of the fact.

With his ego bigger than ever, his failure in the eyes of the other partners, to harness the young talent that he had advocated to them, was a constant and growing thorn in his side. John McDermott didn't do failure and at the moment, *she* - Lauren - was failing him.

Lauren was working harder than ever and it irked Anna to see her put every ounce of energy into the job, for what appeared to be zero reward or thanks from her boss or the other partners. John McDermott had changed his attitude towards his protégée in the blink of an eye. His obvious disgust at her decision to take a sabbatical, even though he had proposed the idea in order to keep her, was being levied against Lauren on a daily basis, with not so subtle gibes and aggressive - sometimes threatening - behaviours. Lauren put on a brave face, but Anna could see right through it and the hurt in her lover's eyes stung. She had been lucky that a blood transplant hadn't been needed and here she was killing herself... again. For what? Anna questioned to herself.

'Hey, go easy on yourself,' Anna pleaded, sensing the irritation in Lauren's voice as she recounted the mounting issues with her boss. They had talked all evening about the situation, which was followed by a restless night's sleep and Anna was feeling the distance between them grow as the man clearly occupied Lauren's mind.

Patiently, she stroked the side of Lauren's face, tried to hold her eyes - to connect with her - but failed. 'You my darling, need to rest. And I am going to see to it that you do,' Anna commanded, poking Lauren in the chest as she spoke, trying to lighten the situation.

'I should be looking after you, remember.' Lauren smiled weakly as her hand brushed lightly over Lauren's womb. She still felt exhausted and inexplicably disconnected from Anna. She wasn't sure which feeling troubled her more. She didn't know how or when the disconnection had taken root and right now she didn't know how to remove the barrier that had been erected.

'How about we look after each other?' Anna asked softly.

'Deal!' Lauren conceded.

'Right... now get packing. We need to get going,' Anna said, motioning to the still empty suitcase lying open on the bed. Lauren saluted in jest and set to work. Both women were working hard to lift the dark energy that had descended on them.

24.

'Hello darlings.' Valerie greeted the two women excitedly as they stepped out of the car and stretched. They had been travelling all day and the sun had long since set over the barely visible mountains, chased away by impending darkness.

'Hi mother.' Lauren pulled the older woman into a warm hug, holding her longer than she ever had done before.

'Hi Valerie.' Anna smiled warmly, leaned in and kissed the woman on each cheek.

'You must be starving,' she said, waving them to follow her into the house. Anna and Lauren nodded at each other, welcoming the predictable first response from Valerie - food and drink were always her safe 'go to' response no matter what the circumstances. They followed the spritely woman into the living room, dropping their bags at the front door. 'Drink?' she asked, heading towards the bar.

'Just water thanks,' they responded in unison. Valerie looked at them both suspiciously over the top of her half-empty Champagne glass.

'Hmm,' she remarked to herself.

The women took the water and wandered into the dining room, sat at the table and tucked into the cold buffet that had been prepared for them. Valerie bubbled as she explained how the preparations for the wedding had gone and how she saw the day panning out. It was to be a quiet affair, family and close friends only she had explained. But, only the best food and wine would be acceptable, of course. The main meal would comprise traditional Corsican cuisine, which included wild boar casserole and a wide selection of charcuterie and cheeses - using the best organic ingredients - and wine from their personal cellar. The table flower displays would be Poinsettias. They, and bouquets of white roses, were due to arrive the next day. Lauren noticed how her mother glowed as she talked them through the details. She especially lit up when talking about Henri. Lauren smiled inwardly, unable to recall seeing her mother so 'in love' before.

'Right, I'm ready for bed,' Anna said, looking to Lauren for support.

'Me too,' Lauren squeezed the thigh underneath her hand whilst maintaining eye contact with her mother.

'Thank you for a lovely supper,' Anna said, moving to stand. 'I'm really looking forward to tomorrow. Please let me know if I can help?' she offered.

'Thank you darling,' Valerie said, standing and taking Anna's hand in her own, pressing it firmly. 'Sleep well,' she said, leaving the table, Cognac in hand.

Lauren paused in the living room as her mother settled into the lounge chair and watched her Cognac swirling in the glass, a frown on her face.

'I'll be up shortly,' she motioned to Anna who was yawning. Pouring herself a Cognac she sat opposite her mother, butterflies invading her stomach. She took a large glug of the burning fluid and caught her mother's eyes. Valerie braced herself in the chair.

'Why did he do it?' she asked, holding her mother's gaze, noticing the glassy sheen appear across their surface. She knew exactly what Lauren was referring to, having expected to have this conversation before now.

Taking in a deep breath she rose from the chair and walked towards the desk at the far end of the room. Slowly opening the drawer, she reached in, pulled out an embossed envelope, and returned to sit next to Lauren on the couch. Handing her daughter the letter, Lauren immediately recognised the handwriting of her full name on the front. 'He wanted you to have this. It explains a few things that might help you forgive him, and forgive me,' she added with a hint of sarcasm. She spoke candidly, her hands shaking as she rested the letter in Lauren's lap. 'I know I haven't been the mother you expected, or wanted even.' She stopped and glanced to the ceiling, clearly finding it difficult to say the words that needed saying. Composing herself she continued. 'When Corry died...' she swallowed deeply, showing a level of emotion that Lauren had never witnessed before. Lauren's heart thumped and she wanted to hold her mother, but waited. 'When Corry died, it devastated us... both of us. We handled it in different ways.' Her eyes searched the darkness through the living room window. 'Your father and I had an arrangement that suited us both.' She held Lauren's eyes with assurance. 'He gave me the children I desired. We took care to preserve the family name - at least tried to - and I gave him his freedom.'

'Freedom?' Lauren asked softly.

'Freedom to be with the person he truly loved,' Valerie confirmed. Lauren's heart hit the floor as she tried to comprehend what her mother was trying to say. 'He and Antoine were in love with each other,' she clarified immediately. Lauren gasped outwardly. 'It's okay darling. I always knew. I blamed him for... for you turning out the way you have. Oh god, I don't mean it that way. I blamed him for your affinity for the same sex. I was young, ignorant, and angry... and then with your sister dying I closed off to the outside world... including Petru and you. The two people I loved the most, and I deserted you both. I'm so sorry Lauren. I've been distant and unfair towards you. I hope you can forgive me.' Tears rolled effortless down the older woman's face and for a moment Lauren couldn't move. Couldn't breathe.

'I...' Lauren stumbled to speak.

'It's okay darling. I don't expect anything from you. I just hope that one day we can have the relationship you deserve. I hope I can make it up to you.' Valerie stood and straightened her dress as she walked to the door. 'I love you Lauren and I want you to be happy. I can see that you are in love with Anna. I hope you never lose one of your children, but, god forbid that you do, always try to keep an open heart.' The door clicked quietly as the older women left Lauren standing, mouth agape, letter in hand.

*

The revelations of the evening had rendered Lauren speechless. For a long time after her mother had left the room, she had just stared at the envelope in her hand, her mind blank. Eventually, she re-filled her Cognac and leaned into the high-back chair her mother had vacated. Still feeling the residual warmth of her mother's body, she opened the letter with shaking hands and a racing heart. *Antoine's* image remained at the forefront of her mind until her eyes began to focus on the words on the paper.

Dearest Lauren,

If you are reading this then you will have discovered that your mother and I had an arrangement that suited us both. I hope you can forgive me and that, one day, you may understand the pressures of the world in which your mother and I have had to live. I pray that you are free to make choices that weren't possible for me, or for us.

You will already know that Antoine was very special to me. We had the best life that we could together. I loved him more than life, and I always will.

Unfortunately, I also did something that cost me and cost us. In anger and frustration, after the death of our dearest Corry, I had a brief affair with another man. I hated myself for it. Antoine was, of course, very forgiving. But I became ill as a result of my selfishness. Antoine and your mother ensured my health for as long as I considered sustainable, but I had already determined that there would be a time I could no longer hide my illness from those who would judge me, judge us as a family. Such judgement would be intolerable to me. With the help of my closest friends I have been able to take my own life to protect those I love, my family, and Antoine.

I truly wish things could have turned out differently my darling, and I can only hope that you have the courage that I did not have. Follow your heart and stay open to those you love.

I will always love you.
Papa

Tears rolled uncontrollably down Lauren's face as she read and reread the letter her father had crafted with his own hand. She pressed her fingers to the dried ink, trying to connect with him. She had no idea for how long she had silently cried, or when the tears had stopped. But now, she was shivering and still mesmerised by the piece of paper in her hand. Finishing her drink in one glug, she coughed at the burning fluid jolting her out of the trance. The clock chimed twice, bringing her attention to the fact that it was the early hours of the morning and she needed to sleep. Slowly making her way to her room, she noticed the slither of light emanating from her mother's bedroom. Approaching the room, suddenly she stopped in her tracks. What would she say to her? Turning around she quietly entered her own room. The scent of Anna warmed more than her body and she released the breath she had been holding, before stripping and sliding under the quilt. She could feel Anna's body heat in the bed. Her own body was colder and she didn't want to wake the sleeping woman. She lay on her back looking at the ceiling trying to reconcile the evening's events. Restless and wide awake, processing her father's words, it was only as the dark night begun to lighten that she eventually fell asleep.

*

Lauren woke to the sun shining brightly through the thin cotton curtains. The sound of people shouting over the banging and clattering of metal assaulted her ears. Her head thumped and her mouth was dry. The realisation that the previous evening had not been some bad dream seemed to pound through her head with every thump of her hangover headache.

A loud crash woke her from her reverie. Clearly wedding preparations were well underway. She picked up her phone. 11.00. *Shit*. It must have been close to 6.30am, maybe even later, before she had fallen asleep. Her eyes felt heavy, her head groggy, and she felt drained... and something else that she couldn't clearly define. The other side of the bed was empty and cold, she noticed, as she reached across to the space, taking in the scent of the woman who had deserted it not so recently. Huffing, she pulled back the quilt, dragged herself out of the bed and stepped into a steaming shower. Quickly throwing on jeans and a baggy t-shirt, she jogged down the stairs.

They had spent the previous day helping Valerie with the arrangements for the day. Finally checking off the guest list, seating plans, flowers and food, Valerie had worked systematically until she was confident the event would run perfectly. Henri hadn't come around and Lauren had teased her mother about not seeing the groom the day before the wedding. She had been surprised how much she had enjoyed her mother's company. They had sung along to the music rehearsal and re-sampled the wine - wine they already knew to be the best. Anna had abstained from drinking of course. Today her mother was getting married - to a man she loved.

Following yesterday's earth-shattering revelation Lauren looked from her mother to Anna. *Surreal* she thought, aware that Anna had no idea about the news Valerie had divulged the previous night.

'Morning darling,' Valerie said warmly, unsure whether to approach her daughter or not, but looking like she very much wanted to. Lauren reached for the older woman and held her tightly for several moments.

'Morning mother,' she said softly, and kissed her tenderly on the cheek.

'Morning sleepy head,' Anna teased, looking radiant in cut-off jeans and sweatshirt. Lounging in the couch reading her kindle, coffee in hand, she stopped and locked eyes with Lauren.

Lauren's breath caught in her chest and heat rushed to her face. How did Anna do that to her so easily? After all that had gone on in the past twelve-hours, Lauren almost felt guilty feeling so turned on, as she absorbed Anna's alluring gaze. Anna patted the seat next to her. Lauren poured a coffee from the resting pot and snuck up close to her on the couch, leaning into her shoulder, breathing into her neck. Anna wriggled at the contact and put the kindle down. Turning to face Lauren she planted a tender kiss on the dry mouth, stroked her face tenderly, assessed her with concern.

'How are you feeling?' she asked, hoping the sleep had done some good and unaware that Lauren hadn't actually slept for very long.

'Much better,' Lauren whispered, smiling convincingly, ignoring the fact that her eyes felt so heavy they might close at any moment. She would explain to Anna later.

'Good, 'cause we need to get ready for the wedding,' Anna said, taking Lauren by the hand and standing them both up.

'But it's not until 3.' A confused look passed from Lauren to Anna as she juggled not to spill the hot drink in her hand.

'Uh huh,' Anna flirted. 'I've got plans for you until then,' she said, raising her eyebrows in expectation.

'Have you now?' Lauren teased back, rising with great effort from the couch.

*

Lauren's mother looked delightful in her soft peach two-piece suit. Standing next to her, the suave Doctor smiled lovingly. His eyes sparkled as he stared longingly into Valerie's eyes. It was clear they had found their match in each other, as they said their vows with meaning. Love oozed from their pores and the space between them closed as they sealed their relationship with a chaste kiss. Anna wiped the tears that had escaped her eyes and Lauren tightened her arm around her. The simple ceremony had been short and poignant and Lauren felt her eyes burn as her mother took the short walk through the guests holding the man she loved close. Her husband. She and Anna remained seated until the other guests had made their way into the living room for the Champagne reception.

'I love you.' Lauren said, sincerity in her eyes, stroking the wavy hair at the side of Anna's face.

'I love you too.' Anna choked through the tears that seemed to flood uncontrollably, in between a light-laugh, as she acknowledged her overly emotional response to the situation.

Standing together, they meandered into the bustling reception room. People were gathering and most of the faces neither of them recognised. Holding hands, they weaved their way through the unfamiliar guests towards a face they knew.

'Antoine!' Anna waved to get his attention. Lauren felt the heat rise in her face as her dark brown eyes caught those of her father's *lover* for the first time.

'Good afternoon ladies,' the gentle man cast his eyes lovingly over the two women. 'You both look... stunning.' He nodded, with a glint in his eyes. Lauren wore dark brown, fitted trousers, with a cream open-neck shirt, which beautifully exposed the top of her tanned breasts. Anna had opted for dark blue fitted trousers with a lilac shirt and dark blue and lilac striped waistcoat. The colours accentuated the steel-blue eyes that had captured Lauren's heart. 'Your father would be very proud,' he said, motioning towards Lauren. 'Finding yourself a beautiful woman to love... who loves you,' he clarified, clicking his tongue in approval and smiled warmly at Anna.

'I got lucky too.' Lauren smiled perceptively and swept him into a hug.

'I'm glad you spoke with your mother,' he whispered before releasing the hold and placing a kiss on her cheek. 'Now, Champagne?' he asked as he pulled Anna into a strong embrace.

'I am too,' Lauren said, inaudibly.

'What was that about?' Anna asked, looking confused.

'Nothing important... just business.' Lauren took Anna's hand in hers and directed them to the Champagne. Anna wasn't convinced and nudged Lauren in the ribs. 'Okay, I'll tell you later,' she said squeezing the artist's hand, grabbing two glasses from the offered tray and heading across the room to congratulate the happy couple.

*

Antoine sat under the eucalyptus tree with a bottle of red Ferdicci talking to the valley. He had carried out his last act of duty to his lover. Valerie was happily married and he was pleased for her... and, strangely he was pleased for Petru too. He had never been a bad husband and always wanted the best for Valerie, even when she rejected their life and the outside world after the death of Corry. The evening was well under way, but he had needed some space and fresh air.

Sipping the wine, he relayed the activities that had taken place at the vineyard - updating his boss - on the latest crop and fermentation process now fully in progress, and the wedding. *It was a wonderful affair Petru, he said. Your daughter looked stunning... and she has a gorgeous girlfriend... and I sense that you would have been a grandfather soon. You would have been proud of her. She is also good with the vines, you know. She has your talent, but she doesn't realise it. Maybe one day she will. I hope so. She reminds me of you and she is also good company to work with. To you my love*, he toasted into the night sky.

Tears flowed as the gentle man continued to speak into the wind, hoping for a response. Resting his hand on the grave of the man he had loved for so long, as if the earth could connect them again on a physical level, he laid his head down and stared into the dark space above him. The man he had supported through thirty years lay in a box below him, in the damp soil. He tried to envision him as one of the stars appearing in the darkness but he never came. *Never would they converse again.* That thought cut him deeply and never more painful than today. The day he would never have - a wedding day. Never would they wander through the vines together sharing their ideas of a revolutionary future - a future together. One that they both knew, deep down, would never materialise. Born in a different time and place, maybe? But, not for him: not now, not ever. Antoine's heart ached with the absence of his dearest friend and lover. He had made a brave choice in taking his own life. But that choice had cost Antoine too. He would have rather cared for his dying lover until the end than lose him so soon. Any amount of time together, no matter what the circumstances, would have been better than this… surely, he reflected. The empty feeling that had haunted him seemed to recede. The vines would always connect them. Comforted by the feel of the earth - his lover's presence below him, Antoine slept fitfully, as he had done for many nights over the previous months. Only now the nights were getting colder. His bones ached more… and still his lover lay, forever asleep.

'Hey?' the deep voice jolted him in his dreams. 'I've been looking for you. I was worried you'd left already.' The young man's light-grey eyes pierced through Antoine's hazy awareness. His heart raced from being startled out of a deep sleep.

'Hello,' the startled man spoke as he raised himself to a seated position.

'Sorry, did I disturb you?' the tall, slender man gestured towards the grave Antoine had been sleeping on.

'It's a long story,' Antoine responded, holding the man's gaze, warmth penetrating his bones all of a sudden.

'I've got all night,' the man smiled as he presented a bottle of red wine and two glasses. He sat, uninvited, and poured them each a glass. The stars reflected in Antoine's eyes as he felt the heat of his vision contact his thigh, sitting so close. 'I'm Chico. Henri's nephew.' He held out his warm hand, firmly rubbed Antoine's cold hand, and smiled. 'Nice to meet you.'

'Antoine,' he responded with a smile - aware of and enjoying the stirring, and unexpected, sensations in his loins.

'Yes. I've heard a lot about you already,' Chico said

flirtatiously, as he raised his glass.

*

'Who is that?' Carla said, pointing at the young-looking dark-haired woman who was stood talking to Valerie.

'No idea. One of Henri's side of the family I assume,' Lauren surmised dismissively. Francesca and Anna followed their gazes. All four women stared.

'Wow,' Anna said as she took in the athletic frame, long wavy hair and stunning - Italian - features. 'She's hot!' The three-women turned and gazed aghast at the honest admission. 'What? She is?' Anna blushed and sipped at her sparkling water. All eyes returned back to the stunning woman who momentarily caught the four-pairs of eyes on her and smiled unabashedly.

'She is hot.' Francesca supported an embarrassed Anna, sipping her Champagne, the comment getting herself a swift slap on the side of the arm from her wife. They laughed and agreed it was okay to observe beauty, from a distance. Closing their circle, they raised a toast… to beautiful women they announced.

'Sharing the joke?' The singsong voice took them by surprise, causing Lauren to choke on the fluid she had just supped.

'No joke,' Carla saved them. 'Just a toast to beautiful women.' She raised her glass again.

'To beautiful women,' the Italian motioned with her glass. 'I'm a big fan,' she added.

'I'm Carla.' She introduced herself before introducing the other three-women in their circle. The intensely dark eyes held each of the women in turn and especially lingered on Lauren. Anna's hackles rose up and she glared possessively at the brazen woman. Lauren shrugged, and smiled helplessly.

'Rosa,' she said. 'Well, Roselyn actually, but I prefer Rosa.'

'Lauren and Anna are together.' Carla said waving her hand between the two women, attempting to calm a potentially volatile situation.

'I never assumed differently,' Rosa flirted openly. 'I'm Henri's niece by the way. Wasn't it a fabulous day?' she oozed sensual as she shook her head softly. Her hair seemed to float in the air, as if in slow motion, before settling itself perfectly around her stunning features. And she knew exactly the effect she had on those around her. 'I'm so pleased for Uncle Henri.' She seemed genuinely concerned for her uncle's happiness, which went some way to forgiving her brashness. The seductive smile continued as she held court with four-pairs of eyes transfixed by her natural ability to entrance. Her eyes still lingered on one pair of eyes in particular though, and Anna was beginning to boil.

*

'Excuse me,' Rosa said as she eyed another guest and swept effortlessly into their path.

'Interesting,' Carla said as the woman left as swiftly as she had arrived. 'So, what do you know about Henri and his family, Lauren?' she asked curiously.

'Nothing.' Lauren said nervously. Her body was still reeling with the impact of Rosa's blatant sexual advances towards her. What shocked her even more than the overt attention she had received, was the fact that her body had responded to the woman's seductive gaze. She hadn't expected that and was still disturbed by the fact, as she held Anna's hand firmly, trying to channel her urges towards her lover. But the image of Rosa seemed firmly entrenched in her mind and directly connected to the throbbing sensation that

245

was causing her to hop restlessly from one foot to the other.

Rosa had moved on again and Lauren was thankful that she couldn't see her. 'I'm just going to the loo,' she said, releasing Anna's hand.

'You okay?' Anna asked.

'Yes, I just need some air... and the loo.'

'We'll be here.'

'Won't be a minute,' Lauren said as she scampered through the French doors, intending to walk around the grounds for a couple of minutes to clear her head, before going to the bathroom. She needed to process what had just transpired and regroup her feelings. Since the illness she still hadn't been able to close the gap between her and Anna and for that she hated herself. Feeling turned on by Rosa's attention was the nail in the coffin. Confused, she stepped out into the chill of the night and breathed the cool soothing air into her lungs. The Eucalyptus tree called to her.

The ground was still warm where Antoine had rested and Lauren sat in the same spot staring out into the same darkness, seeking answers. *What's wrong with me?* The question bounced around her mind. She never doubted that she loved Anna more than anyone she had ever met. *Is this about the baby? Am I still just too tired?*

'Here you are.' The singsong tone caused Lauren to jump out of her skin as her stomach flipped for all the wrong reasons.

'Oh, hi,' she stammered

'Are you okay?' Rosa asked with concern.

'I'm fine. Just getting some fresh air.' Lauren distanced herself as well as she could, though her voice was letting her down.

Rosa stood over her, staring into the darkness. 'It's strange... life?' she confirmed, with a sombre tone.

'Um.'

'You never know what's going to happen next. I mean, your father's here isn't he,' she said, pointing at the ground beneath Lauren. 'And your mother… well there she is in there and married to my Uncle. It's bizarre how people come together don't you think? And how love changes everything.'

'I guess so,' Lauren admitted, as she stared up at Rosa. 'What do you do for a living?' she asked out of fascination with the apparent transformation from flirt to philosopher.

'I'm a surgeon,' she said. 'I work in Paris.'

'Do you always flirt so openly?'

Rosa laughed haughtily. 'I think you are one of the first people brave enough to ever ask me that question.'

Lauren laughed spontaneously, relieved that Rosa wasn't flirting with her in that moment. 'So, is it something you just save for weddings then?'

'Weddings and special events,' she said. 'And special people.' She added, as she looked down at Lauren and winked. *Spoke too soon*, Lauren thought edgily.

'I'm really not available, you know.'

'I know. Just my luck, the best ones are always taken.' She smiled dejectedly before holding out a hand to help pull Lauren up to stand. 'Come on let's go in? You're safe with me. An outrageous flirt I may be, but I'm not into wrecking relationships.' She pulled Lauren up with ease and they walked back towards the house. Lauren glanced back towards the tree and nodded her thanks. She knew it was Anna she wanted and promised to give herself time to adjust to the new life she was carving out for herself… and her family.

*

'So, out with it?' Anna had waited all night to find out what it was Lauren had been unwilling to share with her earlier. Lauren blushed like a schoolgirl caught doing

247

something they shouldn't.

'Out with what?' she responded trying to sound innocent, coming across defensive, still feeling guilty at the flirtatious attention she had enjoyed from Rosa and their subsequent, secret, discussion on the lawn.

'Your news that seems to be a well-guarded secret?' Lauren released the breath she had been holding, which didn't go unnoticed by Anna. 'What did you think I was referring to?' Anna eyed her suspiciously. As their eyes locked together, Lauren's couldn't lie.

'Oh, I'll come to her in a minute,' Anna threatened teasingly, watching Lauren squirm a little at the forthcoming inquisition.

'Oh, says she. You were the one that announced to the room how 'hot' she was,' Lauren began to tease Anna back as she pulled her into her body. Heat passed between them and Anna moaned into the kiss that Lauren pressed firmly to her lips. 'You are the only one I want,' she said as she pulled back and looked into the steel-blue gaze.

'So, your news?' Anna tilted her head, the question still unanswered. Lauren moved out of the hold and took Anna by the hand, leading her into the bathroom. It had been a long night and she would explain the details of the conversation with her mother whilst taking a hot shower.

'Shower,' she nodded towards the walk-in unit, 'and I'll tell you all about it.'

Slipping into bed, Anna was still gabbling about Antoine and Valerie. Anna's sense of compassion towards her family warmed Lauren, whose more immediate response had been anger, frustration and confusion. Standing back, she could appreciate her parents' battle - to carve out a life together, whilst also preserving the family name and reputation in a small place like Corsica. Pulling her lover into her arms she reflected on how lucky she was to be born in a time that was more tolerant of individual choice. Anna wound her arm around Lauren's waist and snuggled into the hold.

'I'm not finished with you about that woman,' she mumbled as she began to doze, and a giggle rippled through them both. Lauren stared into the dark space listening to Anna's rhythmical breathing as it slowed and quietened, before allowing herself to drift into a deep sleep.

25.

'Well, hello.' Rowena beamed a welcoming smile and sat bolt upright as her protégée glided through the door. 'Wow. You look... different,' she remarked. Lauren had gone to London after the wedding and Anna had settled back into her work. Long hours spent at the canvas had been exhausting, but enjoyable. The finished piece was ready for collection, for Corsica - a Christmas gift she had decided, for the person she now considered to be her mother-in-law. It would be there for Christmas Eve.

'I've been busy,' Anna defended, smiling at her agent as she pressed the button on the coffee machine. She savoured the familiar hiss and pop and scent of the roasted beans that wafted across her nostrils.

'I've got a new commission for you, if you want it?' Rowena stood and eased her body around the desk to give the artist a warm embrace. Anna hadn't expected the hesitancy she felt, and tensed at the idea of another project. 'There's no travelling for this one, though that seems to have worked out well as far as I can see,' she teased. 'You going to update me then or do I have to take my daughter's version as gospel?' Rowena quizzed in excitement. 'Talk of the devil.' Her eyes focused on the opening door as Eva sauntered in carrying a box of croissants.

'Oooo great, I'm starving,' Anna greeted her friend by diving into the box. The long working days had resulted in an early breakfast and a snack by 9.30 to get her through to lunch. She was ravenous. Fortunately, she wasn't gaining weight through her new eating regime.

Eva held the box out for Rowena to take one and started to head for the coffee machine, fighting the tingling heat that was rising uncontrollably at the sight of Anna. *Get a grip.*

'Thanks.' Rowena placed the box on the low table before placing a kiss on her daughter's cheek. 'Right, you and I have a New Year sales, tactical promotion we need to get our heads around by close of play today.' She tapped Eva on the arm. 'I need your genius brain and if we can get it nailed by lunch-time, then we can close early for the Christmas break,' she said, nodding at her smirking daughter.

Eva turned and popped a pod in the machine while her mother continued to talk. The urge to kiss Anna deeply surprised Eva and caused untold disruption to both her mind and body. And she was feeling a little embarrassed at her sudden desire for her friend. *Was she really losing the plot?* She hadn't had a sexual encounter for weeks and that was clearly playing on her mind, and body. She had been back to the bar a couple of times but never seen the tall, elegant woman again. No one else compared... except, it seemed, Anna. She breathed deeply while the coffee hissed and popped at her.

'Right. Anna. This proposal?' Rowena focused the artist on the proposition while Eva grabbed her coffee and tucked into a croissant.

Eva studied Anna carefully while she dipped the cake. She looks... different, she mused.

Anna glanced at her phone as it buzzed in her pocket.

Can't wait to see you tomorrow x

A big smiley wearing a Christmas hat finished the text. Anna was lost in her thoughts of Lauren, and spending the Christmas together.

'Earth to Anna,' Rowena nudged her shoulder.

'Sorry,' she said, but she wasn't. Chuckling, she pocketed her phone. 'This project,' she said, feigning interest.

'I'll email you the details now. I think you'll find it interesting,' she said realising she had lost Anna already.

Clicking the keys on the keyboard, 'Gone!' She looked up at Anna and nodded.

'Cool. I'm off Christmas shopping now,' Anna said as she turned on her heels, placed the empty cup on the table and glided out the door. The two watching women stared, heads shaking, as the door closed.

'Well that was brief,' Rowena remarked with a perceptive grin. 'So! What's up with you? You look like you just found out you're on Santa's naughty list, not that that should come as any surprise to you,' she jested.

Eva shrugged evasively. 'I'm fine. Let's get to work.'

*

Lauren searched the display the salesman had put before her. She felt pretty clueless as to Anna's taste in jewellery. She had never seen her wear much, so assumed if she went for anything it would be simple - classic even. Anna's house was decorated in minimalistic style, she recalled, trying to find a link to justify her choice. There weren't any trinkets lying around - no dust collectors, she reflected. Just poignant pieces of art cleverly presented. Lauren needed the piece to represent those same qualities and after much discussion with the expert, she selected the one her heart had chosen at first sight. Tucking the small box into her deep coat pocket, keeping her hand firmly placed on the precious package, she hopped onto the tube back to St James's Park and floated into McDermott, Knight and Davies.

It had been a swift lunch break and she hadn't bothered with eating, so she could find the perfect Christmas present for Anna. Her stomach growled as a reminder that she needed to take better care of herself. She grabbed a couple of biscuits left over from an earlier meeting, and a coffee, and began to work through the daunting pile of case files on her desk. She jumped as the door flew open and John McDermott bounded towards her desk.

'So, where are you at?' he asked aggressively. His demeanour hadn't softened at all in the last week Lauren had been back in the office. It was almost as if a switch had gone off in his head, seeing her in a weakened state, and she was now on the wrong side of him - unable to get back to the right side. It didn't matter how hard she worked, or what results she attained for the company, nothing was going to endear her to him. The fact that she had requested a sabbatical - that he had instigated after she talked about resigning - hadn't appeased the situation. In fact, it was getting worse.

'Here, these are finished,' she pointed to three-files in a pile on her desk. 'I've got a meeting with the client this afternoon on this one and the others are in progress, but not much we can do on them until the New Year now,' she explained as she handed over the completed files. He snatched them from her, huffed and stormed out of the office. Lauren sighed. The earlier excitement and joy she had felt, buying her lover's gift, had been stamped all over by the odious man. She stood and walked towards the glass front of her office. Looking out she stared into space.

Can't wait to see you too. I love you x

The ping of her phone drew her attention from the stunning blue cloudless sky. Hurriedly, ignoring her phone and with all her senses focused on her decision, she bashed the keyboard on her computer. She tapped into the Internet and booked a late afternoon flight out of London. She would be in Paris by 7 and at Anna's by 8. Pleased with herself for situation she had finally set in motion, she picked up the files from her desk and marched into John McDermott's office without knocking.

The reddening face, incensed by the intrusion and the email he had just read, spat at the calm focused lawyer. 'You can't resign now. You've got cases you need to…'

'Sue me.' Lauren cut him short, placed the files carefully onto his desk, turned, walked out the office and shut the door with a soft click behind her, leaving her ex-boss steaming and swearing profusely.

She floated into the street with a grin that was broadening with each step. She had never felt more relieved and content. Follow your heart, her father had said. It was only now that Lauren realised her heart had a lot to say about many aspects of her life - including her work, and she needed to listen. For too long she had been caught in the status trap. Now she was free. Even the sun was shining in the deep blue sky on this crisp winter day. That must be a good omen, she mused. Looking up as she walked at pace, she noticed a part of the sky that resembled the steel blue of Anna's eyes. She stepped down from the curb before looking away from the sky. Squealing breaks… the smell of burning rubber on tarmac… and a furiously pumped horn blasted into the sky, invading the precious space Lauren had occupied with her thoughts just moments ago. She didn't hear the crushing sound of bones snapping like twigs before the darkness descended on her. A shrill scream pierced the atmosphere, as a witness reacted to the sight of a body thrown into the air and hitting the ground with a heavy thud.

*

'We're sorry to disturb you… Ms… Stevens. Rachel Stevens?' The male police officer looked into Rachel's eyes nodding, seeking confirmation.

'Umm... yes... that's me... what's happened?' Rachel looked at the two officers, from one to the other, as they stood with a serious look on their faces.

'Ms Stevens, can we come in please. We need to speak to you about Lorenza Vincenti,' the policewoman stated formally. Rachel's heart sunk and she could feel her pulse pounding in her throat. Lauren wouldn't have liked being called by her full name, but that was beside the point.

'What's happened to Lauren?' she asked with urgency, before the officers had time to take a seat in her living room.

'I'm sorry to say that she's been involved in an accident. She's been taken to St George's hospital in London,' the woman clarified. 'You are her next of kin,' she stated.

Yes, she supposed she was. Rachel pondered the fact. Their divorce hadn't been finalised yet, so she would still be the nominated person officially. What about Anna? Rachel worried to herself.

'Is she okay?' Rachel's voice stuttered as she tried to hold herself together.

'We don't have any other information, Ms Stevens. I'm sorry. She was taken to A&E at about 3pm. We assume you will want to go to the hospital,' the female officer continued. 'Do you need a lift to the station?' she asked.

'Yes. I'll get my coat.' Rachel pulled her coat off the hook by her front door, grabbed her purse and phone, and followed the officers into the police car. She felt the burning behind her eyes as images of an injured Lauren flashed through her mind. Her hands were shaking. Please don't let her die, she prayed. The car weaved its way slowly through the heavy, evening traffic and into Brighton and Hove railway station. Rachel felt impatience rising in her blood. She hated feeling out of control, and she hated public transport even more than that.

'Thank you.' She nodded politely to the two officers as the car came to a stop. Leaping out of the vehicle she ran through the ticket office and stood on the platform. Pacing the platform, cursing to herself, she still had a ten-minute wait for the next train to London.

*

'Fractured left tibia, pelvis, and right clavicle. Concussion and there's a contusion on the right temporal lobe,' the Doctor instructed, as he summed his assessment of Lauren's condition. 'Lucky lady,' he said 'Pressure on the brain has been released. Observations every hour please,' he noted in the file as he handed the patient folder over to the ICU nursing team.

Rachel approached the desk and introduced herself as Lauren's partner to avoid inquisition. Feeling mildly guilty, she reasoned it was the best way to get to see Lauren. She needed to work out how to get hold of Anna and was hoping she could access Lauren's phone.

'I'm sorry. Ms Vincenti isn't able to receive visitors right now.' The nurse said, apologetically. She's not long out of surgery. If you'd like to wait - the cafeteria might be the best place,' the woman offered, pointing Rachel in the direction of the visitors dining area.

Rachel's eyes lowered to the floor. Raising them, tears pressing for release, she spoke softly to the nurse. 'Do you have Lauren's phone? I... I need to contact her parents,' the politician bluffed.

'I'm sorry dear. The phone got broken in the accident. I don't think you'll get anything from it, but you're more than welcome to take it,' she said, looking for Rachel to confirm one way or the other.

Sighing deeply and glancing toward the ward, 'No, if it's smashed it won't help me,' she agreed. 'You have my mobile number?' she confirmed with the nurse. 'Please call me when I can see her.'

'Of course, dear. Hopefully, in an hour or so,' the nurse nodded at her prediction. Rachel stepped away from the desk feeling dazed. She hated the smell of hospitals, even though she had never personally had a bad experience of one, and she hated waiting. She had expected to be able to see Lauren immediately. She needed to see her. *Fuck.* She made her way to the cafeteria and ordered a large latte.

Picking up her phone Rachel made a couple of calls. She needed to track Anna down.

'Valerie?' she confirmed, even knowing to whom the voice belonged.

'Yes.'

'It's Rachel.' She took in a deep breath before continuing. 'There's been an accident. Lauren's okay, but I'm with her at the hospital in London,' she spoke quickly before her mouth couldn't form the words. The sudden gasp followed by silence, worried her. 'Valerie? Are you okay?' The sound of tears, uncomfortable in itself, reassured her that Lauren's mother was still alive.

'Where? When? What happened,' the older woman reeled off all the questions to which she needed answers. 'Can I speak to her?'

'From what I can tell she walked into the path of a transit van. It was an accident. She's not long out of surgery and asleep right now though.' Rachel kept the details brief and painted the most positive picture she could. She needed to reassure Valerie and calm her down, not freak her out with the fact that her only remaining daughter was out of it, having had surgery on her brain to release the pressure of the severe contusion. 'We're in St George's Hospital, ICU.'

'I'm leaving on the next flight,' Valerie said, having adopted a pragmatic and focused stance in her voice. 'Henri,' she heard the woman shout. 'Thank you for calling Rachel. Does Anna know?'

'No, not yet. I don't have her details. Do...'

'We have her agent's details. I'll get Antoine onto it right away.' Rachel sighed in thanks.

'Thank you,' she said, as the phone went dead.

Halfway through her third coffee, mindlessly watching the comings and goings in the cafeteria and flicking through Facebook, Rachel's phone rang.

'Ms Stevens?' the woman asked.

'Yes.'

'You can see Ms Vincenti now... very briefly.' Rachel shot out of the plastic seat, scraping the metal legs on the varnished floor. Heads turned at the noise, but she was long since gone, as she walked at pace back towards the ICU.

Puffing as she approached the desk, her heart thumping in anticipation, she smiled weakly at the nurse, who seemed to recognise her. 'Ah, yes, follow me Ms Stevens. She's not awake, but she has opened her eyes, so you can sit with her for a short while. She's in a private room, this way.'

The kind manner comforted Rachel as the nurse opened the door to Lauren's room and closed it softly behind her. The dimly lit room remained quiet but for occasional sounds emanating from the monitoring equipment. Too many tubes seemed to pour out of or into Lauren from her face, head, and hand. Her eyes were heavily swollen with red and black bruising covering much of the right side. The rest of her face looked paler than her normally tanned complexion. Her vulnerability hit Rachel and she gasped softly, putting a hand to her mouth, so as not to disturb the beautiful woman sleeping. She sat quietly in the chair next to the bed and watched Lauren's chest rise and fall - hoping it would continue to do so.

After half an hour, a nurse appeared and quietly went about her work, checking the equipment and the patient. A short time later another nurse came in and gently recommended that Rachel get herself a rest and something to eat. Reluctantly Rachel complied.

*

Someone's in a hurry to get started today, Rowena commented to herself as she unlocked the door to her office. Bloody lucky I'm even in, she bemoaned as she reached for the phone. They had intended to finish work for the Christmas break the previous day but, typically, her darling daughter had swanned off to do something far more interesting, promising, and failing, to catch up the work by the end of the day. She had gotten drunk, and apologetically had agreed to get started at the office by 7. It was now 7.30 and no sign of the, fast becoming, unreliable Eva. Rowena sighed as she put the phone to her ear. A frantic voice on the other end pulled her from her mental frustrations with her daughter.

'Hello Mrs Adams, it's Antoine here. Antoine Fiorelli...'

'Hello Antoine, I know who you are. How...'

'I need to get hold of Anna urgently.' The normally calm man sounded panicked.

'Of course. Is everything okay?' she asked as she flicked through her contact list on her mobile.

'Sorry, no. Lauren has been in an accident and is in St George's hospital in London. She's in ICU.' Rowena's heart hit the floor.

'Oh my god. Is she okay?' Rowena hadn't even met Lauren but she was well aware of what she meant to Anna.

'She's alive, thank god.' His response was barely satisfactory but it would have to suffice for now. 'I don't know anything else, but I need to get to Anna,' he continued,

259

pressing the agent. 'Lauren's mother will arrive in London shortly, but Anna... she doesn't know about this yet.'

'Of course.' Rowena gave Antoine Anna's home and mobile number and address before falling into her chair. Her legs weak, she couldn't stop her hands from shaking. She felt the tears well behind her eyes.

The door opened slowly and a sheepish Eva appeared, stopping the instant she realised her mother was on the verge of tears and shaking. 'Jesus mum, what's happened?' she asked, running the short space between them to hold her mother tightly.

*

Anna stepped out of the bathroom with a satisfied grin. The buzz and excitement of seeing Lauren later in the day fuelled her. She jumped two steps at a time to reach her loft studio needing to finish the other piece of work she had been crafting over the previous weeks. She hoped Lauren would love it. Enthralled, she picked up the brush and continued to place considered strokes on the canvas. She could hear the house phone ringing but ignored it, deeply engrossed in her creation. She wasn't expecting a call, so whoever it was could wait. The phone stopped ringing and then started again almost immediately. Frustrated at the persistence, and the interruption to her concentration, she stomped down the stairs. The phone stopped ringing and her mobile started ringing. She leapt back up the stairs and reached the device before it too stopped ringing. Breathing heavily down the phone, she was surprised to hear Antoine's voice and especially the urgency in his tone, which caused her to flinch. A wave of butterflies flipped through her stomach.

'Antoine. Is everything...'

'Anna, I'm sorry, Lauren has been involved in an accident and is in hospital.' Anna's stomach lurched at his words. This didn't sound good. Her heart thumped through her chest and got caught in her throat. She could also feel a red rage rising through her blood, crowding her mind.

'No… no… no!' The words were shouted out, hitting her ears, but she was unaware of the fact that they had emanated from her mouth. Panic flashed through her body and she had to sit before the dizziness floored her.

'Anna, listen to me.' Antoine pleaded, trying to sound firm and calm. 'Anna, listen,' he spoke more firmly this time. A short silence separated them, before Anna's sobs filtered down the line. 'I have already booked you on a flight to London but that's at 11.30, so you need to leave as soon as you can. A taxi will be with you anytime now. It's going to be tight, but I have explained the situation to departures and they will hold the gate open for you. Do you understand me?' Anna snivelled out a yes response.

'Thank you,' she mumbled, grateful for Antoine's involvement. She needed to compose herself, she admonished. She had to be strong for Lauren no matter what. Building herself up, her heart started to slow, but the effort required to hold back the tears was too much. She sobbed uncontrollably as she threw a couple of things in a bag. She was waiting outside the barn long before the taxi pulled up.

*

Lauren's eyes drifted open, then closed again almost immediately, the weight of her eyelids challenging every ounce of strength she possessed. Even though the lighting in the room was low it was still brighter than the darkness behind her eyes. She blinked a couple of times, orientating herself and her body, tried to move a fraction, groaned.

'Hey,' Rachel said softly, reaching to hold her fragile hand. Squeezing the limp fingers a wave of emotion flashed through her and tears welled behind her eyes. 'Am I happy to see you?' she purred, holding Lauren's hand protectively.

Swallowing, the dry lips attempted to speak and a glint of something sparked in Lauren's eyes as her hazy focus fixed its attention on the concerned woman holding her hand. 'Hi Rachel,' Lauren managed, and a weak smile formed on her lips. She tried to squeeze the politician's hand but failed to achieve anything more than a flicker of a touch.

'You need to rest, Lou. I'm not going anywhere,' Rachel assured her, as she stroked the curly locks out of her ex's sunken eyes. 'You're doing fine,' she whispered as Lauren's eyes fell shut. 'But you really do need to think twice about diving in front of vehicles.' Injecting humour caused Lauren's mouth to twitch at the sides. A second later she slept again. Rachel just watched and prayed. The nurses came in from time to time, each time their smiles increasing in intensity.

The door opened slowly, out of sequence for the nurses Rachel thought, as her eyes were drawn to the soft hush of the moving door. Quietly, Valerie tiptoed into the room and Rachel stood, immediately pulling her into her arms, holding the older woman tightly. Rachel took the full weight of the slight woman as she nearly collapsed with the intensity of emotion she carried. 'Sit down,' Rachel insisted, helping Valerie into the still warm chair. Valerie's eyes were filled with worry, as she looked her daughter up and down. The older woman looked pale, and suddenly a lot older than her years. Staring up at Rachel, she looked really fragile, the politician thought.

'Will she be okay?'

'Yes.' Rachel affirmed with all the strength she could muster. 'I'm sure she will.' Her eyes scanned Lauren and she tried to raise a smile if only to convince herself. 'I was just planning to get a drink. Can I get you a coffee or something?'

'Coffee... please.' Valerie's gaze was firmly set on her daughter's face. The pain of loss tore through the older woman's heart as memories of Corry's lifeless body flashed through her mind. Tears tumbled down her thin cheeks. The bone china flesh of the older face was gaunt with stress and the dark eyes looked smaller and dull. The shine and sparkle of only a few days ago now just a distant memory.

Lauren stirred in the bed and Valerie jumped to attention, leaning forward eagerly waiting for the next move. Eyes flickered as Lauren won the battle over her heavy lids. 'Mother,' she breathed, as her gaze fell on the older woman, the strain apparent on her face.

'First the fireplace and now this! What am I going to do with you?' she jested as she leaned in. Holding her daughter's face tenderly with a shaking hand, she pressed a soft, loving kiss on her cheek. Lauren tried to move into the gentle hold, but found herself restricted by the discomfort emanating from her leg, hip and shoulder, and numerous tubes.

'Bit of a mess huh,' she responded, frowning, and a little confused at her mother's uncharacteristic sense of humour.

'You've looked better,' Valerie gibed gently. Lauren mustered a smile before seeming to relax even deeper into the bed. The effort required for even the briefest of conversation overwhelming her and she closed her eyes, drifting back into sleep. 'I'll let you rest now, but I'll be back,' Valerie mock threatened, even though Lauren didn't hear her. Slowly standing and satisfied that she had reconnected with her daughter, she left the room and headed for the cafeteria.

*

The journey from Paris to London was torturous, even though the flight and the train into London conspired for Anna and she achieved good time getting from her barn to St George's. She had spoken to Rowena who was clearly beside herself with worry. The agent had offered to go to London with her, but Anna had refused even though, with hindsight, the distraction would have helped deal with the stress of being able to do nothing but sit on public transport. Every part of Anna ached. With the pain of loss already invading her senses, the fight to retain some sense of logical thought had drained her. She had spoken briefly to the hospital before boarding the flight and then again on the train into town. On both occasions, they had given her very little information. From their perspective, she wasn't the next of kin. That person was with Lauren now. Anna's instant indignation at the situation had been tempered as she realised that if it hadn't been for Rachel she wouldn't be on her way now. She would deal with the truth when she arrived.

Her heart thumped through her chest as she entered the hospital building, the medical aromas hitting her senses causing her stomach to lurch. She felt sick and short of breath. Locating the ICU, she approached the desk with urgency, every part of her body shaking.

'I'm here to see Lauren Vincenti. I'm her girlfriend,' she announced to the male nurse, her features heavy with the weight of the pain invading her heart. He eyed her with an element of suspicion and fiddled with the paperwork in front of him.

'Anna!' Valerie called from behind her. The relieved woman threw her arms around Anna, which the nurse took as an affirmation of her identity. 'She's in there,' Valerie pointed to the door before the nurse could interject. Rubbing Valerie's arm in thanks, Anna stepped towards the door.

Her heart thumped and her hands were clammy with sweat, even though she knew Lauren was going to be okay. Turning the handle, she stepped into the dimly lit room. Relief struck her instantly as her eyes caught the sleeping woman, warring with anxiety at the sight of all the tubes protruding from Lauren. *She looks so vulnerable* - the thought burned in her chest. It took every effort for her not to run across and take Lauren into her arms, shake her into the life she had just a few days earlier. She wanted to hold her and never let her go. Beeping sounds invaded the silence and Anna sobbed inwardly at the sight of her motionless lover and the substantial bruising on her face. The compression in her chest was like nothing she had ever experienced before, the weight of it pulling down into her legs rooting her to the spot.

With an overwhelming sense of sadness dominating her senses she flopped into the seat next to the bed, watched the gentle rhythmical breathing of her lover, and thanked any and every God that might have existed for the fact that she had survived.

After what seemed like a lifetime of waiting, Lauren's eyes blinked open and she tried, unsuccessfully, to move her body again. Anna smiled longingly and jumped to the side of the bed. She moved towards Lauren to kiss her and stroke the pale, bruised face.

Lauren's eyes opened fully. 'Is it that time already?' she said groggily. There was no tenderness in her voice and the vacant look in her eyes caused a rush of adrenaline to course through Anna. Her legs weakened, her hands shaking.

'What time?' she asked, frozen, disbelieving of her immediate experience.

'Obs.' Lauren said, her breathing starting to race with the effort it had taken to try to move her body.

Anna stopped, backed off from the intended kiss. Her world flipped on its axis. She stared, transfixed. Her legs giving way and tears pounding the back of her eyes, begging to be released, as the gravity of the situation hit her squarely in the chest. 'Lauren, it's Anna,' she insisted, searching her for some form of recognition. The hazy, vacant response caused the hairs to rise on her arm and an unpleasant shiver to run down her spine. She tried to breathe through the choking sensation in her throat, only able to draw shallow breaths. *She doesn't remember me.* The thought ripped through her heart, coursed through her veins, leaving a pain so deep she didn't know how to move - or whether she would ever breathe again. If she could have moved she would have pinched herself to see if she had died.

'Uh huh. Are you a new nurse?' Lauren queried, matter of fact.

Anna withheld the screaming inside her head. *No... no... no... please Lauren, please. You can't leave me.* 'Lauren, it's Anna. I'm your girlfriend.' She choked out the words, barely able to speak. Walls were collapsing around her and she was running to escape being crushed. But she was failing, and no matter how hard she ran the light ahead was fading before her eyes. She was losing focus and in danger of fainting.

'I'm sorry.' Lauren's confusion was written in the frown on her face as she assessed the woman in front of her. 'I'm married. Rachel. She's outside.' Lauren forced the words out, indicating to the door with her eyes before they closed, again.

Paralysed. Helpless. Anna watched the sleeping woman as grief consumed every ounce of her mind and body. Within five-minutes her world had collapsed. Wrapping her arms around her body she slumped in the chair and sobbed.

She wasn't sure how much time had passed before the nurse entered the room, but it had been long enough for her to start to formulate a plan. The tears had stopped flowing quite quickly and she had sat rocking in the chair for a long time, in silence, wondering what lay ahead for her... for them both, and for their family. She felt numb. Cold. But she was determined to fight for Lauren. She needed to speak to a

Doctor and find out what the medical prognosis was. Clearly, Lauren remembered Rachel and her mother, so why not her?

Reaching into her pocket she removed the manila envelope she had placed there earlier and went to slide it onto the top of the locker next to Lauren's bed. She had taken the photograph earlier that day - two straight lines, confirming she was pregnant with Lauren's baby... with their baby. At the last minute, she pulled it back and pocketed the envelope.

Walking slowly to the door, she turned and faced Lauren. *I'm not going to let you go,* she said to herself. A muffled sound came from the bed at the same moment the thought crossed her mind. She nodded towards the nurse undertaking the observations, feeling an inner strength and calmness she had never previously known, and stepped outside the room quietly closing the door behind her.

To be continued....
in 'Remember Us', Part 2 of The Vincenti Series.

**Follow Anna & Lauren's story
in Part 2 of The Vincenti Series**

REMEMBER US
by Emma Nichols

*Is a perfect ending ever possible,
after such devastation and pain?*

*Or is it best to cut your losses
and move on?*

Soul mates need to be together, but how, when that connection is denied?

As Lauren Vincenti works to overcome her demons and retrace the past, and Anna Taylor-Cartwright begins to build a life as a single mum, will the forces of nature bring them together again, or has too much water passed under the bridge? Can Lauren ever accept the truth and move on? Can Anna ever trust her again?

About Emma Nichols

Emma Nichols lives in Buckinghamshire with her partner and two children. She served for 12 years in the British Army, studied Psychology, and published several non-fiction books under another name, before dipping her toes into the world of lesbian fiction. You can contact her through her website and social media:

www.emmanicholsauthor.com
www.facebook.com/EmmaNicholsAuthor
www.twitter.com/ENichols_Author